DRAMATICALLY
EVER AFTER

DRAMATICALLY EVER AFTER

EVER AFTER · BOOK TWO

ISABEL BANDEIRA

Spencer Hill Press

DRAMATICALLY EVER AFTER

Library of Congress Cataloging-in-Publication Data
available upon request

Published in the United States by Spencer Hill Press
www.SpencerHillPress.com

Distributed by Midpoint Trade Books
www.midpointtrade.com

This edition ISBN:
9781633921009 paperback
9781633921016   eBook

Printed in Canada
Design by Mark Karis
Cover by Jenny Zemanek

EVER AFTER SERIES

To the Veterans of Foreign Wars and its Auxiliary, who gave so much in service and continue to give to the community through programs like Voice of Democracy—with special thanks to the Department of New Jersey, ANMAC Post 6253, and in memory of Mrs. Louise Stagliano. I am who I am today, in part, because of my participation in VoD. Thank you for helping a very shy teen find confidence in her own voice.

My last word echoed just slightly in the bathroom-turned-recording studio and, when I looked up, Phoebe and Grace were looking at me with identical expressions of awe. Alec, in true Alec-ness, was still busy playing producer, his eyes focused on his computer screen and one hand in the air to indicate silence.

"Annnnd, we're done recording," he said, punctuating his words with a dramatic click of his mouse.

"Woah, Em." Grace's stare made me squirm a little bit. "That was amazing."

"If you don't win, the judges are idiots," Alec said with a nod.

I bit my lip and stared at the back of Alec's laptop, perched precariously on the edge of the sink. I still hadn't completely come down from the nervous rush of energy that always ran through my body whenever I acted or did a dramatic reading. Even though I wrote the speech and had read it a million times, it still felt new and wonderful and awful, all at the same time.

"Play it back?" I asked Alec, who frowned.

Phoebe narrowed her grey eyes at me. "Oh, no you

don't. It's perfect. If you listen, you're going to want to record it again." She stood up from her crouched position between the toilet paper roll and the tub and caught me by the sleeve of my sweatshirt. "C'mon, Alec can clean it up and e-mail it to Mr. Hayashi for you."

No way. As much as I loved my friends, they weren't the most unbiased judges, especially Phoebe and Grace, who had helped me turn my improv stream of consciousness thoughts into an actual speech. A speech that needed to be perfect if I wanted to win, or at least catch the attention of the judge from Rutgers. I tugged my sleeve free and ignored her, focusing my attention on Alec. "Play it back or I'll tell Laura about how you made the pretty elf-princess love interest in your game look just like her."

Alec looked from Phoebe to Grace to me, and frowned at the two of them. "Sorry, blackmail wins."

Phoebe groaned and pushed her way out of the bathroom. "I'll call Dev and let him know I'm going to be late," she said as she passed me, Grace following close on her heels.

Grace gave me a little shove as she passed. "Don't question and fix this into oblivion, okay? It's perfect the way it is."

"You're biased because you helped me write it," I said before the door clicked behind me and I nodded at Alec. His lips set in a straight line as he fiddled with his mouse, then my voice filled the room.

It took a second to adjust to hearing my recorded voice—something that never really went away, no matter how many times I did something like this—then, I leaned back against the vanity mirror and mouthed the words along with the recording. There was a missed emphasis in one spot, and something was wrong with my tone in the best part of the speech. I hit the mirror repeatedly with the back of my head. "Damnit, is there a way to chop that section from the last recording and stick it in this one?"

Alec stopped the recording. "You do realize this is supposed to be like a live speech, right? You won't have anyone to remix you if you make it to nationals and have to read this out loud."

"But I need this to be perfect," I said, cringing a little at the whininess I heard in my own voice. None of my friends understood. They weren't trying to get into programs with incredibly tiny admissions rates that were ninety percent dependent on how the admissions people liked a few acted-out scenes. "C'mon, out of everyone, you know what's been going on here. You *know* who's judging for our state. And you know how huge this would be for me." If Dr. Lladros liked the speech and my delivery, there was a big chance she'd remember my name. And I couldn't beat that kind of direct exposure to her, especially after her compliments about my voice and delivery during the Mason Gross summer session I'd attended. Winning state, with her as a judge, would be huge for my application.

He took a deep breath and began speaking carefully, like he was tiptoeing around me, "You're really talented, Em. You don't need some speech competition to stand out. Besides, you realize you're going against all the kids in our state, right? Every speech will probably start sounding the same after a point, anyway, and the judges won't remember any of them."

"And that's why it needs to be perfect."

"No, that's why it needs to be real." Alec leaned forward, pointing at his screen. "This is real, Em. It's good. It doesn't have to be polished, like the fake shiny stuff Grace puts on her hair to make it look like something out of a magazine. This is like…distilled you." He crossed his arms, barely toned from dedicated years of science tests and gaming, and stared me down. "Look, if you don't trust us, the people who've known you practically your whole life, to tell you the truth, I don't know what I can do to help. Because I'm not messing with this."

I tried my best pout at him, but his expression didn't budge. Alec was always the easygoing one in our group. So, when he pushed back on something, I knew I wasn't going to win. "I could just record it myself," I said in a voice I knew was seriously bordering on whiny.

"Go for it. But I won't help you with any technical glitches."

"I'm supposed to be the bossy one."

"Whatever. Are you done with your pity party now? Because we're going to miss the matinee for *Perfect Zombieism Two* if we don't get out of here soon."

I made a dismissive gesture with my hand and hopped off the vanity. I had the awesome ability of storming out of a room with great effect, kind of like Vivien Leigh when she played Scarlett in *Gone with the Wind,* even though the bounce factor of my chin-length curls added an annoying cutesy element I couldn't help. Turning my drama factor to high, I swung open the bathroom door and stomped out into my room.

"Told you Alec would take care of it," Grace said in a slightly bored tone from where she had propped herself on the window seat.

Phoebe looked up from her phone, smiling past me at Alec. "I thought she'd talk you into at least one more try."

"You three are hilarious. This is only my future we're talking about," I said, grabbing a jacket and starting out the door with a massive sigh. "God forbid any of you miss your precious movie for me."

"It's *Zombieism.* You don't want to walk into school on Monday and be the only person who hasn't seen it." Alec pushed past me, keys jingling in his hands. "It would be like all of us turning into Phoebe or something."

"Oh, shut up," Phoebe said, though she laughed as she said it.

A smile tugged at my lips and I fought to keep my tortured expression. "I'd be suffering for my art," I pointed out.

Grace spoke around the hair elastic in her mouth as she pulled her hair into a ponytail. "And I'm suffering for some kettle corn. Break some speed limits, okay?"

We piled out of my house and over the lawn to Alec's driveway. Alec hit the button to unlock his beater Subaru station wagon. "Of course, Princess Grace. And you can pay the speeding ticket later, right?"

"Nope, this is all on Em. I'm not the one who made us late."

I grabbed the passenger front seat door handle before Phoebe or Grace could reach it. "You all suck."

2

Life at the Katsaros house after Dad's former company had layoffs in August had settled into a pattern of job interviews, random statements about how he and Mom weren't made of gold, and constant reminders that he and I had very different ideas of how I should live my life.

One of the positives of Dad being laid off was that he was almost always home when I came home from school, giving me and my baby sister, Chloe, a chance to hang out with him and help out with his projects. Dad always had an artistic eye and, with all his newfound free time, he was able to dive into fun things, like a swirly headboard for Chloe's room or a new mosaic backsplash for the kitchen. We were already halfway through planning an epic lamp he wanted to make for my room. It was nice to have practically unlimited Dad-time whenever we wanted.

But unlimited Dad-time also meant unlimited chances to be reminded that I was on the way to becoming the family disappointment. He was almost always home when I came home from school, asking about my grades, checking in with my teachers, and micromanaging me to get the future he wanted me to have. While Mom's position at Schuylkill

University meant I was guaranteed both getting into an Ivy-without-the-Ivy and a free ride, it also meant daily lectures about applying there and getting a *practical* degree.

And he was on a roll from the minute I walked into the house on Monday.

"You know," Dad said, idly, as he chopped carrots into slices for Chloe's snack, "Another poll came out with Schuylkill University graduates toward the top in jobs and salaries after graduating."

I scrunched my nose and stole a carrot stick from the chopping board. "That's great for Mom. More people will want to go there after that, right?"

"Great for you, too, if you go." I didn't give him an answer, just my usual head shake. Dad dove into the same lecture I'd been hearing since mid-junior year. "I just cannot understand why you don't want to apply when you have the ability to go to one of the most elite universities in America for free."

"Because there are other schools I'd rather go to that have what I want to study."

"With average grades like yours, it won't be easy to get into colleges on academic merit."

"My grades," I said, correcting him, "are *not* that bad, they're Bs. Mostly."

"Not your math grades."

"Teachers need to learn how to appreciate creativity in answers. And I get As in history to balance those out. I'm above average, at least. And you should be happy I want to stay close to you and mom wherever I get in."

"Ephemie, do you see what happened to me because I have no degree?"

"You had a good job and they just had layoffs. Companies do that, even to people with degrees in, like, astrophysics. That has absolutely nothing to do with college."

"But if I had finished my law degree…"

"We'd be living in Athens right now or you and mom would have broken up instead of getting married. And I don't think I'd be really good at speaking Greek."

"…I would have had more on my resume for a more stable position in the company. And it would be easier to find work now."

"I don't want—" I started, but then Chloe popped into the kitchen and both Dad and I shifted into "nothing is wrong" mode. We Katsaros-es might have been stubborn about letting go of arguments and wanting to win every fight, but there was an unspoken agreement amongst all of us that we weren't supposed to pull Chloe into our problems.

"Were you fighting again?"

Partly because she always tried to fix things.

"No, we were just talking," Dad said, then moved over to the stove and held up a pot. "Do you want a snack? I made carrot sticks and tomato soup."

Chloe and I shared a look. She might only be six, but I could already see her people-pleasing instincts warring with a strong sense of self-preservation.

Dad must have seen the look because he sighed and added, "From a can."

"Yes, please."

While Dad busied himself getting bowls together and muttering about how he was a perfectly good cook and how he had two picky daughters, Chloe wrapped her little arms around my waist and said, "When we're done snack and you're done homework, can we finish seeing that old movie? I liked it a lot."

I melted some more, then pat her on the head while detangling myself from her. "You're sneaky, but good, munchkin."

"Movie?"

"Yup. You, me, and *My Fair Lady* later."

She then plopped down into an end seat with a sugary grin and dropped her doll on the other seat so Dad and I had to sit next to each other on the bench at the table. The UN had nothing on this first-grader.

3

I squirmed in the squeaky vinyl diner booth, wishing I'd taken more time that afternoon to look decent. In my ratty yoga pants and Pine Central sweatshirt with no concealer and my curls frizzing out of the claw clip I had found in my purse, I looked like a reject straight out of *Perfect Zombieism*. The look had been okay for hanging out and watching bad sci-fi movies at Alec's house, but here at Carlo's Diner with their big windows looking out on Main Street, I felt like I was on display to the entire world.

Life was a stage, and, even though I wasn't at Grace's level of fashion, I always tried to stay as in character with my personality as I could. And "Em" was confident, flirty, and had a fun sense of style, even when her boyfriend was five thousand miles away in Germany.

The bell over the diner door dinged and Phoebe pushed into the diner, her eyes searching the room before finding us and hurrying over. Even she looked cuter than me in the long-sleeved red archery t-shirt she'd paired with a short teal skirt. Somehow, over the past year, she'd found a way to make her bookish sense of style really work, like a quirky young Judy Garland.

"Heard from Wil?" Phoebe asked as she slipped into the booth next to me, her boyfriend Dev right behind her. It was like she could read my mind sometimes.

I fiddled with my fork. "Just a quick e-mail, but you know how those are. Wil's English isn't that great." I guess the fact that we made out when he was supposed to be studying his English as a Second Language textbook the whole year he had been here as an exchange student probably didn't help. "We're video chatting tomorrow."

Alec sat across from me, flipping open his menu to study it even though we always got the same things. "I never noticed his English was bad. He totally kills it in three languages when we're gaming."

"That's because you never have any deep conversations with him," I pointed out.

"You haven't, either, if what I used to hear coming from your yard was a sample," he countered with a grin. "He probably just sucks at speaking flirt. I'm telling you, you need to take German. It beats all other languages when it comes to sounding cool." He shrugged. "I'm still a little mad I let Grace talk me into French."

"*Nein.* I'll stick to English, thanks. I know the important stuff: *umarme mich, küss mich*, and *ich liebe dich*."

"'Hug me,' 'kiss me,' and 'I love you' aren't exactly useful phrases," Alec shot back.

"Oh, they're very useful," I said. I then added, matter-of-factly, "And French like that might help you impress girls if you ever tried putting it to use. Just not with French girls, because long-distance relationships suck."

Without saying anything else, Phoebe reached over and gave me a tiny, one-armed hug. There were a lot of reasons why she was my best friend, and the way she just knew how not to push things was one of them. I saw her nudge Dev and he looked up from his phone to say,

"This might cheer you up. I was in the office today and heard Mr. MacKenzie say they're going to announce the winner of the speech contest tomorrow morning. Looks like someone in our school got state." I froze, icy fear stretching from my heart like the moment our roles were put up on the board for a play or musical. After Dev's flash mob at the homecoming dance last year, he and the school's vice principal actually talked sometimes. Like vice principals were real people or something. If Dev heard it, this couldn't be a rumor.

"It has to be you." Phoebe's voice got all high-pitched and she squeezed me even tighter. "Nobody else in this school could have done anything half as awesome as your speech."

"Except, oh, I don't know—maybe the whole senior AP English class?"

"Nah. I'm in that class and I can guarantee no one in there has anything interesting to say," Dev said, which earned him an elbow in the side from Phoebe. "Present company excluded, of course." He winked one green-grey eye at her. I'd thought those were contacts until one day I overheard him explaining to one of the other girls in the theatre club that his eye color wasn't *sooo* unusual in India.

Which made me feel better I didn't end up looking stupid by asking a question like that.

Phoebe tossed her wavy brown hair over her shoulder and crossed her arms. "Such a shame most of us aren't 'actors' like you and Em, and aren't cool enough to dress up in tights and poofy sleeves."

He quirked an eyebrow at her. "It was Shakespeare. Literature? And if I remember right, you thought I looked hot."

"Yeah." A goofy smile spread across her face. "But that's beside the point."

Those two were annoyingly cute—like those nineties Bollywood movies Phoebe loved so much. They never even kissed in public, only hugged and held hands and stuff. Wil and I, on the other hand, would practically make our desk chairs spontaneously combust with our makeout hotness. Sometimes, I felt like the Rizzo to Phoebe's Sandy. Well, without the teen pregnancy, smoking, or dressing Phoebe up in leather thing. I was totally okay with Phoebe's shyness because PDA is really only fun when you're the one PDAing, but it was still *weird*.

If it weren't for me, they wouldn't have even gotten together last spring. Still, it didn't mean I had to listen to them as they flirt-fought while I was mid-crisis of the soul. "Now I'm nervous and nauseated. Thanks."

"One sec, Leia." Grace stopped mid-phone conversation with her girlfriend, pulled a Scharffen Berger chocolate bar from her purse, and passed it across the table to me. "Breathe,

Em." I was about to protest about my diet for the fall play when she narrowed her dark eyes at me. "And eat the chocolate. It won't kill you." She was always so put together, a cross between Veronica Lake's blonde glamour and Katherine Hepburn's steel. Popular, with perfect, straight blonde hair, and she and Alec always faced off for the yearly science medallion for our grade. Nothing fazed her and that drove me crazy sometimes. Like the yin to my dramatic yang.

"Right. When I'm a varsity cheerleader with a perfect figure—" But her glare unnerved me and I quickly took a bite of the dark-chocolate-y goodness. I loved my curves and totally rocked them, but my jeans were not going to love me after this. As an acne-prone nervous eater, I would have to avoid any excuse to fall into a vat of chocolate and chips for the next twenty-four hours.

"This isn't the only scholarship out there, you know. If you don't get this one—" Alec broke off when Grace cleared her throat and he cowed under her death glare, "—which is impossible because your speech was awesome, you could apply to different ones. Like the Greek one your Dad keeps talking about." Since we'd been neighbors forever, Alec was practically my brother, down to people sometimes mistaking us for twins despite the fact that we looked nothing alike except for our hair color. The downside was that he knew everything about my family. Including all the Greek community stuff my Dad was always pushing on me.

"Yeah, I'll get started on it. Remind me later to write an essay about how inspired I am by all of Yia-Yia's stories from the old country about her goats."

Alec tossed a balled-up napkin at me. "Doesn't your grandmother live in Athens? I didn't know her apartment building allowed goats."

"See what I mean? I can't even be stereotypical." I twirled my fork in the air. "C'mon. You know I'd lose to all those full-blooded Greek kids who went to Greek school and will apply in both languages just for laughs." Alec opened his mouth and I cut him off, "Ditto the African American Scholarship Mom found. And don't get me started on the church one. 'Yeah, I kind-of stopped going to your church and became agnostic, but, hey, wanna give me a scholarship?' Plus, none of those have the added bonus of judges from my dream program."

Dev paused in the middle of giving his order and said, "Use some of the creativity they're making us channel in the workshop. I'm sure you can come up with something that sounds good." He handed his menu to the waiter. "Veggie wrap with extra cheese, please."

"Right. Because the stuff we come up with in remedial playwriting for actors is the same as writing a scholarship application," I said, trying not to face-palm. Mr. Landry had suggested we take some intensives in New York City and Dev and I were in the middle of a monthly playwriting one that was supposed to make us, as actors, more well-rounded and tap into our creative wells. I still hadn't started writing my play.

"You can't win if you don't even apply," he pointed out.

"French Dip, please." I ordered, and then shot back at him, "I can't lose, either. I prefer that."

"I give up. You're such a drama queen," Alec finally said, laying down the menu and crossing his arms.

"You wrote your speech about drama?" The voice came from over my shoulder and I jumped. Kristopher Lambert stepped into my line of sight, a smug look in his light-brown eyes. "Figures. You should have stuck to acting. Thanks for making sure I have the best speech in the school, Katsaros. I guess we know whose name they're announcing tomorrow." Of course he'd know about the announcement. Kris must live in the office, kissing principal and vice principal butt all the time.

I wrinkled my nose at him, but Grace was the one who spoke, making a dismissive gesture with her hand. "Excuse me, but did anyone ask you to jump into the middle of our private conversation? No. So, go away." Her eyes then widened and she quickly turned to say into her phone, "No, I wasn't talking to you. It's that guy, you know, the one who hates athletes?"

"I don't hate athletes," Kris said, his smile morphing into a grim straight line. "Anyway, good luck, Em. I promise to thank you in my acceptance speech when I win the competition." He tapped me on the shoulder, and then headed over to the counter. "Later."

"Bye, Kris," Phoebe said with a wave and smile.

I glared at her. "Traitor." At least the class president from hell was too far to hear us. I didn't need him to know he got to me with his mind-game ass-hattery.

Phoebe actually rolled her eyes at me. "He was joking, Em. Kris isn't that bad."

"You only say that because you had a crush on him." I had no idea what she saw in him. Even in his out-of-school clothes, from a polo to jeans I swore had a crease ironed into them, he looked like he was applying to the young politician's club or something, and he slicked his dark-brown-bordering-on-black hair into a style that would have made every male actor from the forties jealous. If it weren't for his ridiculous wardrobe and attitude, he had the potential to be hot, but hot probably wasn't "class presidential" or something.

Next to her, Dev stiffened, then tried to look nonchalant. Phoebe bumped him with her shoulder. "Had. Past tense," she said, more to him than me. Big grey eyes met mine and her smile grew wider. "He's probably just as nervous as you. Kris deals with things by trying to sound confident. You deal with stuff by either going all control-freak on us or panicking."

I didn't dignify that with a response.

Grace reached across the table and lay one perfectly manicured hand on my arm. "You'll be fine. And by this time tomorrow, it'll all be over and you can find something new to blow out of proportion."

"Real supportive, Grace." I slumped on the bench and focused on my salad. In twelve-ish hours, I'd know my fate.

4

No one else in homeroom was on edge. This was the downside of being alphabetically incompatible with any of my close friends except for Alec, who kept throwing me sympathetic looks from his desk in the back corner of the classroom. None of the other "late J" to "early M"-s understood why I was bouncing in my seat like I'd eaten two bags of chocolate-covered espresso beans, or why I kept looking over at the TV monitor in the corner of the classroom. Everyone else regarded the morning announcements as nothing more than the start of a school day. Today, for me, it meant learning my ultimate fate.

I fidgeted through the Pledge of Allegiance, then sat and gripped the underside of my hard plastic chair as I willed the sophomore reading the announcements to shut up and let MacKenzie take over the microphone. Finally, the vice principal's face filled the screen and I held my breath as he started to talk. I barely heard half of his words as he went on and on about the speech competition and how it was so prestigious and everything the state and national winners would get. "... and that's why I'm very proud to announce that New Jersey's female representative to the US

Youth Change Council speech competition this year will be Ephemie Katsaros…"

Oh. My. God. First reaction: cringing at my full name. Second reaction: The held breath rushed out of my lungs and I dropped my head onto my desk. I was still too wound up to feel anything beyond relief. This had been a million times more unnerving than any casting.

Alec made a whooping sound that echoed through the classroom, a happy scream that could only be Phoebe's echoed down the hall from another homeroom, and the people sitting around me reached out to pat my back, give me high fives, and grin at me.

I almost missed our Vice Principal's next words. "And, in an incredibly rare but wonderful coincidence, the male representative will also be from Pine Central. Congratulations, Kristopher Lambert."

My gaze shot to the back of the room, where Kris looked as shocked as I felt. But the shock soon smoothed over into one of his more annoying self-assured smiles. Without missing a beat, he started taking in the congratulations like the polished politician he wanted to be. It wouldn't surprise me if he reached up and slicked back his black hair, just in case there was a photo op.

Cassie, one of Grace's friends from the cheerleading squad, leaned over to bridge the space between our desks and whispered, "You know what this means, right?" I had to strain to hear her over the chaos that had descended over our homeroom.

"That I'm up against the most pompous ass in Lambertfield history?"

She cracked a smile. "No. Well, maybe, but also that you two get to spend an entire week together in Boston. Try not to kill him, okay?"

"Crap. I didn't think of that." The finalists all spent a week in Boston, doing live versions of their speeches for the judges while touring the city and taking part in a youth summit. As the New Jersey reps, that meant Kris and I would be stuck with each other through all the summit sessions.

Cassie pretended to think for a second, tapping her finger against her chin. "Actually, if he did happen to accidentally fall into the Boston Harbor, I don't think we'd be too depressed. Just saying." She let out a little laugh, probably at the expression of horror rushing over my face. "I'm kidding. Don't look so freaked out. I'm sure you'll have a great time, even with Mr. Class President over there."

"I—" I had no idea what to say. The bell rang and I shuffled through my backpack just to have something to do. Phoebe was probably already waiting out in the hallway and I needed another moment to absorb it all before getting caught up in her whirlwind of perkiness.

A knock on my desk made me look up and, instead of Alec, there was Kris, his light-brown eyes focused on mine. If eyes could smirk, his were the smirkiest ever at that moment.

"Go Jersey!" He held up a fist as if he expected me to fist-bump with him or something. "Looks like they had to fill their drama queen quota, but at least they stuck to

Lambertfieldians. First and second place are in the bag, right?" Over his shoulder, I could see Alec roll his eyes and point towards the hallway before heading out.

I ignored Kris' fist and, instead, stood up, putting space between us. Part of me itched to tell him where he could put that fist, but self-control won. "Right. I'll see you at the podium." With that, I swept out of the classroom, like Clark Gable after he said, "I don't give a damn," and right into Hurricane Phoebe.

She grabbed my arms and twirled me around like something out of a movie. "Oh my God, you did it." The twirl ended in a hug.

"State. I still need to beat everyone for national," I said into her sweater. My stomach twisted itself again and the wool was already starting to make my face itch. "Including Mr. Ego." Phoebe pulled back to arm's length and regarded me for a silent minute, her lips quirking into a smile. I couldn't help but grin back. "But, yeah, we did it." The excitement finally started to bubble through.

"I told you," Alec said before giving me one of his "I love you, but don't want to show too much affection so people don't think we're dating or something equally gross" restrained arm pats.

Grace hurried down the hall and suddenly we were in a giant group hug. My stomach unknotted and I laughed as Grace started an impromptu cheer right there in the Language Arts hallway. Alec kept going on about how his editing *obviously* helped. We all ignored the warning bell.

I had the best friends in the world.

I was going to Boston.

I bounced on my bed as I waited for Wil to log on to the video chat, trying not to let my nerves get to me. It was already 9:30 in Freiburg, which was so hard to process sometimes. It was always so weird to see the dark street through the window behind him while the sun still shone for me every time we talked.

My tablet dinged as Wil's videochat invite came up and I smoothed my hair one more time before tapping "connect."

"Hi," I said as his face filled the screen, hating how I sounded a little breathless. Nerves twisted my stomach into knots I knew would stay in place until minutes after our chat ended.

Wil's smile helped a few of the tighter knots loosen. Even through the sometimes-blurry connection, I could see the way the lights in his room shone off his hair like a blonde halo. With his square chin, sapphire blue eyes, and longish hair, he looked like a warrior out of Black Forest fairy tales. The perfect leading man. "Hello, beautiful."

I giggled, even though this was our daily ritual. It had been the first English phrase I'd jokingly taught him as an "American tradition." Even after I let him in on the joke, he still kept it up.

"I miss you," I said, hating the needy note that crept into my voice. "You've been so busy, it's like I never talk to you anymore."

"I have been very busy working. Oktoberfest season is very good for tour guides. They are giving me all the English and French tours I can do after school." It was so cute how formal he always sounded. "They know I am saving for December travel."

"December travel? Really?" I tried not to get my hopes up, but he had been working hard enough that he probably had made enough money for a flight back here to see me again. Tour guides always made a killing on tips, at least that's what it said online.

"Yes, I hope to visit my aunt and friends in Dresden."

Or maybe he'd surprise me with tickets to Germany, like he teased before he went back. "That's one of the places with a Christmas Market, right?" Dreams of wandering between the stalls in Dresden's market, eating stollen, and stealing kisses from Wil between sips of hot chocolate as tiny snowflakes fell around us warmed me.

"It is, but Freiburg has one, too, the best one, especially at the Munsterplatz. I will send pictures when it opens in November."

"That's awesome. I can't wait to see what you're always talking about." I took a deep breath and tried to let the excitement from the speech competition announcement wash over me again. A little part of me was annoyed that he hadn't asked anything about the competition yet—I'd messaged him the second I got home from the diner about my nerves about today's announcement, "I have news, too. Big news."

"News?"

The distant way he said it started to bother me, but I pushed away any annoyance. I had to always remind myself that English wasn't his first language and the poor guy was trying so hard. "You know that speech competition I entered? I—"

"Wilhelm!" Someone said something over his shoulder in German. He held up one finger apologetically and turned his head to respond. I could pick out *nein, computer,* and *Em,* but the rest was babble to me. Sharp babble, because a lot of German conversation always sounded so angry for some reason. After another back-and-forth, he turned back to me, a frown marring his features. Wil raked a hand through his hair. "I have to go."

I tried not to let any disappointment show on my face. "Okay." I wasn't going to try to cram my news into a few seconds.

He must have noticed something in that one word, since his expression grew softer. "We can talk tomorrow, *ja?*"

"*Ja.* Of course." I touched the screen, my fingers tracing his cheek. "Good night. *Ich liebe dich.*" I had to have butchered it, but he still gave me a huge smile. That still didn't mean he'd say "I love you" back, but it was worth a try.

"Good night."

The chat screen timed out once he logged off and I stared at my tablet background, my heart sinking right through my grey comforter, through my mattress, and into my grey rug. I reached up to touch the dried corsage hanging by its ribbon off of my headboard, cringing as the edge of one of the rose petals flaked off onto my fingers. This bundle I made of his carnation and my roses from the Junior prom was one of the few physical pieces I had from Wil. Everything else lived in my memory, or in my inbox.

"Life sucks," I said to my walls, just as my door creeped open.

A curly brown pigtail and one brown eye peeked into my room. "Are you done talking to your boyfriend?" a little voice asked, emphasizing *"boy."* I answered with a groan, and my door popped opened all the way, my little sister Chloe rushing in and landing on my bed with a thud.

I had to steady my tablet before it went flying off the bed. "You could have waited until I answered, at least. Or knocked."

Chloe shrugged and, in her usual self-important six-year-old fashion, ignored what I said. "Dad said you're going to Boston. Are you going with Phoebe? Can I go, too?" I opened my mouth to answer, but she barreled on. "If I go, can I wear that funny hat Phoebe bought me? And see where they threw the tea into the water? Can *we* throw tea into the water?"

"Mom!" I yelled in the direction of the open door.

"Mom's on the phone with Uncle Mike." Chloe said, bouncing off the bed and wandering over to my Mad-Hatter desk chair, the back curved to look like it was about to fall over. My uncle was a carpenter and he, Mom, and Dad had spent months making me a room full of awesome Alice-in-Wonderland-like furniture. My light-blue bookshelf curved in and out, a little cabinet peeking out of its side. Meanwhile, the green dresser tilted on a crazy curve that countered my mirror frame's tilt. I loved this room, down to the glittery yellow walls that were a perfect background for some of my classic movie posters. "She said to come bother you and Wil." Her expression turned serious, in perfect imitation of Mom. I wasn't the only actress in the family.

I snorted. Like we would be doing anything that needed a first-grade chaperone. My baby sister's perpetually sticky fingers wandered too close to the yellow fabric upholstery on my desk chair and I rushed over and swung her onto my vinyl beanbag chair. "Oh, no you don't. The last time you touched my chair, I was pulling pieces of lollipop off of it for days."

"I don't have candy today." She wiggled her fingers to show her empty hands. "Anyway, you still didn't answer. I want to go to Boston with you."

"Sorry, kid-lin, but you can't. It's a school thing. Not even Phoebe is going." At her pouty look, I flicked her nose. "Besides, it's going to be boring. We're going to spend every day in meetings. Like school."

Her little eyes narrowed with suspicion. "Every day? No way."

"Yes way. I told you, it's a school thing. It's going to be like when Mom and Dad made you go to my Shakespeare play. You know, like '*There's rosemary, that's for remembrance. Pray you love, remember. And—*'" I put on my best Ophelia-gone-crazy voice and mimed handing her a flower.

"Stop." Chloe made a face. "Ugh, that was so *dreary*."

"Who taught you that one? Phoebe or Alec?"

She crossed her arms and automatically fell deeper into the beanbag. "I have my own smart friends, thank you very much."

"Then, why aren't you bugging them, instead of me?"

"Because I have you right here. And you have nail polish." She waved those sticky fingers at the little cabinet door perched on my bookshelf where I kept everything I didn't want her to touch.

"Boston is going to be awesome. I might actually get some privacy," I said, sighing as I got up and opened the cabinet. "What color?"

Chloe swung herself onto my bookshelf to get a better view of the shelves. "Green."

I added a mental note to ask Dad to put a lock on my cabinet before I left.

From: Em (emkatsaros@dmail.com)

To: Wilhelm (wmeyer@dmail.de)

Re: Hi!

Hi sweetie!

I miss you so much. I hope everything's okay. Since you didn't answer Tuesday's email and your mom interrupted our call, I'm going to dump all my updates in here. How is it going? Did you present your class project yet?

Well, remember the A Doll's House auditions? I got Nora, of course. I know you don't know a lot about acting, but this role is *huge*. It makes me wonder a little if Mr. Landry chose it because he knew how great it would look on my applications. If I can pull it off, that is, because it's a really hard part, you know? And I have a guess about what we're doing for the spring musical, but I don't want to jinx it, so I'll tell you when Mr. Landry confirms it. Cross your fingers for me!

And I definitely didn't get to tell you that I actually won state in that speech competition! They haven't told me the details yet, but I get to go to Boston to compete in nationals. I don't know when yet. I really hope it's early December so I can see all the holiday lights and decorations. They definitely won't put it over any holidays, so it luckily won't mess with any plans I might want to make.

Speaking of holidays and plans, remember when we went into Philly last year and skated at the Dilworth Park rink and it started snowing? And then you kissed me? It was so perfect, until the guard kicked us off the ice. I wish I could go see the Christmas markets with you in Dresden, or that you could come here. Mom and Dad said definitely no to me flying out there because of the whole Dad's job and not stressing the budget thing. I'd love to see Europe. Have you thought about coming here? Everyone misses you, especially me, and it would be so awesome to get us all together again. Maybe we could even road trip up to Boston and I can show you everything I'll see when I'm up there for the competition. I'll be your personal tour guide ;)

Tell me you're flying back here. I miss you so much.

XOXOXOXOXOXO,

-em

Em,

It is good to see your email and all is good. I am very busy here, but good.

The play and competition are very good news. You worked hard and I am happy for you.

I do not know about Christmas. It is a very busy time. I have been saving for Dresden, the train is very expensive—about €120. It will be good to see my aunt and my friends.

Say hello to everyone.

Kindest Regards,

-Wil

5

"I don't want to die, Llamaman," I wailed, and curled myself into a pillbug-style little ball on the ground as the super-hero improv exercise I was doing with Dev dissolved into a ridiculous mess. Dev gave off another llama-call and my sides hurt as I silently burst into laughter, shoving my face into my knees so no one else in the theatre could see. Added bonus: my shaking would look like I was trembling in fear.

"You are safe with Llamaman," he said in a classic super-hero-y voice. Then, a sound just like my grandfather trying to hock up spit filled the air and Dev's next words were muffled as if he had something in his mouth. "Llamaman Spit Attack!"

"Dev, no, no—Cut," Mr. Landry yelled out and, thank-fully, Dev stopped whatever he had planned. Landry mum-bled something about janitors and overtime, then said, "That was good, both of you. Em, I would have liked to see a little more reaction from your character during the second attack. I understand that she was supposed to be shy and afraid, but you don't want to be too static in the back-ground. Even peeking out every now and again or trying to scoot away a little bit more would have given a little more visual interest—do you know what I mean?"

I nodded.

"Great." He clapped his hands together to get everyone's attention. "Good job today, everyone. We're starting *A Doll's House* rehearsals this Friday. Em, since you'll be out, I'd like to walk through some of Nora's key scenes first. It's a complex role, and I want you to study the text while you're out to really understand the character. If she isn't acted right, it'll make the entire play fall flat, so I'm depending on you to make it work. Matt, you'll want to do the same for Torvald, but I can help you through some of the basic characterization next week. Everyone else, read up, we're hitting the ground running with this one. Dev, I'll need you to stay late on Friday so we can figure out your Krogstad. You're all—"

Maya's giggle rang through the theatre and we all looked her way as she grabbed Kris' cell phone and typed something into it before handing it back to him and hopping off the stage. The boy really needed to wait for Matt outside of our practices or Matt needed to get another ride.

Landry didn't do anything more than raise an eyebrow at the interruption, then said, "—dismissed."

I shook my head at Maya's exit, then turned my squint back on Dev. "Were you actually going to spit?"

Dev grabbed his backpack from the pile of bags and shrugged it on his shoulders. "Mr. Landry said to stay in character." He waved at Phoebe, who was leaning against the wall at the back of the theatre. "You okay with getting home? Phoebe and I were going to the library to study but we can drop you off on the way there."

"I'm good, my dad's picking me up. Besides, you two don't need me breaking up the romantic atmosphere of moldy-smelling books and calculus."

"I appreciate that."

"I'm glad you do." I pretended to buff my nails on my sleeve. "Wingwoman-ing for you guys isn't easy."

"I'll be sure to mention that to Phoebe while we differentiate equations together." Phoebe waved again and he nodded at her. "Okay, I gotta go." Dev pat me on the arm before jumping off the stage in a very "Patrick Swayze at the end of *Dirty Dancing*" way.

"Show off," I yelled after him.

"No jumping off the stage," Landry yelled at the same time. Dev just threw us a thumbs-up and a grin on his way out.

I heaved my own overloaded backpack onto my shoulders and headed for the stairs, which Matt and Kris were blocking as Kris flipped through his phone. "...you tell her this time?" Matt asked, eyebrows raised. "This is what, the third time this week? Dude, if you and Maya—"

"Hell, no. I just said I accidentally deleted her number and I don't answer unknown calls. If I'd known she came to your rehearsals and didn't need her to operate the sound board for Spirit Week, I'd wait outside for you just to avoid her." Over his shoulder, I saw Kris delete Maya's number from his cell. "I'll just put up with her until November."

"Typical," I muttered, as I pushed past them with a barely polite "Excuse me."

They didn't stop talking, but I could clearly hear Matt say, "What's wrong with her?" as I made my way down the aisle to the exit.

"Drama divas. I have no idea how you tolerate…"

I pushed through the double doors before I could Kris go on his inevitable "artsy people are useless and overreact to everything" rant. I didn't need to be sucked in to a fight, and definitely didn't need any more stress in my life at the moment.

Boston was going to be bad enough, even without him.

6

Vice principals usually didn't call students out of first period for good news, but it at least got me out of hearing Ms. Singh drone on and on about derivatives. My heartbeat sped up as I hurried down the hall towards the office and clicked through all the possible reasons why MacKenzie wanted to see me. I wasn't failing any classes that I knew of and I hadn't cursed off any teachers like the one time Evan lost it in Chem. Maybe one of my parents were in an accident, like the time Mike Lyons was called out of English, or maybe something happened to Chloe... the pounding in my ears matched the fast clack of my shoes on the floor.

I had to hold back the urge to vomit.

Instead, I grabbed the office's door handle and forced myself to keep propelling forward. Without even saying a word, the office aide smiled at me and waved me towards MacKenzie's open door. Smiling was good, right? This was the nice aide, who I knew wouldn't smile if anyone was hurt, unlike the crankypants old lady who loved to deliver awful news.

"Is everything okay?" I blurted out as I skidded into MacKenzie's office.

The balding vice principal was talking with a guy in a familiar grey sweater, and, mid-sentence, let out a loud bark of a laugh. The boy shifted in his seat as he joined in and I realized why I recognized the sweater—it was the same one Kris had worn in homeroom that morning. Worry about Chloe or my parents was replaced by a new fear when the boy turned around to grin at me and it was Kris. They must have made a mistake when they announced the winners. Kris and MacKenzie were probably laughing over the absurdity of me even thinking I could possibly be a state winner.

MacKenzie cleared his throat and gestured towards the other empty chair in front of his desk. "Everything's fine, Ephemie. Come on in."

"Em," I said in a tiny voice. MacKenzie wasn't the type to take corrections lightly. I dropped into the chair, gently setting my bookbag on the floor next to my feet. Dev would totally make fun of me for feeling so timid around him.

"Em," he repeated, then smiled at me. "I called you in here to—"

Tell me I need to go back to being Eliza Doolittle and forget about playing the part of an upperclass speechwriter?

"—congratulate you on winning the speech competition. All of us here at PCHS are so proud of both you and Kris."

Kris smirked his superior smirk at me, like he'd been reading my mind. "Thank you, sir," he said, smooth as James Bond, while I probably looked like I was in the middle of a fish impression, gaping mouth, big eyes, and all.

MacKenzie didn't seem to notice my mental flail. "The

state committee told me they were impressed by the quality of both your entries. They said they hadn't heard speeches of this caliber in years, and especially not from the same school."

"That's…great," I squeaked out. I still hadn't gotten over the shock of not being told I sucked.

"I have the lucky privilege of filling you both in on the specifics." He slipped on his glasses and looked down at the paper in front of him. "The *US Youth Change Council* will be flying you both from Philadelphia to Boston. You'll spend a week in a youth summit and, on the last day, will both give live speeches to the judges. In your free time, the summit organizers have set up tours of Boston," he read aloud, then looked up to add, "I don't have to remind you that you will be representing not only this school but the entire state of New Jersey. I expect exemplary behavior from both of you." There was the MacKenzie we knew and loved.

"Lambertfield couldn't have better representatives, right, Em?" Kris prodded me with his elbow. "It's a given, considering we're from one of the best schools in the state."

I tried not to roll my eyes at his obvious suck-upishness and, instead, tried to play his game. It seemed to work with Vice Principals, at least. "Class President and Theatre Club star extraordinaire." I gave a mini-bow with a flourish of my hand. "We'll put those other states to shame with our model citizenry." I resisted the urge to stick my tongue out at Kris like a five-year-old.

"Right. Just don't get into trouble," MacKenzie said, then handed us both manila envelopes with our names scrawled across the top in permanent marker. As usual, my last name was misspelled. I looked over at Kris' and took way too much pleasure in the fact that they spelled his first name with a "C." "Those packets contain all of your information, including a parent permission slip. Since you'll be under the supervision of the conference organizers, there's also a code-of-conduct sheet I expect you both to memorize." His practiced stern expression smoothed back into a smile. "Oh, and some important information on prizes. By default, as state winners, you've both already won one thousand-dollar scholarships."

One thousand dollars. That was a drop in the bucket for college tuition, but it would definitely help. And if I won first place at nationals, I'd get thirty thousand dollars, enough to cover freshman and maybe a little bit of sophomore year. Dreams of hanging out on Rutgers' campus and maybe even being a part of their Shakespeare intensive danced through my head. "I…" I paused, unsure of what to say, and defaulted to, "…thanks."

"Eloquent." Kris winked at me, then stood and reached across the desk to shake the vice principal's hand. "I can't wait to show Boston what Pine Central has to offer."

I waved weakly at MacKenzie with my non-packet hand. Kris grabbed my elbow and steered me out of the office and into the hall. Once we were out of hearing, I shook free of his grip. "Eloquent? Really?"

"No, not really. Maybe your sarcasm meter is broken."

"We're supposed to play nice, you know. This isn't one of your elections."

"I am playing nice." He leaned so close to me, I could see the dark-brown ring around the honey brown of his eyes. "If I wasn't, I would've already found a way to get under your skin and freak you out so much that you wouldn't even remember what a speech is. It would be so easy, because this is *my* world, not yours." I blinked and took a step back, which made his eyes crinkle in a smile. "But, like I said in homeroom, I want us to corner first and second place. Do you realize how awesome that would be?"

"It would be more awesome if you stayed three hundred miles away from me instead."

Kris snorted and turned to walk down the hall. "Keep dreaming, 'theatre club star.'"

I sucked back the urge to throw my bookbag at him and collected myself. There was no way he was going to psych me out.

I kicked the nearest locker and headed back to pre-calc.

The second time I was called down to the office that day, I was more worried about another extended "make nice" session with Kris than any potential family disasters. But when the aide waved me into MacKenzie's office, the other chair was empty and the vice principal's desk phone had been pushed to the center of his desk. He gestured for me to sit and followed it with the cheesiest thumbs up ever. The man was the epitome of the middle-aged balding vice principal trope. "Okay, she just walked in."

"Is this Ephemie Katsaros?" The older woman's resonant

and strong voice sounded familiar through the speaker-phone, but I couldn't place it.

I slipped into the chair, my forehead crinkling as I stared at the phone. "This is Em."

"Em, this is Dr. Lladros. I was one of the judges for our state for the Change Council speech competition."

My eyes grew wide and I found myself bracing my hands against MacKenzie's desk as I leaned closer to the phone. I pulled on every acting bone in my body to keep my tone as even as possible. "I know who you are. Thank you so much for picking me."

"You earned it. Your delivery was beautiful and you really managed to capture the attention of the entire judging panel in a very memorable way." She didn't let me finish my squeak of thanks before saying, "You were at the acting intensive at Mason Gross this summer, weren't you?"

"Yes."

"I thought your name sounded familiar." I held back an excited squeak at those words. Dr. Lladros remembered my name from the workshop. Of course, there weren't a lot of Ephemies in the world and especially not people my age, but still. "Anyway, I really wanted to call you to congratulate you on winning at the state level and look forward to seeing how you do at nationals. I can only imagine you'll get better with the coaching they provide during the competition."

"Wow. Thanks. I'll do my best."

"I expect you to. I hope you and Kristopher know there is an entire team of judges cheering you on back home. I'll be watching the awards ceremony and I think you'll both do New Jersey proud."

"Thank you." I stared at the phone for at least a full minute after she hung up, completely unsure of what had just happened. When it actually hit me, a thrill ran through my entire body, followed by a cold splash of dread. Now I definitely couldn't lose.

MacKenzie pulled the phone back towards himself. "That was a nice surprise, wasn't it? Usually judges don't bother to reach out like that. Sounds like you made a good impression."

"Did she talk to Kris, too?" I asked, and my voice sounded distant, like I was detached from my body.

"No, she just asked for you."

"Okay," I whispered to myself, then stood and picked up my backpack, still feeling like I was in the middle of an out-of-body experience. "Okay." I started towards the door before realizing the Vice Principal was still sitting there. I stopped at the threshold and turned around to say, "Thank you."

"You're welcome. Stop at the desk on your way out and they'll give you a pass."

"Thanks."

7

"Hey." Alec poked his head into my bedroom. "Do you want some company?"

It was around four, which meant he probably just got out of Science Club. "Done taking science tests?" How he could take physics and chemistry tests for fun was beyond me. I waved him into my room and grimaced as he dropped so hard onto my beanbag chair the seams squeaked in protest. I rolled onto my stomach and inched to the side of my bed so he could see my face. "Dad let you in, didn't he?"

Alec wiggled deeper into the chair, trying to get comfortable. "Your dad loves me. And I bribed him with Mom's mac and cheese."

"Huh?"

"I told her about his cooking experiments and she thought she'd save you guys from starving to death."

Thank the mac and cheese gods. Mom wasn't the biggest fan of traditional gender roles, but had learned early on in their marriage that cooking was one chore she and Dad could never share. Dad's "I'm bored, so I'll help make dinner" moods he'd gotten into the past few weeks had confirmed that with each ever increasingly disastrous dinner.

And Alec's mom's cooking was the best in Lambertfield, if not all of New Jersey. "Your mom's the best."

"She's pretty awesome. So." He picked up one of the books Phoebe had lent me and started flipping through the pages like it was a flipbook, filling my room with a whirring sound. "Your dad seems upbeat."

"He's always upbeat unless his soccer team loses or he's telling me how I'm going to end up penniless in some New York City crack den apartment if I decide to just pursue acting. Which, by the way, was his mood last night."

"That's really specific."

I put on my best Dad expression and shifted into Dad's heavy accent. "Ephemie, the arts are important, but you need something to pay the bills. Look at your cousin Vasilis. He's trying to be an actor, too, and he can't afford dinner most of the time."

"I can't understand Greek, but I've seen your cousin's videos online. He kind of sucks."

I waved my hand in a "that's beside the point" motion. "You know Mom and Dad. It's all about doing what's safe and practical."

"That's not always a bad thing, you know."

"Well, look at where safe and practical got Dad. The people who sat around in the office doing nothing only to leave exactly at five on the dot got to stay but people like him who busted their asses every day for, like, ten or twelve hours got laid off." I could hear the bitterness creeping into my voice and took a deep breath before saying, "Sorry, I'm just—"

Alec's lips set in a straight line and he tilted his head in exasperation at me. "C'mon Em, you don't have to pretend everything's okay with me, you know. It's already stupid how you do that with Grace and Feebs. Besides, your parents tell my mom everything, anyway." He pulled his sketchbook out of his backpack and handed it to me. "Here, weigh in on my character designs while you freak out."

I faked a long-suffering sigh and took the book from him before saying, "Whining isn't going to suddenly make my parents the 'follow your dreams, we totally support you' types. And whining isn't going to bring Wil back from Germany. Besides, you know Grace would just try to give me advice to fix things and Phoebe would hover and worry." I quirked up one corner of my lips and pretend-fluffed my hair. "I need to project an aura of pure and utter confidence to the world."

"I can see through that aura-thing."

"That's because you're practically a Katsaros. We've got good BS-meters."

He put down the book, and crossed his arms. "Since I have this awesome BS-meter, I can tell something's up. What happened in the meeting with MacKenzie?"

"Ugh." I flipped onto my back and spoke to the ceiling. "It's just...Kris."

"Why are you letting that bother you so much? You're going to be going up against a hundred other kids, so who gives a crap about one guy from our school?"

I heaved a giant sigh. "Because that one guy does

everything possible to not just win but destroy his opponents. He said as much to me today. I'm positive I'm going to be his special target during this competition."

"Okay, Kris can be a jerk, but you're exaggerating."

"Lani was in tears halfway through the student council president debate," I said, though I shouldn't have had to remind him.

"Lani was also in tears when they ran out of burrito bowls last Friday."

It took everything in me not to face-palm. "You know; you really lack an emotional sensitivity gene. If you saw her crying, you should have swept in like a knight in shining armor and given her your burrito bowl. That's how you get dates." It was nice to focus on something that wasn't about Kris for a few seconds.

"Em." Alec did not sound amused.

A plan formed in my head. I could invite Lani to sit at our lunch table next week… "She's actually really pretty and freakishly smart, except for the political thing. You two would be really cute together."

"Em…" He said in a warning tone. "No."

"Sorry. But you have to admit I do my best match-making when I'm stressed about stuff." I paused, and then everything I'd been holding back all came out in one long stream of worry. "Fine. About Kris destroying people. You realize he doesn't even need a freaking scholarship, so I don't know why the hell he even bothered to do this competition except to screw everyone else over. And he's going to waltz into Boston and mess with my head for an entire week to make me lose just for laughs. And because Mom and Dad are all about college because '*college*,' without scholarships, I'll have one less argument I can give them and then I'm going to have to go to Mom's university because it'll be free and *practical* and because they don't have a decent theatre program, become an accountant or something…"

"Hey, my mom's an accountant." Alec swiped at me with the book, but missed.

"Yeah, but she wants to be and I don't. Your mom's a perfect example of what happens when artists don't put all their focus on their art. She wanted to be a ballet dancer, but was trying to be practical and study stuff, and boom, no ballet career."

"Yeah, but she always says she was happy with that decision. She didn't love ballet enough to try to scrape by when she didn't get into any of the big companies. You're different. You'll do anything to be on stage, even if it means living in a crack den in New York."

I tilted my head back over the edge of the bed so I was looking at him upside down and the faux-serious expression on his face made me crack up. "True." I waited until the stitch in my side stopped hurting from laughing and said, in a much softer tone of voice, "Half of this started because of what happened with Dad's job. God, imagine if I could get that first-place scholarship? It would pay for at least an entire year. Mom and Dad at least can't say anything freshman year if I'm going for free."

"That's a really big thing to pin your hopes on, you know. You'd have to beat the best speeches in the entire country. And military base regions. And US territories."

"You don't think I can do it?"

"I'll let Grace calculate the odds against you. And, honestly?" I froze and waited for his next words. Nothing good ever followed the words "and honestly." "Your speech is really good and your voice gives me chills when you read it, but you're not into speechwriting. You're a performer, not really a writer. There are probably people at nationals who live and breathe this stuff and have speeches a million times better than yours."

"Et tu, Alec?" Behind the mock hurt in my words was the bitter taste of bile. Grace was usually the one who carried the sledgehammer of painful truths.

He powered on. "If you win and get the scholarship, that's awesome, but you might not. And that's okay, just go on student loans. Your parents will get over it."

"You don't know my parents."

"Actually, I do. Remember, practically a Katsaros?"

"You don't get it. Your mom is all about letting you follow your dreams."

"To be fair, she's also really happy I want to double major in computer science and graphic art. Actually, she's *really* happy that I didn't just decide that I don't need to go to college and move to, like, Japan or Korea to try to work in gaming or animation or something."

"Well, *my* Mom and Dad don't believe in putting yourself

in debt. I'll probably be ninety and they'll be haunting me from beyond the grave with 'See? You shouldn't have put yourself in debt for a dream.' Even if I end up doing great." I raked my hands through my hair in frustration and muttered a curse at the massive frizz I probably just caused. "Winning this would be awesome. It would be like wasting free money if I don't use the scholarship." I absently flipped to the next page in his sketchbook and held it up to him, pointing at my favorite character sketch on the page. "I get it, I really do. I don't want to be stuck with crappy loans, either, but I also don't want to go to Schuylkill University only because it's free."

"I just don't want you to go into this expecting to get first, or even place in the top ten."

"I'll keep looking for more scholarships. And Rutgers is a state school, so that should help if I get in. And it's not too far to commute, so that will save money." I shrugged and added, "I have to do really good in the competition, anyway. That professor said she'll be watching out for me. If I win, I'll impress her, get an extra leg up on the gajillion other people applying for a spot there, get the scholarship so I can take away mom's and dad's argument as to why I should go to SU, and everything will be perfect." I flipped to another page in his sketchpad and stopped at a drawing of a super-creepy little girl that looked like an evil Victorian doll. "This one for level two. It would scare the hell out of anyone."

"I was thinking of making that one's attack be spiders swarming all over the player."

"You're going to give small children nightmares. I love it."

"You know, if I pull off this game, I just might decide to drop out, start up a game company, and then mom and your parents can talk about me being the creative disappointment of the 'family,' instead." He grinned, taking back his sketchbook and dropping it on the floor.

"You're a sciencelete, which makes you perfect in their eyes. You'd have to do something like decide you're going to become a hermit and live off nature deep in the woods before you ever reach my level."

A laugh boomed out of him. "Speaking of, you might want to start your homework. You're the one who's going to be missing physics for a week and I'm not helping you remotely while you're in Boston."

"Hmph." I side-eyed him as I pulled out my tablet and physics notes. "Killjoy."

"Plus, you need to stop blowing things out of proportion with Kris." Alec used the book he'd been flipping through to poke me in the shoulder. "Just ignore him. Meanwhile, I'll keep an eye out for more scholarships. You'll be okay no matter what happens in Boston."

I wanted to hug him.

I sent about the tenth text to Wil and waited. His fastchat status was green, so I knew he was online. "C'mon, Wil," I muttered, then sent another chat request.

His face finally popped up on the screen, his brow furrowed and lips set in a straight line. "I cannot talk right now."

"But we were scheduled to talk fifteen minutes ago and you've missed our last two chats. I miss you."

His expression didn't soften like it usually did when I said I missed him. "I have no time. I have school and other important things I must do."

"I should be the only important thing in your life," I said with a grin. At his pained look, I added, "I'm joking, you know."

"I just came home from a nighttime tour and have not had dinner. I need to finish this paper so I can eat."

"But I've been sitting here trying to get you for the past fifteen minutes. I deserve some of your time, too. We have a schedule and you keep breaking it without even bothering to text me about rescheduling."

"The schedule is not working. I do not like feeling like I'm tied to the phone because of you. I feel like I cannot have a normal life because you always demand my attention."

My smile faded away and lead started filling my lungs. "That's not fair," I said, softly.

"What is not fair is feeling like I have two mothers. We need to stop—" He said something in German but didn't bother to translate.

I narrowed my eyes at him, wishing I had a voice translation app on my tablet. "Stop what?"

"Stop talking. I do not want every minute of my life scheduled by a girl on the other side of the world."

The lead grew until it filled my stomach and my limbs. "Are you breaking up with me?"

"Maybe that is a good idea."

I cringed as he said it, then forced myself not to show how much his comment bothered me. "Maybe you're an asshole." His expression didn't shift and I decided to elaborate in slow, perfectly enunciated words so he couldn't misunderstand. "If you do this now, we're over for good, do you understand? This isn't going to be like our other fights, where I forgive and forget and we get back together."

His only answer was to disconnect the chat.

8

Phoebe carefully led me to the currently deserted "sit and knit" corner of the yarn shop and pointed me at the worn, over-stuffed couch covered in fuzzy afghans. "Sit, I'll be right back."

I dropped onto the couch and was automatically swallowed by it, like I'd fallen into a cocoon made of wool and eighties paisley. Phoebe hurried back in from the back room, carrying a package and two mugs. She dropped the package onto the yarn-covered coffee table, but handed me the mug and then snuggled next to me, tucking one of the afghans around both of us. "Drink."

She was just adorable. I looked over at her in amusement and sniffed at the mug. "This tea smells like a peanut butter cup."

"Mmmhmm. Cassandra gets it shipped from that Canadian tea store she loves." I took a sip, and while I was still trying to process the weirdness of tea tasting like chocolate-covered peanut butter, she said, "Okay, start."

My amusement at Phoebe in caregiver mode faded away to nausea. "Wil broke up with me this time."

"Ouch. I'm so sorry, Em."

"Does he think he's the only one stressed with this

long-distance relationship crap? I had to set up all of our chats and keep track of time zones and schedules, but God forbid he show up to anything in the last few weeks. He's acting like *I'm* the one imposing on *him*." My hands started shaking, so I put down the mug before I could spill its contents all over myself.

"That's not fair to you." Phoebe said, her tone soothing.

I felt my lips slide into a straight line as I nodded. "I won't let him off easy. When he comes back to his senses, it'll take a few apologies before I let him get back together with me this time."

Phoebe's fingers twisted in the holes of the afghan, like she was trying to avoid what she was about to say. "You know, every time you two broke up in the past, you were the one who did the breaking up. Are you sure it's not different this time?"

"I am." I ignored the giant stone that had settled in my stomach, souring the tea in my mouth, and added, as convincingly as I could, "Wil and I are stronger than a little fight."

She twisted the edge of the afghan even more. "I don't know, you two never really talked after your fights, you just made out and everything was okay. You can't exactly do that when he's on a completely different continent."

"Since when did you become a relationship expert?" Her words made the stone in my stomach multiply, but I pushed her with my shoulder and said, "Don't worry, we'll be fine. The two of us have an epic romance, like *Sleepless in Seattle*, just with actually knowing each other first." I pictured a romantic reunion at the top of the Empire State Building, where I'd be wearing the scarf he bought me last year and he'd be holding a giant bouquet of yellow roses, snow falling around us as we embraced with the New York city skyline shining around us.

Phoebe raised an eyebrow at me, but instead leaned forward to grab the bundle from the table. She handed me the wrapped package. "Here, I made this for you for Boston." As I pulled the off-white sweater out of the tissue paper, she added, "October can get cold up there."

The sweater was mostly sleeves and long, wide strips with a button—it looked like one of those cool modern wrap sweaters I'd pointed out to her in a magazine a few weeks ago, but she'd need to teach me how to wear it. "I need to keep breaking up with Wil. I swear, every time I do, you make me something."

Phoebe smiled over her mug. "It's because you're knit-worthy. And the knitworthy get all the things." She tilted her head to the side until it was on my shoulder. "Promise me you'll forget about trying to fix things with Wil until after the competition is over? You already have enough to stress about, you don't need this, too."

"You're sweet. I'll be fine."

"I know. But sometimes it's nice to let others worry for you, okay?"

"I promise." But I crossed my fingers as I said it.

"Grandpa Mike and his friends called Nana Betsy the Belle of the USO." Mom pointed at a faded picture of our great-grandmother in a very forties outfit and hair standing in front of a door marked "USO" before carefully turning the page of the yellowed scrapbook. Chloe had pulled the book out of the shelves in the living room and had brought it over to Mom after dinner. She was curled in Mom's lap, holding the book, and Mom smiled down at her, adding. "He was head-over-heels, crazy-in-love with her."

"And she never let him forget it," Dad chimed in, with a laugh. "'Honey, you love me more than anything, right? Then get me my glasses." His imitation of Nana Betsy was dead-on, at least from what I could remember, except with Dad's accent, it sounded even funnier. I was leaning against him on the sofa and both of us shook with laughter. I'd heard these stories a million times before, but, even though I had homework, I couldn't turn down another chance to hear them again.

"You take after her, Em." Mom reached over to smooth a hand over my hair, gentle enough that she wouldn't crunch my curls. "Definitely in the personality..."

"Hey! Nana Betsy was awesome."

"...but she was also a wonderful singer. Some say she might have been as big as Ella Fitzgerald if she hadn't decided to work in the factories during the war, instead."

"Who's that?" Chloe asked.

Mom took the scrapbook out of Chloe's hands and deposited it and my sister on the coffee table before getting up and walking over to the sound system. "Only my favorite singer ever." She poked at the screen before smiling over at my sister. "I think you'll like this one." *A-Tisket, A-Tasket* came over the speakers and Mom grabbed Chloe's hands and started bouncing her around the room in time to the music. "This was your grandmother's favorite song."

"She could have been just like Ella, you know," I said as I watched them swing around the room. "I've heard Nana's recordings."

Mom frowned, but didn't stop dancing. "A lot of girls wanted to be her, but you know, there's only one Ella Fitzgerald. We don't hear about those other girls."

"But—" I started, trying to get a word in as Mom barreled on with an all-too-familiar lecture.

"Nana knew her dreams weren't as important as taking care of the people at home. There are only a few spaces in the sky for supernovas in jobs like that, Em. It's not a guarantee and there are a lot of failures. She had to choose and she chose reality."

I folded my arms and looked over at Dad for support. "If you don't try, you don't have a chance to succeed," I said. It hit me that I was repeating Dev's advice to me, but I didn't let myself get hung up on the irony.

Dad nodded. "That is very true. You can try, but you have to make sure you can support yourself. Dreams are nice, but they don't buy dinner."

"Some do," I said, and started inching forward on the couch. If this was going to turn into another lecture about studying something practical in school, I was out.

"What about me?" Chloe piped up after quietly watching us for a minute, "Do I take after Nana Betsy?" Mom laughed, twirling her around as the band picked up pace.

Dad was the one who answered. "No, you're more like *Papouli* Christos." At Chloe's disappointed face at being compared to our grandfather on Dad's side, he added, "Nana Betsy was a butterfly, like Em, a lot of love and color and excitement everywhere she goes, but very fluttery sometimes. *Papouli* Christos was steady and reliable, more like a dove, like you." His answer only made her pout stick out a little further and he added, "He was a famous diplomat and peacemaker, you know. You're very good at bringing people together, just like him."

"A butterfly sounds like a lot more fun."

Dad was right, though. For someone as young as she was, Chloe was always the one fixing things with us and with her friends. I didn't completely agree with the butterfly comment, though. "Well, you're a very colorful dove," I said, getting up and joining her and Mom in some silly swing-like dancing as another song came on. "There's definitely some butterfly in those feathers."

"I like that." She pulled Dad off the couch so we were all dancing. Chloe really was like Papouli Christos.

"So do I."

9

My face hurt from smiling for the camera. The County news-paper photographer had been taking individual pictures of Kris and me all over the school for over an hour. He'd just finished getting a few of me perched on the low wall by the school entrance, pretending to read a piece of paper that was supposed to be my "speech." He waved at me to relax and, as I hopped down to the ground, said, "Can you grab Kris? I'd like to get a few of the two of you together."

"Sure." I wiped wall-dirt off my buttand made my way over to the flagpole, which Kris was leaning against casually while tapping at his phone. They'd gotten some super-patri-otic shots of him there earlier, looking as if he'd just hoisted the flag up the pole. It was almost too cliché, even for him. "Hey, Kris," I called out as I approached, "they want both of us now." Even though I knew he heard me, Kris didn't even look up from his phone, just kept tapping away at the screen like I wasn't even there. I felt my fist clench enough to wrinkle the paper I was holding, and I tried again, letting annoyance drip into my tone. "Kris."

He kept his eyes glued to his phone, his lips in a straight line, and held up a finger in a "one-minute" gesture.

"Well, Mr. Class President, when you're done with whatever is more important than three people sitting around waiting for you to grace us with your presence, we'll be over at the entrance." When he didn't say anything again, I huffed and made my way back to the photographer and reporter. "I tried, but—"

Before I could finish, Kris' voice piped in from behind me. "'Ready for my closeup, Mr. DeMille.'" I turned and saw that he had a major shit-eating grin on his face as he slipped his gaze over to me. "Or is that your, line, Em?" he asked, like he hadn't just pointedly ignored me a minute before, or just basically insulted me with a *Sunset Boulevard* misquote of a line said by a delusional actress.

"Cute." *Not.* "Done texting?"

He made a big show of slipping his phone into his back pocket, then turned towards the photographer and journalist. "So, what do you have planned for us next?"

"Considering you're both state winners, it would be nice to showcase you together." The photographer said.

"Especially since the two of you seem to get along so well. That will make for a great story," the reporter added with a smile as the photographer squinted at the position of the sun and the school's covered entryway, camera up as if he was checking his next possible shots.

"Em and I've been in school together since kindergarten. It's awesome that we both get to represent our state like this," Kris said before I could answer, his response as polished as the overpriced watch on his wrist.

"I love that. Mind if I quote you?"

While the reporter and Kris chatted, the photographer started moving us around, positioning us back-to-back and saying, "Okay, now cross your arms." I followed his instructions, posing like a pro since this super cliché position was used in promo photos for practically every play or musical that involved a rivalry.

While the photographer clicked away, the reporter had propped her cellphone on her notepad and was scribbling notes while shooting questions our way. "How does it feel knowing you have to compete against one of your classmates?"

"Technically, we already competed for state," I pointed out.

"Not really, considering we only compete against own genders on the state level. You haven't gone against me yet," Kris said, turning his head to smile down at me. It was the same smile he turned on every time he was trying to get something out of someone. Even though I knew it was all for the cameras, I wasn't totally immune and had to catch myself as my own smile softened more than it should. Kris scrunched his nose and twitched his eyebrow up the slightest amount in a smug look before turning to grin at the camera again. "I think it's going to be fun. I still haven't heard Em's speech, but you know Pine Central students are the best at everything we try."

I let the photographer move me around, this time arranging my hand on my hip and linking Kris's arm through mine while we were still mostly back-to-back. When he told us to look at each other, I met Kris' eyes with a challenging smile of my own and said, in a voice that would give Glinda the Good Witch a run for her money, "And we're also super competitive. I can't wait to kick Kris' butt when we get to Boston." At the flicker of surprise in his eyes that I wasn't going to play the perfect PR game he'd been playing, I added, "It's *definitely* going to be a lot of fun."

We stared each other down and neither of us noticed when the photographer had stopped taking pictures. "That's the shot," he said, stopping to flip back through the images on his camera and pointing one out to the journalist, then turning the camera to show us. "You're both really photogenic. You look great together."

I untangled myself from Kris and stared at the screen, shifting uncomfortably at the story the image was projecting. The photographer had caught the moment between us when I'd basically told Kris I was going to crush him, but instead of looking like we were smiling while plotting each other's murder, it had a perfect combination of competition and fire. I didn't like the buzz it caused in my veins—we looked incredibly hot, and I didn't know a photo could lie so much.

Beside me, Kris was also frowning at the picture. "I don't know. Don't we look a little—"

"Perfect." The reporter cut him off with a smile. "We'll check the other pictures, but Kyle's right," she nodded at the photographer, "that's exactly what we need for this article. Two friends from the same school, fiercely pitted against each other in a national competition but cheering each other on at the same time. I love it."

"Okay," I said, not able to completely hide my unconvinced tone, and just barely heard Kris make a snorting sound he covered with a cough. For once, it sounded like we were in agreement about something.

10

"Toothbrush?" Grace said, reading off a list, and I waved my little zipper-bag of tooth care at her before tossing it into my suitcase. "Brush?"

"I'm a curly. No brushes for me." Instead, I grabbed my shower comb and tossed it in after the zipper-bag.

"Right." Grace hopped off her perch on my desk and came over to inspect our progress. "I think we're ready for clothes now."

Alec's head shot up from the game he was playing on his phone. "Whoa. If you girls are going to start throwing underwear around, I'm out of here." He inched my smooshy chair closer to the door.

"Relax. I'll take care of that later so I don't offend your delicate sensibilities." I snorted then started rolling my pajamas into a packable log.

"Please do."

Phoebe looked up from her book. She'd been reading on my bedroom floor for the past hour, lost in one of her imaginary worlds. "You know what? Being truly immortal would suck."

The rest of us turned to stare at her. Well, at least I

stared. "Where did that come from?" I was probably going to regret asking.

She waved the book in the air so we could see its girl-in-a-dress cover. "Genevieve is immortal in this book. Nothing can kill her. Imagine what it would be like when the world actually ends? She'd be the only one left, unless she can make more immortals."

Grace calmly turned the packing list that had come in my information packet to the next page. "Even worse, when our sun goes supernova, she'd be floating around in space naked because all her clothes would get burnt off in the explosion. And since no one can hear you in space, she won't even be able to talk to herself," she said, like responding to Phoebe's comment was the most normal thing in the world.

I opened my mouth to stop this geekfest, but then Alec jumped in. "That's nothing. What'll happen to her when the universe starts shrinking back in on itself?" he asked, a grin spreading across his face. "I hope this character isn't claustrophobic."

Dropping my head into my hands so no one could see the smile starting to snake across my lips despite my best efforts, I said, "You all do realize you're talking about someone in a book, right?"

"Actually, Grace and I are talking about physics."

Grace's girlfriend, Leia, shot me a sympathetic look, but her lips were pressed together and I could tell she was trying to keep from laughing. "Okay, back to packing," she said in a tight voice before letting a giggle escape. We were the least nerdy people in the room. Grace, in her cheerleader uniform, was a stealth geek, but a geek nonetheless.

My phone buzzed and I pulled it out of my pocket, swiping my finger over the fingerprint recognition button to unlock my screen. Wil had posted a picture of a busy city street from his car dash while stopped at a red light. Right at the very top of the picture, the Pine Central lanyard I'd given him was hanging from his rearview mirror.

Leia peeked over my shoulder, then looked over at me, her brows narrowed in confusion. "I thought you two broke up."

"Yup." I nodded while flipping on the translate function: *So happy to think of a nice day special person.*

Leia snaked her arm around me and took my phone out of my hands, then stepped back before I could get it back. "So why are you getting," she glanced at the screen, "Photogram notifications for his posts?"

I glanced over at the other three for help, but they were in a heated debate about whether or not immortality extended to clothes if the person was wearing them. I looked back over at Leia, who rolled her eyes in solidarity before gesturing back at the phone, prompting me to say something. "Because we're just on a little break and I want to keep tabs on him. Why should I turn off notifications when we're getting back together soon, anyway?"

She put one hand on her hip in what Phoebe called her "teacher pose" and nodded. "Okay, and what if you don't get back together?"

That comment made my heart lurch, but I waved it away. "We will. It's not a real breakup, just a bump in our love story. Every good one has rough patches." I grabbed my phone from her before she could do something drastic, like unfollow him. "Besides, just because I'm not dating someone doesn't mean I'm not friends with them. I mean, I follow your Photogram and Phoebe's, even though her feed is just yarn and fancy pictures of the books she's reading."

"Hey, I heard that," Phoebe said, midway through flipping pages in her book to find something to support her argument, "and bookgrams are a real thing."

"Okay. Just remember what people post online is a really carefully chosen set of things they want others to see. And online doesn't always reflect real life." Leia's expression grew extra serious, and her tone soft. "Don't pin your hopes on a few pictures and bad translations."

My pride wouldn't let me show how much that last sentence affected me. Leia didn't always give advice, but when she did, it was like getting hit by a nice asteroid. "Believe me, I won't."

"Good. Because the great Em Katsaros, speechwriter and actress extraordinaire, should never have to keep tabs on anyone." Before I could say anything else, she nodded and smiled in a way that let me know she was done advising me. "What do you think? Since they're busy over there, should I start helping you pack? Because I think you should rock a pair of jeans for the semi-formal thing." She reached for my red-and-orange Pine Central hoodie, her reddish-black angled bob sweeping forward with her movement.

Pursing her lips but also sharing a smile with Leia, Grace nudged her away from my suitcase. "Conference gala: Semi-formal attire required," she read aloud from the packing list, looking pointedly at her. "That's the Betsey Johannsen dress you bought at the outlets, Em. Belt, heels, and clutch," she ticked off on her fingers while I grabbed all those things from my closet and stuffed them in the bag.

The heels were a nightmare to pack and I jammed them between my jeans and socks. Considering Grace had borrowed them from her mom and those shoes cost more than everything else in the bag, I was surprised she didn't cringe. "I still can't believe you pulled this off on my parents' budget." The dress was designer, the last one on the clearance rack and exactly my size and style. The jeans were more expensive than any other pairs I'd ever owned, but Grace had somehow found a pair for ninety percent off.

"Please. I'm like the Yoda of shopping *and* I'm in AP calc. I can work with a budget," Grace said, pulling the headband I had been planning to wear with the dress out of my bag and tossing it onto my desk. She rifled through the things on my dresser and pulled out Nana Betsy's black rose pin. "Put this in your hair, instead. It'll be different and dramatic, but still really pretty."

"Phoebe asked you to do this as payback for her make-over, didn't she?" I glared at my best friend, who dipped her head even deeper into her book.

"It could be worse—it's not like I'm threatening to

restock your entire makeup bag. Besides, the gala is the night before judging starts. You need to make a memorable impression since the judges might actually be there," Grace said. A sweater joined the pile in my rapidly overflowing bag.

"Thanks for giving me something else to freak out about. It's not like I'm not already panicking about losing, you know."

"You already won state. You'll be fine," Alec said. "And if you don't, you'll still be fine. We don't give a crap if you come in last."

"Not helping," Leia pointed out.

Alec threw her a stinkeye and mumbled something about girls and drama.

"Em, you totally own the stage. Even for band. I don't know why you're freaking out." Phoebe closed her book and looked me directly in the eye. "You're the most confident person I know. Don't let me down."

I shook my head, cold fear starting to make its way through my veins again. All of them had no idea how much of my confidence could be an act, sometimes. "This is different. If I screw up on stage, I can improv to the next line, or pretend I'm playing the right notes. If I screw up during the speech—"

"Keep going and don't let it phase you. You're an actress. Become one of the great speechmakers. Like..." Leia waved her hands in the air while thinking, "Lincoln. Be Lincoln."

"Four score and seven years ago," I intoned in a deep voice and pretended to adjust an imaginary top hat. "Kris probably doesn't have to pretend to be Lincoln, though I bet he wants to *be* him."

Grace cracked a smile. "The only thing Kris does is project confidence. I bet, deep down in his shriveled little politician heart, he's just as terrified as you are. He just doesn't show it," she said. "It's like cheering. When Millbrook is crushing our team, I still need to sound like I think we have a chance, even though there's more possibility of me falling for the quarterback and having babies with him than our guys ever scoring a touchdown on their defense."

"That was a visual I didn't need," Leia said with a mock cringe.

"Don't worry. I only go for cute brown-eyed girls. And Millbrook's quarterback is an idiot, anyway." She paused in her packing to reach over and squeeze her girlfriend's hand.

Leia's laugh filled the room and she turned to me. "Hands off, she's all mine." Right. I was the only other girl in the room with brown eyes. Those two had been together for so long, they had such an easy way with each other, like being together was as simple as breathing. I felt a twinge of jealousy followed by the awful realization that Wil and I hadn't had the chance to get to that.

"Don't worry. She's too high-maintenance for me," I said in the lightest voice I could manage.

"Hey!" Grace tapped me on the head with a rolled up t-shirt. "Don't bite the hand that will make you look amazing."

"I didn't ask you to," I said, reaching for my rolled-up yoga pants and pointing them at her like a fencer. Worry about Kris and the competition slipped to the back of my mind as I lunged forward, aiming for her head in a move I learned from the theatre-club weapons choreographers.

Grace ducked as the yoga pants nearly messed up her perfect cheerleader high ponytail. "You're representing our state. We get enough bad press as it is from media idiots who think we're just bad accents and big hair. I can't risk you having another flapper fiasco. It's just a public service."

"'Flapper fiasco?' You realize that was only once, and only because my regular clothes were soaked. And I totally made that dress work." Grace was never going to let me live down having to wear one of my fall play costumes at school freshman year because one of the bus drivers hit a huge puddle in the school lot, tsunami-ing dirty water all over me *and* gym bag. "It's not like I'm Phoebe, with her book costumes."

"Em!" That made Phoebe jump up and grab her own weapon. She pelted me with a few pairs of balled socks before picking up my jeans. The three of us circled each other with rolled-up clothes, our "swords" landing with deadly accuracy until we dissolved in a pile of giggles.

I reached over to tug on Alec's foot until he joined us on my grey carpet, pulling Leia with him. "I love you guys." Half of my suitcase was now scattered all around us and Phoebe still shook so hard with pent-up laughter that she was clutching her side.

Chloe popped her head in my doorway and made a face. "You are all so weird."

11

My little sister was clutching my hand so hard, my fingers had gone numb. Mom scanned the list in her hand, her ancient history professor horn-rimmed reading glasses perched on the tip of her nose. "You have the list I made of everyone's phone numbers, right? In case you lose your phone?"

I tried not to roll my eyes. Standing in the middle of an airport was not the place to get a lecture from Mom about respect. "I'm pretty sure I have our home phone number memorized." *Since first grade*, I added mentally. But at Mom's laser-stare, I cowed and said, "Yes, ma'am." I pulled the little notepad she filled for me out of the front pocket of my carry-on and waved it.

"Good. You can't rely on technology all the time." Mom slipped her list into her purse and reached out to hug me. "Call every night and don't get into trouble." Her own curls, tighter and darker than mine, brushed against my cheek and I breathed in her uniquely Mom-smell of rose perfume and the coconut oil she used in her hair.

Dad eventually extracted me from Mom's arms and gave me a quick hug of his own, his Dad-smell of eucalyptus soap and coffee engulfing me. "I am so proud of you. Kick some butt, *manari mou*." I didn't even cringe at "my little lamb," Dad's old nickname for me. His short beard scratched my cheek and I had to blink to keep from tearing up.

Chloe wrapped her little arms around my waist as far as they could go and sniffled into my shirt. I squeezed her tight, then untangled myself from her before she could burrow deeper into the hug—I didn't need to show up in Boston with a six year old's snot and tears on me. "It's only a week, you know." Chloe looked up at me, eyes big and cheeks wet, and my heart melted a little bit more. It would be her first time away from me since my sixth grade camping trip, and she was only a baby back then. "I promise I'll call a few times just for you, okay? I can't wait to tell you all about Boston," I whispered to her, and Chloe nodded, pressing her lips tight together like she was trying her hardest to look brave.

I had pictured looking a lot cooler for my first solo plane ride, sweeping into the security line dramatically with my roller bag behind me, like on TV or like the twenty-some-thing girl a few people ahead of me in line. She looked so bored and composed, like she travelled all the time. Instead, Chloe expected me to wave every time I inched closer to the ticket inspection person, and Mom called out reminders every few minutes. I made it through security and turned to give them one last wave before entering the terminal. They were all craning their necks around the crowds to see me. They were a spectrum, running from Mom's dark-brown skin to Dad's pale olive complexion, with Chloe the in-between transition. A little lump lodged itself in my throat and I swallowed it back, giving a little wave before turning in the direction of my gate.

At Philadelphia International, little planes apparently took off from gates as far as possible from security. I rushed through the airport, triple-checking my gate and the time on every monitor I passed. Out of breath, I dropped onto a seat at my gate and looked around. I had spent so much time before security hugging and stuff that people were already getting ready to start boarding. I stared at my ticket, trying to figure out my group number. They might have already called the number and I didn't know.

Someone tapped me on the shoulder as I rotated the ticket, trying to decipher the printing. "Looks like someone was running late," a familiar voice said and I looked up to see Kris breezing past me and handing his phone to the gate attendant at the door to be scanned. "Have a good flight, Ephemie."

My mood plummeted.

Some people have all the luck on airplanes. Girls from school would tell stories of the hotties they'd sat next to during flights. Grace had even sat a row down from a movie star the last time she and her parents went on vacation. My parents met on a flight back from Greece, when Mom was finishing up her doctoral studies and Dad had been visiting family. Mom said Dad had even offered to switch seats so she could sit by the window.

On this flight, I got to be across the aisle from Kris.

At least it was one of those planes that had rows with one seat on one side and two on the other, and Dad had reserved me the single seat. I didn't have to squish next to a businessman shoving his elbows over the armrest or listen to a talky seatmate. But, damn, the aisle was too narrow to be a decent barrier to Kris' ginormous ego.

I flipped though the safety card and airplane magazine and tried to ignore him. Phoebe had lent me one of her books, but I really wasn't in the mood to read, especially not some weird story about ghosts trapped in mirrors. I made it until we reached cruising altitude, then pulled out the movie version of *Golden* on my tablet to keep me company. Which Kris, of course, had to comment on as soon as he caught a glimpse of Liam's chiseled body in full Leprechaun battle armor.

Kris leaned over the aisle, poking at my screen. "Wait a minute, you're watching *that*?"

I hit pause and graced him with a side "why are you bothering me?" look, perfected from years of being a big sister. "What would you prefer? A recap of the latest congressional debate?"

He actually looked up at the ceiling and shook his head, pressing his lips together like he was trying to keep from laughing before looking back at me. "I didn't peg you as a fan of the most ridiculous movie ever."

"You know, it's really sad how genre films, especially those geared towards a young female viewership, get panned, even if the cinematography and acting are groundbreaking,"

I said in my most superior tone, nose high in the air, then added, "Like this movie."

"Groundbreaking, really?" His finger pointed in Liam's general direction and met my eyes with his own amused ones. "Aren't leprechauns supposed to be, you know, little?"

"Like you're an expert on Irish myths."

This time, Kris snorted. "Better than whoever wrote it. Plus, what about what he's wearing? There's no way anyone can fight in something like that. And why are you girls so in love with that guy? He doesn't look like anything special."

My death glare silenced him and I turned up the volume to my headphones to drown out any more of his comments. I spent the rest of the flight trying to pretend he wasn't there.

12

"Ladies and gentlemen, this is your captain speaking." As the voice came over the PA system, I tugged my headphones out of my ears and looked up. "We've run into a little rush hour traffic jam at Logan airport, so we're going to be circling for a bit until a runway frees up for us. Right now, we're still looking at an on time arrival, but I'll update you if anything changes." A groan came up from most of the other people in the cabin, but I just popped my headphones back in. I could totally handle a few more minutes of Liam's abs.

By the third circle, though, my stomach didn't let me focus on anything but staring straight ahead and keeping the complimentary pretzels from coming back up again. I leaned my head back against the headrest and tried taking in calm, nausea-clearing breaths.

"You don't look too good," Kris said over the aisle. "Can I help? Like maybe switch seats or get you water or something?" I turned just enough to narrow my eyes at him and survival instinct must have kicked in because he quickly buried his head in his magazine.

By the fourth circle, I started losing circulation in my hand from trying to push on the pressure points in my wrist.

I'd already finished two ginger lozenges from the old lady in front of me. When it didn't look like that was helping, I unbuckled my seatbelt and swung my legs into the aisle. Maybe I could make it to the bathroom before losing my lunch and pride in front of everyone.

"I'm sorry, Miss, but you need to stay in your seat." The flight attendant said as he blocked the aisle.

I took in his practiced smile and countered with a tight-lipped frown that was more about keeping everything down than being polite. "I need to go to the bathroom." A part of me hoped I sounded smooth, like I travelled all the time, and not like I was desperate.

"And I need you in your seat. No exceptions."

"I'm not responsible for what happens, then." Giving him the staredown didn't work and I sat back down, reaching for the airsickness bag as a bubble of air pushed up from my stomach. "Oh, crap."

The next few minutes were a blur of sick, getting pity stares and "poor thing"s from the little old lady in 4A, and trying not to look in Kris' direction. Even after nothing else could come up, I clutched at the bag like a lifeline until the flight attendant pried it away from me in his last pass through the cabin. "I warned you," I hissed at him when he took the bag with only two gloved fingers.

The plane taxied to a landing and I kept my forehead pressed against the window, waiting for the plane to stop moving and praying for a close gate. I just needed to get onto solid ground to tame my protesting stomach. The seatbelt sound dinged and I heard the clack of every single person on our flight unbuckling their belts at the same time, followed by the shuffle of people standing and opening overhead bins.

A gentle hand touched my shoulder and I peeled myself from the bulkhead, a wave of shock followed by suspicion rolling over me when I saw Kris' concerned face looking down at me. "You okay?"

I pinched the bridge of my nose for a second to ward off the headache that threatened to join the leftover waves of nausea and nodded. "I'm fine." Sweat had coated the back of my neck during landing and now I was freezing on top of feeling like crap.

"Right." Kris grabbed my bag from the overhead bin and carefully tugged on my arm to pull me to standing.

"Hey, that's mine."

"And I'm carrying it. Or do you want to stay on here until they fly back to Philly?" I made a face at him, but let him propel me forward with his arm around my waist and hand on my elbow, barely touching but close enough to keep me upright and moving. I could feel the heat coming off his body and resisted the impulse to sway towards him.

"How adorable are they?" Some woman a few rows back said loud enough for me to hear and I turned to give her a dirty look.

Instead, I came eye-to-eye with Kris, amusement written all over his face. "What? You don't think you're adorable? Because I know I am."

"Oh, shut up."

He twisted his nose and let go of my arm for a second to fan the air between us. "We need to get you mints or gum or something."

I clamped my mouth shut in horror and faced forward again. "Thanks. Make fun of the sick girl."

We made it out into the terminal and Kris nudged me in direction of baggage claim. Even with his annoying commentary, he still supported me so carefully that I didn't pull away. He probably had years of practice helping little old ladies cross the street in exchange for votes or something. "I'm trying to help you here. If you didn't have me, you'd be all alone and sick in a strange airport."

"Whatever."

"I'm your class president and a Scout. Consider it a moral imperative for me to make sure you at least get to baggage claim without throwing up all over that outfit I'm positive you wore to impress our competitors. Let me guess, you're imitating that one actress from the fifties? Audrey something?" Those last sentences carried a bit of his usual arch superiority.

Everything he said was true. I'd worn my striped top, jeans, and ballet flats in an attempt to echo Audrey Hepburn's classic style, but he didn't need to know he was right. "Whatever," I repeated. I stepped onto the escalator, clutching the handhold as my breakfast threatened to join my lunch. Apparently, I wasn't ready for motion yet. I stumbled off the escalator and Kris' hand was right back on my arm, steadying me. "Thanks," I said grudgingly.

A perky redheaded guy holding up a Youth Change Council sign came up to us. "You two must be New Jersey." At my blank look, he pointed at Kris and our two bright blue Change Council carry-ons. "We have your pictures, and those bags are impossible to miss. Besides, you and Vermont were the only ones supposed to arrive in this terminal."

I bit back the urge to ask redhead if we were going to spend the week being referred to by our states and instead dropped onto one of the non-moving baggage carousels. Kris, in typical Kris fashion, smoothly shook Red's hand. "You guessed right. Kris Lambert," he then tilted his chin in my direction, "And that's Em Katsaros."

Miracle of miracles—he used my nickname. I gave Red a weak wave. "Hi."

Red checked something on his clipboard "I'm Daniel Walsh, but you can call me Dan. I'll be one of your coordinators this week. Think of me like a guidance counselor and tour guide rolled into one." He pointed his clipboard at one of the other carousels. "Your bags should be coming in on that one."

I started to stand, but Kris put a staying hand on my shoulder. "I'll pick up your bag for you. Just sit there until you feel better." To Dan, he added, "We circled the airport for a while before landing. Em's still feeling sick." He dropped both our carry-ons onto the floor by my feet.

He was already working on being a kiss-up, but not moving for a little while sounded like a good idea. The thought of walking still made me a little woozy. "It's the yellow bag with green dots."

"That's a huge surprise," Kris said, flashing me a wide grin. Phoebe was right—he did have a nice smile, even when he was being a jerk. "Now, if you said pink, I'd be shocked."

Damn, he was too perceptive sometimes. Or was my love of yellow that obvious? "Go fetch my bags, lackey," I said with a dismissive wave.

As they walked to the carousel, I could hear Dan say, "It's great to see two people from the same school. That almost never happens in this competition. It's also nice to see that the two of you are friends."

"Yeah, Em and I are like this," Kris held up two crossed fingers and winked over his shoulder at me. "You won't have any problems with rivalry from us."

Forgetting my stomach, I narrowed my eyes at him and stuck out my tongue, my knuckles turning white from how hard I clenched the edge of the carousel.

13

I dragged my things down the antique-lined inn hallway, studying the doors for my room number. Red said that my roommate, the girl from Montana, was already checked in. I tried to curb my inward horror at sharing a room before getting there—it was one thing to be in a hotel room with one of my best friends, like Phoebe or Grace or even Alec, but a stranger was a different story. What if she snored or had already claimed the better bed and filled the closet and took over the bathroom so I'd be living out of my suitcase for a week, sleeping on a lumpy mattress in the darkest corner of the room?

The sound of a flute hitting high G carried down the hallway and when I stopped in front of my door and slid in my keycard, the music continued in perky little staccato notes from under the doorway. I opened the door to a slurred phrase that sounded a lot like Dvorak and made my head spin with its complexity. The girl sitting by the window finished with a flourish and laid her flute on her music stand before standing up and giving me a brilliant smile. "You must be New Jersey."

"Em," I said quickly, dropping my bags on the hardwood

floor. The room was a turn-of-the-century dream, from the two narrow four-poster beds to furniture that looked like it had been there since nineteen-twelve. Diamond-patterned golden wallpaper and satiny curtains finished the look. I thrilled at the antiques scattered throughout the room. I squinted down at the paper Red had handed me with my room and roommate information. "And you must be Anne from Montana."

"Ann without an E. Perfectly plain and practical, and no extra Es," she said, then added, sheepishly, "I always start with that because you won't believe how many Anns with 'e's are out there. In case, you know, you'd ever have to write it out, which we probably won't have to, but it never hurts to let people know. But, anyway, enough about my name." She bounced over to pick up my tote bag full of competition stuff and dropped it onto the coffee table next to hers to give me room to move. "It's so nice to meet you. Sorry if I'm a little chatty. I feel like I know you already from your bio sheet." Her long skirt swirled as she walked, and bangles like the ones Dev brought from India for Phoebe jangled with every movement. Even her hair glowed in the light from the window, the light-brown waves tumbling down her back and past her butt. She looked like a cross between Galadriel and Arwen, as if Cate Blanchett and Liv Tyler really were elves and she was their love child. I was rooming with a Midwestern fairytale princess.

I weighed the idea of pretending I'd read her bio, too, or pretending it got lost in the mail, but settled for the truth.

"I haven't had a chance to read your bio, so I'll have to take your word for it," I said, feeling a little guilty for expecting the worst. Ann hadn't taken over, after all. Her nametag hung on the bed closest to the door, leaving me the one by the window, and a quick peek into the bathroom showed she had only taken a little corner of the counter. But her personality was overwhelming, even for me. "You play flute?"

"Yeah, I hope you don't mind if I practice. I couldn't take off for an entire week. Did you bring your flute? I saw that in your bio, too. We could try some duets."

I pulled the crumpled bio sheet out of my carry-on and skimmed it—first chair in her state youth orchestra. No wonder she was practicing. My flute rarely saw the outside of its case when I wasn't physically in band. "I didn't bring mine. I thought I'd take the week off. You know, rest my hands?" I wiggled my fingers at her and made a mental note not to discuss anything orchestral with her. This girl already made me feel like a total slacker. She'd probably crush me in flute trivia.

"Makes sense. I'd take a break, but my teacher would kill me." She bounced onto her bed. "Isn't this place amazing? I read in our binder that the people who own it block it off every year just for the Change Council. And they don't charge the competition anything except for food."

I tried to keep from narrowing my eyes at her. "How long have you been here?"

"About two hours. Dan said you and the Vermont kids were going to be the last ones to get here. So I thought I'd read the binder. It has all of our speeches in it, you know."

That made my competitive heart skip a beat. "Really?" I left my things where I'd dropped them and pulled the big navy and grey binder out of the competition tote bag. Dropping onto the edge of my bed, I flipped through—we were alphabetical by state and I stopped on New Jersey.

"I like your speech; it's different from a lot of the others," Ann said, not noticing my frown at the word "different." While talking, she had somehow managed to twist her hair up into a bun and hold it in place with pen from the night-stand. "I think it's going to be tough to beat the boy from Louisiana, though. If his delivery is anywhere near as good as his writing, it's a killer speech."

We are integral pieces of a process born over two centuries ago from the hopes and blood of— I looked up from skimming Kris' speech. I had to admit, it was pretty good, even if it was about getting involved in the political process to make change happen. "You must read really fast."

"I only got halfway through, but I'll read the rest tonight. I want to get all my angsting over with tonight so I can spend the rest of the week enjoying Boston. I've never been this far east before."

"Mmmhmm," I didn't look up this time, focused completely on picking out any possible suckitude in his speech. Nothing. Crap.

"The best part of all of this is that I can be anyone I want to be here, you know? I grew up with everyone at my school. Here, I don't know anyone and no one has any preconceptions about 'Ann' and I love that. It'll be so much easier to make new friends."

"Must be nice to be you," I said under my breath. She didn't have to deal with sharing the competition with her greatest antagonist. When she tilted her head in confusion at me, I closed the binder and went over to my suitcase. "Sorry, I think I'm still a little sick from the flight."

"Right. I didn't mean to talk you to death. I'll just go back to practicing and let you rest." Ann went back to her spot by the window and picked up where she had left off, New World Symphony filling our little room.

I picked up my tablet to call Wil and let him know I made it, but then I changed my mind. I was just too tired for the emotional rollercoaster that was bound to happen if he wasn't ready to make up. Really, he knew I was travelling—he should have been the one to make sure I got to Boston safely. His Photogram account was full of really good signs that our relationship was going to smooth right back to where it was, like pictures of places we'd talked about him showing me if I ever visited him, but I was still waiting for him to do his part and swoop in with an "I'm sorry" and some big, romantic gesture, like Romeo climbing the balcony or Lloyd holding up his boombox in *Say Anything*. Until then, I needed to think about me. And sleep.

Less than an hour in Boston and I'd already thrown up in front of my nemesis, chickened out about making up with my boyfriend, and alienated my roommate. Go, me.

14

The only positive to rooming with a morning person who decided to wake me up at six in the morning was that I had time to diffuse my hair dry so it didn't stick up all over the place. I stifled a yawn as I followed Ann into the Inn dining room, pausing to check my reflection in one of the giant mirrors set in the doors. My nametag kept getting caught in the folds of my awesome Grace-approved drapey cardigan, so I pulled off the tag and tied it by the lanyard onto my zipper pull. That pause was enough to separate me from Ann in the buffet line and, by the time I was through, I found myself balancing two plates and scanning the room for somewhere to sit.

Old Em would normally go up to the table with the cutest boy and set my flirt-gun to stun, but that was pre-Wil. I had to remind New Em that I already had problems dealing with one long-distance boyfriend and I didn't need to add another one, even if there was so much adorable accent potential in the room. With my normal seating strategy out, I was totally adrift until a waving hand caught my attention.

"Em, over here." I followed Ann's voice and hand to a

table that was, surprise of all surprises, right by the front of the room and only a few feet from the podium.

"Thanks." I set my plates down and looked around the table at the other six people sitting with Ann. "Hi, I'm Em."

They all introduced themselves, but my brain could only lock on the states. Another Montana, two New Yorks, the boy from Louisiana who had the most delicious accent on the planet, a girl from Alaska. My gaze fell on the boy to my left and I froze at the familiar face peeking out from the most relaxed look I'd ever seen him in. Kris' hair, which was now in messy soft waves, kept threatening to fall into his eyes as he smiled up at me. My appetite suddenly disappeared. "Forget your hair gel?" I couldn't keep the snark out of my voice.

"Actually, I did. Want to lend me some of yours?" He reached over and flicked one of my curls, which was frozen in a perfect spiral.

"No, I think I'll do you a favor and force you to waver from your Kennedy-wannabe look. It'll be good for you."

New York watched our conversation like we were the first match of the French Open. "You two know each other?"

"Unfortunately," I said, while at the same time Kris said, "Yeah, it's a pretty awesome coincidence."

I glared at Kris, and said as I sat down, "We go to the same school."

"You know, neither of you sound like you're from New Jersey," Montana-boy said around a mouthful of croissant. Boys.

I raised one eyebrow, a trick that totally came in handy in situations like this, and put on my most nasally voice. "Oh my gawd, you mean we don't sound like this?"

"Yes! Why don't you sound like that, Joisey?"

Kris and I shared a look that was equal parts annoyance and tolerance, for once on the same page. "Because it's an unfounded stereotype created by people not from our state who think they're comedians, not to mention it's a parody of ethnic accents in parts of the state." he said.

I blinked in surprise at his calm but definitely not super political let's-gloss-over-stuff-so-you-like-me answer. "What he said," I said in my own accent again. That nasal thing made my throat hurt. "It's annoying."

Louisiana, forkful of bacon hanging mid-air, nodded empathetically. "I guess it's like people expect me to sound like Gambit from *X-men* or something. I don't go around calling people "*cher*"all day." He managed to fit all the bacon in his mouth in one shot.

I propped my elbows on the table and leaned forward with the grin Wil always said was my 'heartbreaker' look. "You can call me anything you want in your accent." I shoved back the little guilt-angel propped on my shoulder with a toss of my hair. There was absolutely nothing wrong with a little innocent flirting, after all. Wil hadn't called to make up yet, so technically, we *were* on a break. And I needed something to entertain me, considering I had to spend an entire week trying not to strangle Kris.

Louisiana laughed and choked down the bacon before

taking a sip of his orange juice and saying, "Maybe I'll reconsider the '*cher*' thing just for you."

"Please don't," Kris said, and I had to restrain myself from dumping my tea on his not-so-artfully messy hair.

The girl from Alaska looked from Kris to me and seemed to take a deep breath. I bet she regretted picking our table. "I don't know which part of this week I'm looking forward to the most—the conference or the tours. I've never been to Massachusetts."

New York girl paused her own flirty attempts mid-hair-twirl, though hers were, for some reason I couldn't figure out, aimed straight at Kris. She directed her next words at him, too. "Boston's awesome. My brother goes to MIT and I've been up here a few times. There are some great party spots I can show you."

"I seriously doubt our advisors will let us out to party," Ann said, a little bit of amusement combined with eye-roll in her voice. She nudged me with her shoulder and grinned.

"Exactly." A tall woman with cropped black hair and wearing a grey business suit said as she passed our table on the way to the podium, looking like Pearl Bailey taking center stage. New York girl straightened up immediately. The room fell silent as she continued over the microphone. "While we want all of you to have a good time, everyone needs to understand you will all be under constant supervision by the conference staff and, for your safety, you need to stay in groups where we can keep an eye on all of you. Anyone trying to break the rules outlined in the binders you were given will be disqualified from the competition and sent home." Her teacher-look softened and she smiled at the suddenly sober faces around her. "But enough with the rules. My name is Ms. Shawnee and I'll be your lead advisor for the week."

Kris pushed away his breakfast plate and leaned forward on his elbows in a perfect show of kiss-upped-ness. I countered by sitting back with a bagel in my hand and trying to look like I was relaxed and paying attention at the same time. Ms. Shawnee went through the usual "congratulations for making it to this point, we're proud of you" shtick, then got to the important part of her speech. "Judging will be on the last day. You will be divided alphabetically by state or territory and will individually go before the judges to read your speeches. Up until that point, you'll be working with mentors to polish your speeches. We're confident that, with their guidance, your speeches will go from great to amazing." She smiled widely at all of us and all the heads at my table bobbed in agreement, so I nodded, too.

Ms. Shawnee stepped alongside the podium, still close enough for the microphone to pick up her voice. "This morning, we're going to start you with a walking tour of Boston, and, after lunch, we're diving right into the conference. Any questions, feel free to ask me, Dan, Rosie, or any of the inn staff." She pointed to the back of the room, where Red stood with a pink-and-blue haired girl, both of them in Change Council long-sleeved t-shirts. "We're excited to have you all here. I hope you have a wonderful experience."

As we stood up to leave, Ann put down her coffee cup with a clank and leaned over me to stare at Kris' shirt. I had to scoot back to keep from getting a face full of braided bun. "Wait, do you volunteer for *Noelle's Song*?" I twisted my head to look and realized I had totally missed the familiar music-note logo on this t-shirt.

Kris tugged at his shirt. "I do. I'm on the teen advisory board."

"But why?" I couldn't help but ask. "You're not involved in any of the music programs at school. You hate music." *Noelle's Song* had been formed to help fund music programs in the schools when one of the girls at our school who had been a first chair violinist and a soprano in the choir died of a genetic heart condition. Definitely not the type of charity I expected Kris to be interested in.

He huffed at me, giving me a pretty annoyed side-eye at the same time, before saying, "I don't hate music. And Noelle Winslow was my cousin."

Noelle. *Oh.* "Oh, right. I forgot you were related to half the town," Lambertfield's founding family didn't spread out much beyond the town borders.

He poked me in the arm, lips quirking in a not-quite-smile. "I bet you were expecting me to say I do it because it looks good on a college application, weren't you?"

I wasn't going to give him the pleasure of showing him how right he was. "Possibly."

That not-quite-smile turned into a self-satisfied grin. "Actually, it really does, but it's also a pretty amazing group.

We're in fifteen states so far and my aunt says there's international interest, too." His voice then grew softer than I ever expected from him. "Noelle would be really happy if she could see what we've made happen."

"We just started a chapter in my town," Ann said, breaking the heavy silence that fell between us after Kris' last sentence. She finally stopped leaning over me and walked around to sandwich Kris between us. "The music budget was just cut in a few of our schools, so we've started fundraising and collecting used instruments for them. I teach flute to some of the city kids who can't afford to have lessons. Plus, the Scout troop I lead has been working on informing the community about how important the arts are for schools so we can start lobbying our local officials. The webpage for NS is really great about giving tips about that."

Holy cannoli, I *was* rooming with a saint.

Kris grinned at her, puffing his chest out like a peacock getting ready to show off. "I actually wrote that part of the webpage." He held the door open for us, and added, "That's awesome what you're doing. I'll have to get you in touch with Aunt Rose. She'd love to spotlight your chapter in the newsletter." He slowed his pace to keep alongside us as we shuffled out the front doors of the Inn and towards the busses "It's really important to showcase successes so the different chapters can learn from each other." New York girl pulled him aside to ask him something and Ann and I hopped on the bus, her grabbing a seat next to the guy from Louisiana.

Ann leaned across the aisle and said, "He's so nice."

"That's because it's early. His ego is bound to start suffocating us in t-minus three hours," I said, turning to the girl next to me, who had shortish, curly hair like mine, except hers was the color of fire. "Hi, I'm Em." My eyes went straight for her badge—Pennsylvania.

"Lia, from Philly."

Kris finally stepped through the doorway and I watched as he paused at the top of the aisle. His eyes swept the bus, stopping for seconds on the empty seats, like he was sizing each one of them up. After a few seconds, he seemed to nod the tiniest bit and made his way, super confident, over to the back where one of the advisors was talking with some of the southern kids.

"Figures," I muttered, and when Lia raised her eyebrows at me, I tilted my chin at Kris. "We go to school together. He's so politician-y, even out of school."

She scrunched her nose, peering at me through thick lenses that made her blue eyes look huge. "Okay, I see that. But, really, if you guys didn't already know each other, I'd be a little worried that you were paying attention to something like that."

"It's impossible not to. Kris is a little like a bug bite— you can forget it's there, but the second anything touches it, you're itching like crazy."

She pressed her lips together, but the corners of her mouth still turned up slightly. "So, go scratch that itch." After saying that, her grin escaped and she waggled her eyebrows suggestively.

"Ew. No. My interest in Kris is purely competitive. I've seen too much of his seedy political underbelly. I'll let you and everyone else swoon over him."

She gave me a wary look. "Okay."

"Trust me, you'll see what I mean when he really gets going."

15

The rest of the morning, though, Kris just kept acting like he was on the campaign path instead of at a conference-competition. In a weird show of regional magnetism, all of the Midatlantic states seemed to clump together and we ended up in the same tour group along with Ann and the girl from Alaska. He'd charmed them all, flashing smiles and doing his whole "look people straight in the eye and pretend you care" act whenever anyone talked about anything. I knew his game was charm, throw the person off guard, and destroy, but I didn't think he'd try that with over a hundred people. Apparently, I was wrong. By the time we reached Faneuil Hall, I was about ready to shake some snot *into* him. It was either that or arrange my own personal Boston Massacre right at the site of the original.

Every ounce of annoyance flew out of me in a whoosh as we entered the Great Hall. Our tour guide barely had a chance to give a quick history lesson before we broke free and fanned out all over the room. We were speechwriters, political nerds, or history geeks and this place had enough history to suck in all groups. I made a beeline for the front of the room.

"Susan B. Anthony and Frederick Douglass spoke here," I said, *sotto voce*, as I made my way onto the stage and stared out at the other students milling about the hall. I closed my eyes and imagined the room like it had to have been over the centuries, packed with crowds waiting to hear fiery speeches from people trying to change the course of the country or argue for civil rights. I took a deep breath and tried to absorb some of the greatness that had to have soaked into the walls and floors of the building.

My eyes shot open when the wooden floor of the stage vibrated as someone else came near.

"And Samuel Adams. Speeches that changed our country's history were made in this room." Kris added as he stood right next to me. There was enough awe in his voice—as much as I knew had to be in mine—that, for once, I didn't even mind the intrusion. "You know they're going to have the awards ceremony here, right? Imagine how awesome it would be to get to read your speech on this stage."

"I am a vital component in the fight to 'make the world better.'" My voice carried through the hall thanks to years of practice in theatre, but the one sentence got lost in the din of a room full dozens of conversations. Kris' eyebrows drew together and he tilted his head, making me laugh. "That's the first line of my speech. I'm surprised you didn't read them all yet to scope out the competition."

His brows drew together for a second. "I don't need to scope out anyone because I know my speech is awesome." And the Kris I knew and despised was back, down to trying—and failing—to slick back his hair with one hand. "I know this isn't your thing, but here's a tip—these competitions are all about confidence, I'm confident I'm going to be up there again later this week. If you're not confident with your speech, might as well drop out right now, because everyone else will run with that and crush you." While I stood there trying to think up a retort, he tapped me on the arm with his rolled up tour brochure and jumped off the stage. "Later, Em." With a wave of the brochure, he walked off to join some of the guys checking out a painting back by the entrance. Within a minute, a comment he made had the whole group breaking into laughter. Probably something about my speech.

"Jerk." I reined in the impulse to stomp off the stage in a Scarlett O'Hara-esque huff and instead channeled Grace Kelly, gliding over to another group checking out something on the completely opposite side of the hall. No use in letting him know how much he bugged me.

"You're wrong." It wasn't even day two of the conference and Kris and I were already at each other's throats. The conference room was silent as a-hundred-plus sets of eyes focused smack-dab on the New Jersey section, all because Kris had jumped at the chance to tear me down the second I had opened my mouth about the latest presentation. "There are a ton of problems with voluntourism." Kris shot my way, turning his chair to face me so he didn't have to keep looking to the side.

I didn't let his stare unnerve me. "Stop calling it that," I said, trying my best to keep my tone calm. "Everything has problems. But there are a lot of positives to volunteering in other countries, too."

"Students—" Ms. Shawnee looked like she was about to jump in and break us apart, but the presenter, who had just given us a presentation on international volunteer opportunities, was watching us with a smile on her face. When Kris and I both looked her way, she waved at us to continue.

"Sorry, my mistake, I thought you wanted to help people," he said, his tone bordering on sarcastic. "You're talking about positives like sweeping in for a few weeks or a month to swing a hammer or play with kids and have great photos to post on Photogram while locals and full-time people from the organization waste time instructing each batch of volunteers how not to build a substandard building, right?"

Now, I was fired up. I'd scooted my chair back so far that I was literally on the edge of my seat, practically on the verge of standing. "No, like being more aware of the problems in the world around us, empowering us to make change in the world, and building connections with people in other places."

"All while taking away jobs that would normally be paid? Instead of having some rich kid on spring break help build a school or something, the organizations can pay local workers. People's lives aren't your tickets to personal growth." Kris' eyes met mine and there was the littlest bit of amusement playing in them as he lobbied that last sentence my way.

"Oh, please, not like you like the organizations, anyway, based on what you said when we talked about NGOs."

The presenter cleared her throat and said, "Remember, this is a place to share ideas, but they don't have to be concrete. There are no perfect answers and we want to respect everyone's point of view."

Kris nodded as if he had heard her, but never broke eye contact with me. "At least even those are more efficient when they're staffed with locals. I'd rather fund them and, by supporting local labor and buying local goods, stimulate their economy while building or doing whatever they'd have volunteers doing, rather than fund someone's feel-good self-discovery trip."

I curled my fingers under my chair to keep from getting up as heat wove its way up my neck. "And while you're trying to find those goods and labor and organizing things, we'll be delivering all the things we collected to people who really need them. Because, you know, you saw how well things went here in the US with organizations and government after Sandy and Katrina and the Baton Rouge floods, and I can keep going on. Even here, you need volunteers and donations if you want to help people right away when they actually need it."

"I never said volunteers weren't important, but voluntourists are another breed." He waved his hand dismissively. "Don't even get me started on drives to collect stuff for disaster zones. We end up spending a fortune shipping crap that might not even be what people actually need, instead of buying from somewhere local. But, you know, filling drive boxes at school with old t-shirts and sneakers makes everyone feel better than intensive fundraising."

"But at least we're doing something instead of sitting on our asses and talking crap about helping others."

Ms. Shawnee stood up and cleared her throat. "And, I think we need to take a break. Em, Kris, remember, we want to keep the language a little more…G-rated in our debates, okay?"

Kris smirked at me and I gave him one last glare before loosening my white-knuckled grip from my chair. At least I'd had the last word.

16

"Alabama. I almost passed out when he said hi to me this morning. A face like that combined with that accent should be illegal," the girl from Washington, Adrienne, said, fanning her face with her binder. Since the inn was made up of a row of historic homes tied together through knocked down walls, us girls had our own buildings, totally separate from the boys. We had gathered in the sitting room of our part of the inn, spread out all over the floor and antique furniture. One of the other girls had gotten a platter of cookies from the kitchen and it was already half-empty. While some of the other girls were comparing state facts and others were pulling a Phoebe and reading, the group of us closest to the fire had moved from rehashing the day to a debate on accents. And guys with accents.

North Carolina made a face. "I don't know what it is with everyone falling all over themselves when they hear a southern accent. I mean, yeah, of course *I* think it's nice, but it's not like we're all southern belles and gentlemen or something." As she spoke, I couldn't help but try to tune my ear to the little details in the words that just sounded so gorgeously smooth. I could use that information in the future.

"It beats all the other boring accents. Imagine someone who looks like him talking with a Shore Boyz accent?" Wisconsin chimed in, then looked over at me. "Sorry, Jersey."

"Apology accepted, cheesehead," I said around a mouthful of cookie. I couldn't resist a jab at her, though. "Dontcha know?"

"Speaking of Jersey, what's up with you and him? You two nearly tore each other's heads off in the conference today. I thought Ms. Shawnee was going to explode when you got into the NGO debate."

I looked up from my spot on the hearth to see who asked the question and Colorado waved her cookie at me. I let out a puff of air and tried not to roll my eyes. "He's a jerk and was trying to piss me off. It's what Kris does best. Just ignore him."

"I don't know," Colorado continued, taking a bite of her cookie and saying with a verbal shrug, "he seems nice enough to me."

"Definitely nice. Super polite, too. And, ohmigosh, those *eyes*. He could just look at me and I'd be happy," New York said from her spot on one of the footrests. The other girls were starting to sound like Phoebe back when she crushed on him, like they were totally blind to his many, many faults.

Hawaii nodded. "He was at my table for dinner and I thought he was actually really sweet. He even switched places with Lee so she could see the speaker better."

"Does he have a girlfriend?" New York plopped down right next to me, holding out a cookie like it was some sort of bribe. "C'mon, spill. We don't have inside info on any of the other guys here."

"This is supposed to be a competition and conference, not a dating service, but, no. Kris only loves Kris." I may have taken the cookie anyway, but I wasn't going to play Twenty Questions about the thorn in my side. "Can we please stop talking about him and maybe move on to Louisiana? Now, that's some Southern goodness right there." North Carolina let out an exasperated groan.

"Seriously, Feebs, he's doing this to mess with my mind." I paced the tiny inn bathroom, phone held out so I could see my best friend's reaction on its screen. Out in our room, Ann ran through scales at a demonic pace. "Like a speech competition freak-out mind trick or something."

Phoebe shook her head and let out a laugh. "I think you're overreacting. I'm pretty sure Kris isn't doing some diabolical evil-villain thing."

"Don't laugh. I'm serious. He's not acting like himself. It's really weird." Like this was his good twin or something. "And then, just when I think that maybe he's too busy to bug me, he'll just say something perfectly calculated to piss me off."

"Maybe you don't know him as well as you think you do."

"Right. We've only been going to the same schools since first grade. No, really. I know he's doing this all to trip me up so I lose this competition." I glanced up at my reflection and twisted my nose at the Pebbles Flintstone-y way my little ponytail stuck up on top of my head. "But I have a plan."

The screen flipped around crazily and then settled on a blue-green bedspread and a pile of yarn before focusing again on Phoebe. "The last time you had a plan, it involved dressing me up and shoving me at guys."

"And now you're dating Dev, so I was right, wasn't I?" Without waiting for her to answer because I *was* right, I perched on the edge of the bathtub and twirled an invisible mustache. "So, I'm going to give him a taste of his own medicine."

"Em, really, I think you're overreacting…" she began in her "I live in a world of fairytales where magical teapots and candlesticks talk to me and think everyone is nice" voice, but I cut her off.

"I'm not going to do anything to hurt him or, like, kiss the judges' asses until they like me and hate him. Actually, I'm going to be really, really nice to him."

Phoebe's brows knit together in the same expression she got when we talked about things like music or pop culture. "And how is that…?" She trailed off then tried again after taking a deep breath. "Maybe I'm missing something, but that doesn't make any sense."

"If Kris thinks pretending to be this nice guy will throw me off my game, let's see what happens when I do the same to him and he's exposed to the full power of my flirt. He'll be so confused, he won't know what to think. And then

I'll kick his ass in the competition." I pretended to buff my nails on my shirt and looked at her triumphantly.

"I don't think that's a good idea," she said slowly.

"Please. You know I'm an awesome actor. And it's not like he's not trying to do that to me. He said as much right outside MacKenzie's office."

"Em—"

"Fee," I said, imitating her.

She rolled her eyes at me and shook her head. "You shouldn't mess around with other people's emotions."

"Trust me, this will be fun."

"Trust *me*, you just have this weird perception of Kris as evil incarnate. He's actually really nice with a little bit of an ego, that's all." She pursed her lips for a second, "Not like you're any better on the ego end. 'Awesome' actor?"

"It's true, don't deny it." I pulled my hair out of the ponytail, fluffed it like those actresses in the forties, and smiled. "Plus, you're so wrong about him. You still think of him like the book version of Liam, which he's not."

"I do not." She then giggled. "Liam's taller and has a tattoo. I don't know if Kris has one, but it would only make him hotter if he did."

She was kind of right, but I wasn't going to let her know that. "Eww. I bet Dev wouldn't be too happy to hear you say so."

"Whatever. Dev doesn't have anything to worry about. But, speaking of boyfriends, I bet Wil isn't too happy with your plan." As much as I loved Phoebe, sometimes talking to her was like talking to my mom. The guilt part, not the hot guy part, because that would just be wrong on so many levels.

"I haven't been able to talk to him yet."

"You guys did make up already, right? From the way you were talking…"

"Technically, no, but haven't you been paying attention to his posts? He wants me to see how much he misses me."

Phoebe's eyes narrowed in confusion. "He's only posting in German, except when he's tagging Alec in something."

I waved away her worries. "That's what Translator is for. Trust me, we're good."

"But you haven't talked to him?"

At her frown, I added, before she could jump to any conclusions, "It's really hard with the time difference." The lie tasted bitter on my tongue, but I pushed it back with the guilt monster that had just jumped on my back. It wasn't my fault he wouldn't answer my calls. "I'm sure he'll support me bringing Kris' ego down a few pegs."

"Just…be careful," Phoebe said softly. "You might be good at acting, but you're too good a person to manipulate anyone."

"Thanks, Jiminy."

"Whatever, Pinocchio."

17

"Okay, let me get this straight: Your mom's an ancient history professor so you like ancient history, you love US history, and you love classic movies?" Ann was cross-legged on her bed and had a pen and notebook out like she was ready to take notes. "That's a millennia's worth of things right there." We'd changed into our pajamas and she still managed to look like she'd stepped out of Rivendell in her light-green tunic top and leggings.

"No one said I had to confine the stuff I like to one specific century." I fluffed my hair. "I simply have broad interests, dah-ling." Compared to Ann's perfect posture, I was sprawled on my stomach on top of my bed and had propped myself up on my elbows. My own pajamas were decidedly non-elvish plaid pants and an old long-sleeved Tee I'd stolen from Alec. "Your turn. What do you do when you're not playing the flute or saving the world with all your volunteer work?"

"You make it sound like the only thing I do is volunteer."

"And play flute," I added, pointing at her flute and music stand with a grin.

"I'm a black belt in aikido," she said, smiling at my

expression. "It's in my bio, if you ever bother reading the binder they gave us." I scrunched my nose at her, and she added, "Between that and orchestra and Scouting and Noelle's Song and school, I don't have a lot of free time."

"You make me feel like a slacker." Even hearing about all her activities made me tired.

She waved dismissively at me. "Are you thinking about college?"

"Yup. I really want Rutgers, which has this amazing theatre program." *If I can get in and keep Mom and Dad from guilting me out of it*, a little voice reminded me, but I pushed on. "I want to train as much as I can under the best, and it's so close to New York City. It even has a one-year residency at the Globe Theatre in London. Can you imagine?" Ann's grin grew extra-wide and I looked at her suspiciously—I didn't think there was anything funny about my answer. "What?"

"I swear, you lit up so much when you answered that question. No history, though?"

"Maybe as a minor, but acting is my dream. I want to focus on making it happen." I picked at the stitching on the quilt on my bed. "How about you?"

"I'm actually thinking of spending a year as a part of a volunteer corp. They have a program where I'd live with the other volunteers in a city or town in the US and work with the poor and marginalized." I was about to comment, but Ann put up a finger up in a "wait" gesture. "And then I think I want to become a music teacher."

"Music teacher is a little bit anticlimactic after all of your volunteer stuff," I pointed out with a grin.

"Well, I didn't want to sound too selfless. I'm saving some of that for tomorrow."

She and I lasted about two seconds before we both cracked up. I got up and pulled back the covers on my bed. "Good idea. And, with that, I'm going to sleep before you recruit me into one of your volunteer things."

"That reminds me. We're doing soup kitchen—"

I flicked off the lamp next to my bed and pulled the covers over my head. "Good night, Ann."

Ann snort-laughed, then I could hear the shuffling on her side of the room, followed by her lamp switching off. "'Night, Em."

EmmieBear: @BookishArcher The plan is afoot!

BookishArcher: @Emmiebear The plan makes no sense

EmmieBear: @BookishArcher The plan is pure genius because the person who came up with the plan is pure genius

BookishArcher: @EmmieBear *watches as the plan-maker BLOWS EVERYTHING OUT OF PROPORTION* Really?

EmmieBear: @BookishArcher You love me. You know that.

GCorreaCheer: @EmmieBear @BookishArcher What is this plan you two are talking about?

BookishArcher: @GCorreaCheer I'll tell you about it later. Em's being Em again @EmmieBear

EmmieBear: @BookishArcher @GCorreaCheer Yes. And I'm being brilliant.

GCorreaCheer: @EmmieBear @BookishArcher I do not want to read some news story about you getting kicked out for setting a certain someone's suitcase on fire or something

BookishArcher: @GCorreaCheer @EmmieBear She would never do that

EmmieBear: @BookishArcher Thank you @GCorreaCheer

BookishArcher: @GCorreaCheer It's too subtle @EmmieBear

EmmieBear: @BookishArcher Look who gets all snarky when she's typing instead of talking @GCorreaCheer

GCorreaCheer: @EmmieBear @BookishArcher I know, isn't it cute?

BookishArcher: @GCorreaCheer @EmmieBear Stop calling me cute! We're picking on Em right now for her crazypants plan

GCorreaCheer: @BookishArcher @EmmieBear Right. Priorities.

GCorreaCheer: @BookishArcher @EmmieBear Speaking of, I need to go warm up. Grab me during halftime, Feebs.

EmmieBear: @GCorreaCheer @BookishArcher *Is totally not bummed to be missing a Saturday night football game*

BookishArcher: @EmmieBear Rub it in, why don't you? @GCorreaCheer

EmmieBear: @BookishArcher Oh, go make out with your boyfriend under the bleachers before the game starts. I have plotting to do @GCorreaCheer

BookishArcher: @EmmieBear Em.

EmmieBear: @BookishArcher: Feebs. Lecture later. 😘 now.

DevTheGreat: @BookishArcher @EmmieBear I wholly approve of this suggestion

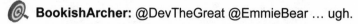 **BookishArcher:** @DevTheGreat @EmmieBear … ugh.

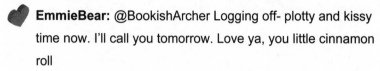 **EmmieBear:** @BookishArcher Logging off- plotty and kissy time now. I'll call you tomorrow. Love ya, you little cinnamon roll

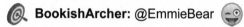 **BookishArcher:** @EmmieBear 😉

18

The dining room was practically empty when I made it downstairs on Sunday morning, so I grabbed a muffin and coffee and headed towards the sitting room. Hanging out on a comfy sofa near a fireplace that the inn staff seemed to keep going twenty-four hours a day sounded like a great way to pass the hour until all the church people got back from their services. Just as I stepped out into the hallway, I froze as a familiar figure came my way.

It was clear Kris hadn't found his hair gel. But that didn't stop him from looking like he'd stepped straight off of the Neitan Markus website, from his unmistakably designer jeans to the fitted grey henley that probably cost more than my entire outfit combined. Not the stiff button down shirt and slacks I'd expected, but still posh casual. Of course. "Morning." I stepped aside to give him direct access to the dining room door, but he leaned against the doorframe, instead, and yawned.

I stopped myself from only saying, "Good morning" and going on my merry way. There was no time like the present to implement plan "Murder Kris with Kindness."

The handle of my coffee mug dug into my hand and I balanced some of the weight on my muffin plate while pasting on a smile. "No religious observation for you this morning?" They'd set up vans for the past two days to take us to services for any religions that might have weekend worship. Kris was Presbyterian of some sort and should have been with the bunch that went this morning.

"Not this week." He shrugged and poked his head into the dining room. "Is that bacon I smell?"

"The muffins smell better," I said, waving my plate in front of him as seductively as I could. "I'm surprised. Aren't you, like, the president of your church's youth group or something?" I leaned back against the wall and the button of my off-white wrap sweater dug into my back. But I didn't mind- it was cozy, my best friend made it for me, and the way it curved around my waist and hips looked awesome.

"I decided sleeping in would be nice today. My mom would kill me if she heard me say this, but I think I can deal with taking a Sunday off. You didn't go?"

"Nope, I'm agnostic. No weekly deity worship for me."

He raised an eyebrow and tilted his head, like he was studying me. I waited for the judgmental look theist people like him gave me when they found out I wasn't on the same religious page as them. But, weirdly, his expression wasn't exactly what I expected. After a second of just watching me, he pointed with his thumb into the dining room. "You aren't eating in your room, are you?"

I choked back the urge to say a simple "no" and instead said, "I wanted to eat in the sitting room. It's not so cold in there—the dining room's freezing."

"I'm surprised. You'd think this would be pretty warm." He reached out and skimmed the sleeve of my sweater with his fingers. I barely felt his light touch through the thick wool, but it was enough to make me freeze in place. "I've never seen anything like this sweater." His gaze followed the line of the sweater as it curved around my waist and, at that moment, the sweater felt way too warm. "I like how it has the button in the back."

My mouth was suddenly dry and it took me a second to find words. "Phoebe made it for me."

He nodded, almost like he was approving my wardrobe choice. His eyes met mine and I could see the gold flecks in them despite the dim morning light. "She did a really good job. It's different, in a good way, kind of like you."

I snapped out of my Kris-charm-bubble—hunger must have weakened my immunity. "I'll let Feebs know." I said, my tone short. I clamped my mouth shut before any more of my annoyance at myself could turn into snark against him and awkward silence took over.

Kris didn't seem to notice, or if he did, he was too polished to let it show. "Okay, bacon's calling, so I'm not going to keep you standing here." Taking a posture like a cartoon character floating after a really good food smell, he ducked into the dining room and I held back a laugh.

This was Operation: Be Disturbingly Nice, not Operation: Pretend Kris Is Hilarious.

"Damnit."

The sitting room was deserted. I grabbed the armchair closest to the fireplace and settled in with my coffee, pulling *A Doll's House* up on my tablet. With all of the inn's Victoriana surrounding me, it wasn't hard to imagine myself in 1870's Denmark, and I started mouthing Nora's lines, trying to get into her head. Act One Nora was light and flirty and naïve, this woman who spent her whole life doing and being everything the men in her life expected her to be, but her little rebellious streak slipped through once in a while. That would be interesting to balance, especially as that already started evolving into something deeper by the end of the act. I sat back in the chair and focused on picking the streusel top off my muffin, popping it into my mouth like Nora's macaroons. I was halfway through destroying the best crunchy bits and mouthing Nora's "I'm damned" with a giggle when a familiar voice broke into my thoughts.

"Cozy. The guy's building in this inn doesn't have anything this awesome." Kris dropped into the other armchair, one hand balancing a plate, the other holding a glass of orange juice.

"You have the gym," I pointed out as I slipped my tablet onto the coffee table, adding, "Why are you here?" Okay, that wasn't too rude.

"The only people left in the dining room are the weird guy from Oregon who only eats chicken nuggets and the girl from Nevada who was actually doing homework."

I scrunched up my nose. "Seriously? Who does that? I thought for a second about bringing my homework, and then the get-a-life fairy smacked some sense into me."

"I *know*. So I thought this sounded like as good a place as any to hang out for a while." He put his plate on the coffee table and I noticed it was piled high with waffles and bacon. "I like my breakfast with conversation."

"That's devil's bacon," I pointed out, and laughed at the confusion on his face. "Because you skipped church for it."

"Well, if I'm going to Hell, at least the trip will be tasty." He rolled his waffle around the bacon and made it into a wrap-like shape. Boys.

My phone buzzed and two messages popped up at almost the same time. The first from Grace was punctuated with about a million frowny faces. *Just heard from Phoebe about your "plan." Bad idea. Call me.* Not a huge surprise—Phoebe probably called her right after we hung up. The second, from Alec, was a lot more straightforward. *This is the stupidest idea you've ever had. Focus on your speech.* Phoebe worked fast. I deleted the notifications and shoved the phone back in my pocket. Both of those could wait.

Kris took a bite of the waffle-roll and chewed dramatically for a few seconds with a look of exaggerated bliss on his face. "Why are you agnostic, anyway?" he asked after swallowing. At least he didn't talk with his mouth full.

I bristled at his question. "That's a very personal question," I said, my voice stiff and alien. Non-plan me would have told him to bugger off, but plan-me had to be at least a little bit civil.

"I'm curious."

The coffee mug suddenly became my best friend as I clutched it in both hands, the hot ceramic burning my palms. "I'm not in the mood to have someone try to convert me or bring me back into the fold or whatever else you're trying to do." My annoyance trigger was held by a hair and I braced myself for a pushy lecture from yet another religious know-it-all.

He surprised me with his next sentence. "I'm not trying to convert you, honest. I'm just curious."

I took a sip of coffee and used those seconds to study his face. There really wasn't anything but interest there, but Kris had perfected the ability to look like he cared over years of campaigning for class office. "I don't have any evidence that higher beings exist. And until I do, I'm pretty happy not affiliating myself with any of them but also not doing anything to piss them off, either."

Kris leaned forward, his elbows resting on his knees. "What if not picking a side is already 'pissing off' a deity?"

"Or deities," I corrected him. "Not everyone is monotheistic, you know."

"Fine. What if you're already making a deity *or* a bunch of deities mad?"

"See, my point exactly. I'll make my decision when I

see some evidence." I dismissed his question with a wave of the mug.

"If you ask me, our very existence, when all the probabilities are so stacked against it, is proof."

The mug went down and I curled my fingers in the sleeves of my sweater to keep him from seeing how much he was starting to aggravate me. I twisted the chunky knit around my thumbs tight enough to almost cut off circulation. "I told you, I don't want to be converted. So if that's what you're trying to do, quit wasting your breath."

He responded by shaking his head, then pushing back the hair that fell over his forehead. It made him look much more earnest and approachable than his usual stiff hairstyle. "Seriously, no ulterior motive here. You do your thing, I just love a good debate, like the one we had in the summit yesterday."

"That wasn't a debate. That was me arguing with you because I was right and you were wrong." His eyebrows went up and eyes narrowed in a skeptical look until I backed down. "Okay, I'll play, but you should know it's way too early to think." I propped my elbows on the chair arms and steepled my fingers. "Tell me why I should care about someone or something I can't see and doesn't seem to want to involve itself in our lives?" I'd said this a million times to so many people, including my parents, that it just rolled off my tongue with barely a thought.

He took a moment to polish off his breakfast in two quick inhales, then, with a nod, asked, "I disagree about not getting involved in our lives, but since you're all about evidence, remember that religion, with all the messages about love and hope and charity, gives us guidance and inspires people to be their best."

This answer was easy. "Balanced out by religious wars and persecution. Those people apparently didn't get the memo. Besides, I'm a pretty good person and I'm not religious. I don't need some guy in a pulpit telling me to be a decent human being. Or do you think I'm not a good person?"

"I didn't say—"

Before he could finish, I cut him off. I was on a roll and, weirdly, kind of enjoying this back-and-forth. It was better than caffeine. "Why doesn't this divine being stop all the bad in the world?"

"Maybe we're supposed to be the ones who do that. You know, go out and do good? Sometimes the miracle isn't that something magically appears, but, instead, that we, against all common sense or human instinct, sacrifice our time or comfort or lives for others. Strength or courage coming from the divine in our lives and ourselves." He let the thought hang in the air before leaning even further forward and adding, "I'm guessing you don't believe miracles or divine interventions are possible."

"I haven't seen any. Plus, let's talk about your cousin. Noelle volunteered with sick kids and used to go into Camden and Philly to help out in freakin' soup kitchens, but she still died because of some weird heart problem. If anyone deserved divine intervention, it would have been her." The memory of her collapsing during field hockey practice in gym rushed back, even though it had already been two years. I had the same question back then.

"You're right." His usual confidence had melted to be replaced by two soft, sad words.

I opened my mouth to challenge him some more, but his quiet answer threw me off. I took a quick sip of coffee to put myself back on-balance. "I'm sorry. I didn't mean to bring her into this." Looking back now, I could see the family resemblance. Noelle had the same eyes. Funny, I knew Kris was related to a bunch of our classmates, but I never put two and two together with him and Noelle.

He smiled, which was something I didn't expect. "Don't be. For someone who said she was too sleepy to debate, you really went for the jugular." He scratched the back of his head then tilted back until it hit the back of the chair and he was staring at the wood ceiling. "I pretty much said the same thing to my dad at her wake. It was really, really hard to understand how I could keep believing in anything, you know, when someone like Noelle could just…" He took a deep breath, his shoulders rising and dropping with the effort before he continued. "But hope is a pretty awesome thing. And I know she's watching all the good the charity is doing in her name and smiling. Her mom and dad could have given up and let the sadness take over and everyone would have understood, you know? But, their faith and hope helped them and, instead, they turned this really terrible thing into something that's giving hundreds of kids the gift of music in their lives."

I shifted uncomfortably in my seat, his unpolished and unguarded tone throwing me off. This was a side of Kris I'd never seen before. "Miracles must exist if you have a soft spot for a music charity, even if it was because of your cousin. What's next? Joining orchestra? I think Osoba might find you a seat playing triangle or something." My attempt at a joke hung in the air and I hoped it would break the cloud that hung over us since my stupid outburst. I wanted to mess with Kris' mind, but not by dragging a dead girl into the conversation. That would make me no better than him.

"Right." He rolled his head to look at me, his soft smile morphing into a grin. Regular Kris was back with a vengeance. "And I just got you to admit that miracles exist. Which means I win this debate."

My brows drew together and I shook my head. "Whoa, you said I was right. I won fair and square."

"I said you were right about Noelle deserving divine intervention. Not about the possibility that a higher being might not exist." He reached over to poke me in the arm playfully. "I almost never take on a challenge I can't win."

"You're aggravating." Still, a smile tickled the edge of my lips and I pressed them tighter together.

His next words surprised me. "And you love debating."

I turned my focus back to the ceiling. I wasn't going to say no, but I also wasn't going to give him the pleasure of seeing me watch him gloat. "It actually feels a little like improv."

"When we're back at school, I need to get you on the

debate team." He tugged again on my sleeve and I pulled back far enough he couldn't reach me anymore.

"I dunno," I said in my lightest and flirtiest tone, "Do you want an artsy theatre and band person messing up your perfect season?"

"You'll help fill our diversity quota. Two socially awkward hobbies in one."

A snort escaped from me, though I tried to keep it back. "Excuse me, but you obviously don't know anything about band or theatre if you think we're socially awkward. We're so much more socially awesome than anything you belong to."

"I don't know. Debate club away meets can get pretty wild."

"I'll believe it when I see it." I popped a piece of muffin in my mouth to give me a second to think. "Does all the debating we did this morning mean we'll be in total agreement during the conference today?"

"I doubt it."

"Yeah. I thought you'd say that," I said, finally cracking a smile.

"It's more fun that way, Em." Amusement curved around his words, emphasizing my name in a way that sounded like it flowed naturally off his tongue but must have come from a ton of practice. There he was, turning on his fake charm again.

"I thought you'd say that, too."

19

I had resorted to reducing my cookie to crumbs and alternating eating a few bites of it with sips of coffee to keep from falling asleep. The morning's speaker didn't seem to notice as he droned on and on about the time he spent coordinating interns and volunteers in some major election campaign with some politician I'd never really heard about but had half the group on the edge of their seats. Maybe if I draped myself across the table and begged for mercy, they'd let me escape. Or they'd kick me out of the competition, which would be bad. Instead, I popped another chocolate chip in my mouth and leaned over to say to Kris, "All this talk about campaigning and stuff must be like a wet dream for you political types."

He narrowed his eyes and put his finger to his lips in the universal shh symbol.

"*Kiss-ass*," I mouthed, then rolled my eyes when he shook his head and pointed forward at the speaker. I flipped to an empty page in my notebook and pulled out my sparkly green pen so he could see what I wrote even from space. *Why's this guy important, anyway? I'm so bored.* I shoved my notebook right over his when he was mid-note.

Kris squinted at my writing, then scrawled out in boxy black letters that were like night and day to my curvy, swirly script, *He only worked on one of the most important gubernatorial campaigns of our generation. If you actually pay attention, you might learn something.*

I pulled back my notebook and added. *Or I might fall asleep. If I hear one more p-word, I'm going to stab myself with my highlighter.* His eyebrows knit together and I added, *Pundit, politician, pollster…*

His lips turned up the tiniest amount in the corners as he reached over and scribbled, *…Pain in the Posterior Princesses from Lambertfield who are Politically Puerile?*

"Oooh, big words," I whispered without looking at him, which earned me a tiny kick under the table.

Up in front, Ms. Shawnee cleared her throat and narrowed her eyes directly at us. I pretended to be cowed as I bent my head over my notebook and wrote *See what you did?* But Kris refused to look over at me. Instead, he started furiously taking even more notes. So, I went back to doodling and trying to act like I was listening to the presenter.

I just couldn't understand why this was supposed to be so interesting. Politics was so full of dry rules and slimy people who were really good at exploiting them for their own good. *Still boring. At least history is full of people with passion who fought and spoke out and ran into burning buildings to save old paintings. Nowadays, they just debate and don't do anything but sit in their private jets and take campaign money from the highest bidder. Or block anyone trying to make change because it's easier than admitting their party might be wrong.* I wrote around my sketches, not expecting Kris to see it.

He must have noticed me writing out of the corner of his eye, though, and reached over to write: *So be the one to make stuff happen. Your speech says that's what you want. Don't blame politics.*

Touchy. I wrote, but couldn't help smiling. He read my speech. So much for that confidence he claimed to have. After that, I went back to my really bad attempt at drawing Rapunzel trapped in the White House, her hair taking over the rose garden. By the time the speaker finished his presentation, I had added a fire-breathing dragon wrapped around the Washington Monument. I clapped just to be polite then closed my notebook. We could leave our things in the conference room during lunch, but I didn't need any of the advisors seeing my "notes."

"You don't sit still and pay attention very well, do you?"

"Please. You've seen me in class; I'm a model student. This was just brain-numbing." I looked around to find someone else to support me on that, but from the way the guy from New Hampshire and both New Mexicos pretended they weren't listening, I was probably in the minority.

"You could learn a lot of things from that talk. We have a powerful system where one person can make a difference. Being educated in how our country works can only help you when you're trying to make that difference." It was like Kris had that little lecture memorized. Maybe he thought it up while the guy was talking about lame ducks.

Instead of responding to what he said, I just tapped his arm as I headed out. "Ever see *Mr. Smith Goes to Washington*?" When he shook his head, I added, "Jimmy Stewart, Jean Arthur? Won an Oscar? Every politician thinks it covers the ideals of their party?" When he still looked blankly at me, I smiled and said over my shoulder as I walked away, "It's your kind of movie. Political Boy Ranger leaders, just up your alley, Scout-boy. Trust me."

"Hey, you." Grace's face and then her bedroom came into focus as she adjusted her laptop screen. Her room always looked like a picture out of a magazine thanks to the interior designer her mom had hired to design the layout. But, then again, Grace, herself, always looked like she stepped out a magazine, so it probably had less to do with the designer and more to do with her. Perfect and practical and currently unhappy with me, at least from what I could tell through the screen.

"Hey." I tried a little wave, hoping that would make her smile.

"How's the conference going?"

"Good, actually. I like the set-up. They have people come in to talk about different topics, and then we have discussions and debates afterwards. It's weirdly fun." I loved how Ms. Shawnee and the other conference people let us debate and discuss without stepping in or speaking down to us. "I'm not a fan of the guy they had talk to us this morning, but we're supposed to do some role-playing in a little bit and I can't wait to crush Kris in it."

Grace's brow furrowed and she leaned forward, close enough to the screen that I could see the sharp edge of her eyeliner. "See, that's a problem."

"What's a problem?"

"You focusing on 'crushing' Kris instead of actually enjoying the experience."

That explained the unhappy expression. I tried to look nonchalant, but it was hard to lean back and cross my arms when one arm had to hold my tablet out. I settled for tilting my head and only crossing one arm in front of me as casually as possible, using it to prop up my tablet arm. "I'll enjoy the experience when I know he isn't trying to mess with my head."

"I know. Phoebe told me about your ridiculous plan. Please tell me you were messing with her."

I twirled one of my curls around my finger and resisted the urge to shrug. Boston's autumn humidity worked wonders on my hair. "I don't know why you're so worried, it's a great plan."

"If you're a crazy manipulative jerk, which is something you're not," Grace said, her voice tight and eyes narrowed. At that, she was up and pacing, which I knew wasn't a good sign.

Suddenly, the wall was *very* interesting. Victorian wallpaper was just so geometric and flowery. "He started it," I said, knowing I sounded just like Chloe when she was in trouble with Mom and Dad.

Grace shook her head and pursed her lips. "Look, I despise that guy as much as the next person, but don't you think you'd be better off actually focusing on the important parts of this, like learning from the conference and giving the best speech possible on Saturday? There are almost a hundred other people you're up against and you can't let Kris bother you so much."

She was right, and the thought of competing against all of them made my nausea start up all over again, but—"Maybe if I didn't have to see him every waking minute. It's not that easy to just avoid him, you know. They stick us together in *every* freaking thing, like we have to be tied at the hip just because we're from the same state, and he's been so…" I searched for the right word, landing on, "duplicitous the whole time, as if I can't see through his tricks. I know what he's up to and I'm not going to let him get away with it."

"You can't control every situation. Sometimes, you need to let go of things." Oh, God, there she went into lecture mode. Next up was probably going to be something about how I needed to trust in my own skills and not let outside influences faze me. If she ever decided not to go into math or science, Grace would have a great career on the self-esteem speech circuit. "Are you sure there isn't something else behind this? Usually your 'plans' happen when you're in control-freak mode. And you only do that when something else in your life is off."

I put all of my effort into keeping my expression care-free and light. "Everything's perfect. Well, except for this Kris thing."

She stared me down for a second, then unconvincingly *mm-hmm*ed. "Also, I think we need to talk about this Wil situation."

"There is no Wil situation." I resisted the urge to pretend I heard Ann calling for me and run away. I didn't need Grace's logic cutting into my love life.

Drawn-together brows joined her pursed lips, and she started looking a little like my grumpy Aunt Melody. "Yes, there is. He's totally ghosting you and you're in denial. You need to stop tagging him on Photogram and Snapbook. It's not healthy."

"No, he's just giving me space so I can focus on the competition."

Grace's finger started a rapid tap-tap-tap on the side of the screen, making the picture shake. "Please, Phoebe and Alec might buy that, but you know I don't. He's unfollowed you on every social media platform and won't answer your texts. If that isn't ghosting, what is it?"

"He didn't unfollow me on Photogram. He even favor-ited one of the pictures I posted from Old North Church." My heart had swelled at that sign, like he wanted me to know that he was checking in but giving me space. "This is just a temporary thing. You know, like last year. Wil and I will get back together when I get a chance to actually focus on fixing this." Which might happen if I didn't have to spend every waking hour explaining the situation to all my friends.

"You know, there is such a thing as mistake favoriting." The tapping grew harder. "Em, this isn't good. You don't want to be with someone who doesn't want you one hundred percent."

"Oh, Wil wants me."

"Em."

"Grace." Our eyes locked in an epic stare-down. "Look, he maybe he did unfollow me, but half his posts are about me, at least from what I can translate."

"You deserve someone who won't play games or string you along. Someone who won't let go unless it's the best thing for you. And, honestly, someone who will call you on your bull."

I cleared my throat. "That's why I have you in my life." I glanced at the corner of my tablet to check the time and jumped to standing. "I gotta go. They're starting in a minute and me being late looks worse than any plan you might think is insane."

"It's not insane, it's a waste of time and effort based on a completely inaccurate theory. And it's taking away from the important thing you need to focus on, which is this competition."

Like I didn't know. I resisted the urge to tell her how much I was trying not to freak out about the competition and, instead, let out an Oscar-worthy sigh. "Whatever, zen-master Grace. Call me tonight if you want to keep lecturing me. Any last words of wisdom before I hang up on you?"

"Don't do anything I wouldn't do."

"Mmmhmm. I'll take that under advisement. Bye." Halfway through her own "'bye," I hung up, dropped my tablet on the desk, and sprinted for the conference room.

Emmiebear: @WilOfHyrule Calling you later, can't wait to chat! <3

WilOfHyrule: Working on many Christmas plans!

Auto-translated from German. Undo?

WilOfHyrule: Someone special will come to Dresden, cannot wait to show the city.

Auto-translated from German. Undo?

WilOfHyrule: Should I be afraid that I miss cheesesteaks? They were unhealthy, but I liked sharing them with friends.

HokageAlec: @WilOfHyrule Dude. Of everything over here, you're still craving cheesesteaks?

WilOfHyrule: @HokageAlec I dream of cheesesteaks. I would go back just for a cheesesteak, though I miss many things from America.

HokageAlec: @WilOfHyrule Don't say it too many times on here or Em might try to shove one in a care package.

HokageAlec: @WilOfHyrule You don't want to see what week-old cheesesteak looks like. Trust me

20

"I tried calling him, but his mom picked up and said a whole bunch of stuff in German I think meant he was out, so I just texted him," I said to Ann and Lia as we stepped off the bus. I still felt crappy from my marathon phone-email-text session that afternoon. After talking with Grace, I just needed one quick reply from Wil to prove she was wrong, but he just wasn't answering. Worry twisted at my stomach but I tried to push it away. I had enough on my plate. I needed to get into Nora's head so I could blow Landry away when I came back to rehearsals. I needed to keep an eye on Kris and beat him at his own game, and I needed to focus on Boston and being awesome.

Lia looked a little in awe. "I can't imagine dating anyone who didn't live in my zip code."

"Wait until you get to college. It might be harder to avoid that than you think," Ann said to Lia, a bit too practically for my tastes. That part of her, along with the whole uber-responsibility, reminded me a little bit of Grace. "Still, it must drive you crazy that you two don't even speak the same language."

"Well, he knows English, but people usually don't talk

much when they're making out," I pointed out as we walked through the doors of the bigger-than-usual colonial building and into seventeenth-century Massachusetts. I paused, letting the history of the place settle in around me like an anchor—it was my favorite part of walking into any older building, like I was the Greek god Chronos or someone in a fantasy film and could, in that moment, touch time. The place was awesome—meat was roasting in a giant fireplace on my right while rows and rows of wooden tables filled the room. Another fireplace towards the back of the room held a cauldron that looked like it came straight out of the scene with the witches in Macbeth. Apparently, the building around us was some sort of inn that had been converted completely to a themed restaurant, down to servers in costume. "This place is so cool." A woman in a cap and striped gown rushed by us carrying a large, grey pitcher, giving me flashbacks to my interpretation job last summer.

Ann reached out to touch the giant stones that made up the inside wall and her fingers traced the edge of the rough wooden beam that started along the wall and travelled up to the low wooden ceiling. "Yeah. Did you see the sign out front? The original structure goes back to 1670."

"This building was around during the witch trials. Who knows what kind of ghosts might be hanging out here?" The guy from Vermont peeked over my shoulder as we followed Red and Rosie to a long set of tables on the side of the room and I laughed and swatted him back. "Careful, Jersey. I heard they like latching onto unsuspecting tourists and going home with them. Especially tourists who laugh about stuff like ghosts." He tilted so his face was in the flickering shadows of the faux candlelight.

I laughed again, turning around when we were midway to the tables and grabbing Kris' arm, pulling him away from one of the girls who was droning on about a hay bale out front and her allergies while he tried to look sympathetic. Luckily, he was only a few steps behind me. It was the perfect opening to up the ante. "That's okay. Kris will watch my back. "

Kris looked relieved to be free of allergy girl's clutches and mouthed a "thanks" before poking me in the side with his elbow. "I doubt you need me. You're not the damsel in distress type."

He caught me off guard with that compliment. "I'm glad you noticed."

"Plus, if I saw a ghost, I'd push you towards him to give myself a chance to escape," he added.

"That's the Kris I know and despise." I winked at Ann, who stifled a laugh. "I was starting to wonder if you had a good twin."

"You bring out the best—I mean, worst—in me." He headed in the direction of the first of the empty tables designated for our group.

I let go of his arm and tilted my head curiously at him. "You're not going to do that room-surveying thing you always do?"

He paused, looking back at me with curiosity. "What room-surveying thing?"

"You know, when you stop in the door and figure out who the most important people are in the room so you can go be by them?"

His brows almost made a straight line, pulled in by the frown that grew across his lips with my words. "I don't do that."

"Almost every single time." He looked like he had no idea what I was talking about, and I nodded to emphasize my point.

"No, maybe I stop because I'm trying to find someone familiar in the room. If I don't know anyone, I try to figure out which group of people looks open to having someone else join their conversation." He had paused and was checking out the tables now that more of our group had sat down. "Dad always does…" he blinked, then, at my pointed look, said, "Oh."

A giggle escaped at his clueless expression. "This is hilarious. You really didn't realize you were doing it? Wow."

"Son of a career politician. I guess it was unconscious." He ducked his head as a sheepish smile spread across his face. With a shrug, he pushed his hair out of his eyes and followed me to one of the tables with a lot of our regular regional group and Ann, where he ended up sandwiched between me and New York girl.

"I'm never letting you live this down, you know," I whispered, and he responded with a light jab to my ribs with his elbow.

Our server, an incredibly hot college-aged guy in

breeches and a red waistcoat knocked on the table to get our attention. At least, the attention of the guys and any girls who hadn't yet seen him. How could anyone *not* notice his tight-fitting pants or his romance-novel-cover-worthy long brown hair, which he had tied back in a low colonial-ish ponytail? "How do you fare, sirs and ladies?" he asked in a somewhat British accent.

I couldn't help it. I itched to take on a character that would fit into this amazing place. I'd spent time at a lot of historic sites, but there was something magical about being somewhere "new." Who knew what stories and scandals and romances *these* walls held? I straightened myself up as if I was wearing a pair of stays, pulling from my memory of the ones I wore from July to August while interpreting the daughter of a merchant from the islands.

"Very well, thank ye, sir," I said, with a bow of my head. That earned me a weird look from Kris and a smile from Historical Hottie.

"And from whence have you travelled to come to this fine establishment?"

Ann was the first to speak up. "Montana."

Historical Hottie made a show of tilting his head in confusion. "I have never heard of such a place. Mont- ana?"

Ann's eyebrows drew together in confusion.

"'Tis out west," the guy from Maryland said, getting into character, too. If I counted right, there were at least four of us at the table who were seriously into theatre and you could tell by the way we were lighting up. Maryland had transformed, too, his body language mimicking our server.

"Far, into the backwoods," the girl from Virginia added in a serious near-whisper, as if she were a proper lady surprised anyone would admit to not being from a colony.

"Ah, now I understand." Historical Hottie smiled at Ann and made a mini-bow with a small flourish of his hand. "I am glad you will be able to enjoy civilized company now that you are back from the wilderness." Ann blinked at him while I tried not to laugh. Historical Hottie winked at me, then kept up a steady stream of banter for five-ish minutes with all of us acting types while the rest of our table just watched.

When he left to get our first course of stewed pompion, I turned back to the table with a grin so wide it almost hurt, as if the edges of my lips were trying to reach my ears. "That was awesome."

Kris twirled his fork on his metal plate, making a scraping sound. "You theatre people are really weird."

New York nodded, reaching over to pat him on the arm. "I agree."

Lia shook her head. "It's fun. You should try it." Maryland nodded in agreement.

"Oh, no, Kris is too cool to do anything fun," I said, keeping my voice light and teasing instead of how I'd normally make digs at him.

"I don't know if talking in a funny accent to a guy in tight pants would qualify as fun," Kris said.

"Well, *that* could be a lot of fun in the right context."

I couldn't help it. He had given me such a great opening and I was still me.

"Seriously?" New York said, sounding a little annoyed. "*Seriously?*" She looked at Kris as if to say, *And this is what your state sent to our competition?*

Virginia blushed for me, but looked like she was holding back a giggle. "That was wrong on so many levels."

I reached over, stilled Kris' spinning fork, and put it back on the table, issuing a challenge. "It's only us here. No one's taking a video," I paused, then thought it might be good to add, "yet. How many chances do you get to eat in a historical place with people acting like they're straight out of the seventeen-hundreds?"

"We live right outside of Philly. That's every other restaurant in the city during Welcome America," he pointed out. "Isn't that basically what you did all last summer, anyway?"

"Whatever. Try it. Say 'tis.'"

"'Tis a stupid idea."

I straightened up again into my colonial lady persona and tilted my chin so I could look up at him through my lashes. "My heart 'tis aflutter with the dulcet tones of your voice." It was hard to keep a straight face, so I hammed it up instead, exaggeratedly batting my eyelashes and putting my hand over my heart. "Pray, speak again, dear sir, so I may bask in your words."

He narrowed his eyes at me, but his serious expression was starting to crack. "M'lady, you are insane." His really bad accent had me torn between letting him off the hook for humanitarian reasons and egging him on.

Of course, I picked the latter. "Bestill my heart, he speaks."

Historical Hottie came back just as I finished saying that and, as he dropped bowls of what looked like pumpkin mush in front of us, said to Kris, "Are you courting this lady?"

He blinked confusedly, and shook his head. "What? No. Just...no."

I didn't appreciate the distaste in his tone. "We *did* travel together. It was a rather long and trying journey." I turned my eyelash-batting colonial harlot persona on him and earned a grin.

"Scandalous!" Virginia shrieked, back in her own character. I watched "I'm always confident" Kris squirm in his seat from the attention. If my plan to out-nice him into losing failed, I'd have to remember how much he seemed to hate being in situations that forced him out of his element.

"It's obviously not like that," Kris muttered while trying to shut me up with a death glare. "We're..."

I wasn't going to let him break out of character, or at least break me out of character. An idea flashed into my head and I couldn't help it, "Cousins." Kris would get the in-joke. He used it all the time with all of his real, if distant, cousins in school. His snort confirmed it.

"Since you are not taken, I hope this offers no offense." Historical Hottie swept forward and, keeping his eyes trained on mine, picked up my hand and kissed it. He slid his hand back until my fingers dropped from his hold, giving a bow before starting to walk away with a wink at Kris.

My heart gave a little flutter and I let out a sigh. One of the other girls at the table whispered, "Lucky." Yes, he was probably a college acting student playing a part and probably did this at every dinner to someone at the table he served, but still, I was human with hormones. Phoebe was going to die of jealousy when she heard about this. I turned to Kris, positive I still looked a little goofy and definitely out of character. "And that is why the guy in tight pants with an eighteenth-century accent wins every time."

"Do you realize how ridiculous that sounds?" Kris asked.

I waved one hand dismissively at him. "You're just jealous that someone from colonial America has more game than you."

"Doubtful."

"They were just so polite and poetic back then," Virginia said, putting her hand to her forehead in a fake swoon.

Kris looked at the other guys for help, but they all made "it's all yours" gestures at him. "Considering they probably smelled like livestock and B.O., they needed *something* if they wanted anyone to get close to them."

"You know, George Washington had a favorite cologne. Assuming he doused himself in that stuff, chances are he smelled like livestock, B.O., and lots and lots of citrus," I said, almost without thinking, then decided to toss a little jab his way, "They still sell it. I'm surprised you don't have a case of it. 'Eau de Founding Father: a must-have for every aspiring politician.'"

Maryland opened his mouth, closed it, and opened it again. "Okay, I bite. How do you know something like that?"

"Em's really into history. She just tries to look cool by hiding under all her acting stuff," Kris said. When I frowned at him, he raised his hands: "What? We're in the same class. It's pretty obvious. You practically drooled when we started the Revolutionary War module."

As if liking history and acting were mutually exclusive. "Anyway…" I blew air through my lips, "weren't we talking about colonial guy having more game than you?"

"This is the most ridiculous conversation ever," New York said with a shake of her head.

"I agree one hundred percent, Marina," Kris said, turning one of his bright smiles on her, his face glowing in the candlelight. It was weird how he actually knew New York's name, just like he seemed to have memorized everyone else's name in the competition already. I was lucky if I remembered their states. "Unfortunately, it looks like Em thinks tonight's dinner needed a debate and decided Mr. Tight Pants had to have an advantage over modern humans to support her side of the argument. But, she's going to lose to my defense of modern courtship rituals." Kris cleared his throat, turned towards me, and tugged on one of my curls. "Ahem. Excuse me, miss. I like your hair. It's so twisty, it's like playing with a spring."

"Ha. Funny." I swatted his hand away, almost knocking over the wooden bowl of chowder one of the wait staff tried to put in front of me. I gave the lady an apologetic look before turning back to Kris, who had triumphant little smile playing cockily over his lips as he took a drink of water from his big pewter mug. I pulled up as much colonial language as I could remember, then innocently twisted that same curl around my finger and leaned in close to him. "Sir, I'm afraid I'm somewhat of a loose woman at the moment. Pray, will you help me tighten my stays?" I was rewarded when his ears turned bright red and he nearly choked on his water. I sat back, satisfaction buzzing through my body at his reaction. "Eighteenth century wins again."

Kris finally stopped coughing and shook his head at me. "I thought this was between a modern, normal human being and colonial pants. Not a game of 'let's see what totally inappropriate thing Em can say next.'" His voice still sounded rough from all the coughing.

"True. But I couldn't help it. It's easy to push your buttons." A sentence came into my head and I didn't even bother to filter it. "I like pushing your buttons."

"Obviously." Vermont put down his soup spoon and looked from me to Kris and back again. "Are you two really related? Because your conversation is creeping me out."

I let out an involuntary snort. "Hell no. Our town might be small, but thankfully, I'm not a Lambert."

"You just wish you were," Kris said back at me with a crooked grin. He then moved the conversation on to the

conference that afternoon, talking about NGOs and govern-
mental policies with Ann, Maryland, and New York as the
rest of us dug into our dinners and talked about the latest
episode of *Vampire Teens*. For two people from the same
town, we were so incredibly different.

After dinner, one of the actors led us all on a lantern-lit tour of the inn and its grounds. The building was so cool and eerie with its sparsely furnished rooms and paintings of people hanging on the walls. While half our group ogled a fancy travel writing box, I stared down the hallway and shivered as our guide told the story of a girl who died in that room on her wedding night. Vermont leaned in and whispered, "See, I told you: Ghosts."

"Why would a female ghost want to latch onto me?" I pursed my lips and took a step back, pretending to look him up and down. "If I was a ghost and had to pick between me and a hottie farmboy from Vermont, I'd pick farmboy any time."

"I'm not a farmboy. That's such a stereotype," he muttered. "But I'll take the hottie part."

"Good." I pushed him slightly towards the hallway. "Now, go, flirt up a ghostly girlfriend." Vermont shook his head, then headed towards Lia and Ann, probably to see if he could scare the crap out of them better than his fail with me.

"You're evil," Kris said as he came up beside me. We made our way outside and the guide led us over a narrow wood and stone bridge towards a building with a waterwheel attached to it. "Sometimes, I wonder if most of that is an act."

The rough wood of the bridge handrail dug into my palm as I clutched at it with every step. A good ten feet below us, a creek or river or something churned over rocks. It definitely didn't look like it was deep enough to cushion a fall.

"'All the world's a stage and all the men and women merely players,'" I quoted between shallow breaths. We reached the other side and I tried not to let relief show on my face. "Everything we do is an act—a part of this carefully constructed story we have about who we are and what we want the world to see about us. You do the same thing, every time you pretend to care about people right before the class president elections." *Be nice, Em*, the plotty voice said in my head.

"That's not an act. Maybe I do take extra time to talk to people I don't usually hang out with in the beginning of the year, but do *you* know everyone in our class?" Before he could answer, he added, "Who aren't in band or theatre?"

"I know a few cheerleaders and football players," I said, and my defensive wall shot up.

"There are over three hundred of us and I want to make sure I understand what everyone wants and needs from the school, even if I don't hang out with them." He ran a hand through his hair and his smile turned infuriatingly smug. "Of course, if it gets me votes, I'm not complaining."

That last comment proved my whole point. "Of *course*," I parroted him, my voice dripping with sarcasm. "Because that's what you care about, anyway."

Kris stopped short and grabbed at my sleeve so I had to back off the path to keep out of everyone's way. He didn't look too happy. "Last year, the student council brought back Spirit Week and I was the one who suggested we add the hallway decorating and music competitions to include you artsy people." At "you," he stepped even closer and pointed his finger at me so I had to press up against one of the fences surrounding the fields to keep from getting poked in the nose. "I spoke with alumni and businesses to get all those extra tablets and e-readers for our library because we didn't have enough. All stuff I learned by talking to people. It's not an act."

I debated slipping through the rails, but instead closed my eyes and took a deep breath. "Sorry, I didn't mean to assume you didn't care. It's just, what normal person does that? Memorize everyone's names and campaign for votes?"

"Someone who wants to make a difference." Kris seemed to realize how close he'd gotten and backed off. He started walking again and I had to pick up speed to catch up to him. Damn my shorter legs. "We're both here because we wrote speeches about how we can make positive change in the world. You can't put the kind of words and passion into a speech that gets you this far unless you believe what you wrote. Or was that all an act for *you*?"

"No." A breeze blew over us and I crossed my arms, pulling my sleeves over my hands at the same time. I had no idea how he could still be comfortable in only that henley.

Even some of the other boys—okay, only the ones from the southern states—were wearing sweatshirts or jackets. "I mean, I really want the scholarship, but my speech means a lot to me." Wanting the scholarship was an understatement, but he didn't need to know how badly I wanted to win. Still, because I'd failed miserably so far with plan "Be Freakishly Nice to Kris" between Historical Hottie and arguing with him about class presidency, I bumped him with my shoulder and said, "Truce? We're both real and awesome. Since we keep getting stuck together here, we can't fight all the time, right?"

"True and truce. Unless we're debating, and you're on the wrong side." He looked at me out of the corner of his eye. "Is that why you've been civil to me today? It's been a little *Twilight-Zone*-y, to be honest."

"I'm civil all the time, I just don't fall over myself around you like you want me to. Besides, our state gets enough flak from bad comedians. It doesn't need us giving it a bad name, too." This time, I was the one who invaded his personal space, smiling up at him. "Besides, I think I've been a lot nicer than just civil."

"Right. Thanks for making fun of me back there with that loose stays thing."

"It's not my fault you have a dirty mind and interpreted that in a modern context. Besides, it's an all-day summit tomorrow. I'm sure you'll have a lot of chances for payback." The organizers always sat us next to each other because of the state thing, but I'm positive they regretted that decision daily.

Kris' teeth were bright in the moonlight. "I can't wait."

One of the reenactors walking from the barn to one of the other outbuildings caught my eye and I watched her silhouette in the moonlight, time freezing as if the hands on a clock suddenly whirred backwards two hundred and fifty years. The entire farm around us took on a surreal feel that buzzed across my skin, like I really was a time traveler.

"You really do like history, don't you?" he asked, breaking the spell and dragging me back into our time.

I turned back to Kris, who was watching me with an amused expression, his features softened by the moonlight. "I love history." I closed my eyes, remembering back to the exact moment I fell head over heels in love with the past. Even though it was years ago, that initial "this is right," key fitting perfectly in a lock feeling rushed over me again. "Do you remember our fifth grade field trip to Philly?"

"When Andrew threw up on the bus before we even left town so we had to smell it the whole way there?"

My eyes shot open and I scrunched my nose in disgust. "Thanks. I'd blocked that part out."

Kris was trying to feign a disgusted look, but he couldn't completely make his grin go away. "I wish I could."

"You know how we did the walking tour? I remember being in Independence Hall and realizing that I was actually standing right where our country was born, and it was a real place that had been filled with real people. It was such an amazing feeling. I've been to Athens when we visited my grandparents and watched the sun set from the Temple of Poseidon and we went along with mom to Koobi Fora when she took some of her students there on a research trip and I touched stone tools from two million years ago, but US history will always be my first love because of that moment."

We started walking again and I tilted my head up at the sky and the red moon filling it. "I obviously wouldn't want to live in it because they didn't have women's rights or civil rights and there was the whole rampant cholera and scarlet fever thing. And I wore stays enough last summer that I'm totally not interested in wearing corsets every day, because that's just plain body torture."

"You're not making a good case for the past, you know," he said, with a small laugh, close enough that his arm shook against mine, but I didn't mind.

"I know. But even with that, it's all just so interesting to me. Not the wars, but the stuff they never really bother to take the time to teach us, like the everyday details of how regular people lived." I looked over at him. "Mom always says that if you want to really learn about a culture, don't look at how the big people in charge lived. The real story is in the food the regular people ate, the traditions they followed, and how their lives were lived in their huts or tents or cottages. A lot of superstitions or religious laws came from things they did to keep safe or healthy." I stopped myself, realizing I'd gone into lecture mode, which was something that usually only Alec, Phoebe, and sometimes Grace could get out of me. I squirmed inside at the realization, and pulled my attention back to the field, hoping the re-enactor would come back out—she'd probably been my history overload trigger, anyway.

"I guess I never thought of it that way." His eyes met mine again, and I could read a little surprise in them, as well as something else I couldn't really see in the dim light. "How come you never get this deep in school?"

"Like I said, we all have our roles. Everyone expects me to be this happy, flirty person, not someone who spouts off history factoids all the time," I said before I could stop myself, realizing how true it actually was—even my best friends didn't always see more than Em Katsaros, flirt extraordinaire—then quickly purged the sullen tone from my voice. "Besides," I added, literally trying to shrug it off, "I'm positive you don't care about revolutionary contributions of colonial women with spinning wheels or what it's like to touch a letter from two hundred years ago."

"I can tell how much this means to you. I—" He started to say something else, but then New York came over and ran her hand down his arm to grab his hand and tug him towards her.

"Kris, come with me to the waterwheel building." She used a giggly tone that made the hairs on the back of my neck stand up, like a cat rubbed the wrong way.

He gently untangled himself from her clutches, smiling tightly. "Sure, I'll be there in a minute. I'm just finishing up talking with Em, okay?"

New York looked from him to me and back to him again, totally oblivious to the uncomfortable vibes coming off Kris in waves. "Sure, see you soon."

As soon as she was out of earshot, Kris let out a breath and said, in a low whisper, "Okay, that was awkward."

I snorted, looking at him out of the corner of my eye and trying my hardest not to grin. "You know, if you stopped flirting with every single girl to get what you wanted, maybe stuff like this wouldn't happen."

"I do not do that."

I reached out to lightly touch his arm and moved in front of him so I could look soulfully into his eyes. Ignoring the jolt that ran through me as his eyes widened in surprise, I pulled up my best Kris impression and said, "Oh, New York girl, please tell me more about your overpriced purebred puppy when you get back. Oh, while you're up, anyway, can you ask the servers to bring me an extra roll? Thanks."

He broke our gaze by stepping back and looking at New York's retreating form. "You're taking my words completely out of context. She asked the whole table if they wanted anything. And her name's Marina."

I made a "whatever" gesture with my hand. There were over a hundred people in the competition and I was lucky if I could remember a quarter of their names. "And the other girl who made you squirm earlier today?" I took a deep breath and straightened back my shoulders before morphing back into Kris, overconfident smile and all. "Wow, One of those Rectangular States I Can't Keep Straight, that dress looks really nice on you." I imitated slicking my hair back and artfully left my hand at the back of my head, pretending to scratch it. "Hey, I totally forgot my packet and have no idea what's next on the schedule. Can I borrow yours for a sec?"

He snorted at my imitation. "You borrow my schedule all the time. Half the time, you don't even bother to ask."

"Yeah, but I don't flirt to get it. And since you wanted to know why this stuff keeps happening to you, well, there's your answer."

He shook his head. "I really don't do that."

I mimicked his tone again, but nodded, instead. "You really do."

"By the way, her name is Amber, from South Dakota. And we really need to work on US geography for you."

"If they just redrew the map to make some of those states look remotely unique, maybe. Until then, chances are I won't be able to ever tell Colorado from Utah," I said, dropping my Kris imitation and becoming myself again.

"Colorado and Utah look very different on a map."

"Rectangles, all of them. Meanwhile, New Jersey is blessed with plenty of curves." I waved my hand down the side of my body and giggled as I poked him in the arm in reaction to his groan. "C'mon, if you don't want to be roped into a bad romantic situation in a dark building, we can head over to the barn, instead. New Mexico and New Hampshire seem to be pretty immune to your charms, so you should be safe there." I poked him again and added, as he rubbed his arm with an indignant expression on his face. "Just watch out for New Hampshire. That state has a few curves of its own."

22

Worry flooded through me as I scrolled through my texts and emails, coming up with nothing. Not one message or favorite from Wil overnight, only a Photogram post of raindrops in a puddle with something that translated as "Autumn storms and Autumn feelings," making me wonder if he was sad, too. It was hard to figure out some of Wil's artsier posts sometimes. Or maybe Grace was right and the favorite had been a fluke. I curled my free arm around my waist and squeezed tight. After all the Kris exposure, I really needed a little bit of support from Wil. Not silence. I didn't like how Kris made me want to rant all the time, or confused me with his all too obvious fake niceness. I needed Wil's perfect leading man stoic support, the big silent shadow behind me always willing to hold me up.

It was easy to know how to act around Wil.

"Em?" Ann poked her head into our bathroom, where I'd gone for privacy, and frowned at my pajamas. "You're going to be late for breakfast if you don't start getting ready."

The part of me that went back to hitting the refresh button over and over again wanted to tell her to bugger off, but I slowly put down my tablet and rubbed my eyes.

"You're right. I'm just catching up on a few things with Wil."

Ann stepped inside, already changed into jeans and a flowy top that looked straight out of *The Lord of the Rings*, and her braid had sparkly beads twisted into it. I pat down the massive frizz that had been my curls.

"Maybe he's too busy to talk?" She asked gently, propping herself up on the counter.

I couldn't help the cold lead feeling that kept growing in the pit of my stomach, but I switched off my tablet and forced as bright a morning smile as I could manage before coffee. "I'll catch him later."

"You're amazing for handling this time zone thing. I'm still trying to get used to east coast time." She checked her phone and hopped off the counter. "Speaking of, it's really getting late. Do you want me to wait while you get ready?" I could tell she was just being her usual, crazily nice self—in the short time I'd known her, I learned Ann hated being late for anything.

Thank God for years of forced stage smiles. I knew mine looked genuine as I padded out to the room to toss my tablet onto my bed. "No, that's okay. I'll catch up with you downstairs. Save me a muffin."

"Are you sure?" She already had her folder and keycard in her hands.

I nodded, heading over to the closet to pull out a pair of jeans and an orange-y red top. Might as well *look* confident even if I didn't feel it. "Looking fabulous takes time. I don't want to disappoint any of the Southern boys, you know."

Ann shook her head and laughed, one hand on the door-knob. "Just get down there before the announcements start, okay?" With a wave, she headed into the hallway, leaving me alone in our room.

Deep breaths. I could worry about Wil later. I needed to be focused—perfect. I had to stop letting Kris throw me off my game and I needed to blow everyone away at the conference, even if it didn't really count towards our actual judging. I needed to prove to everyone that I belonged there as much as anyone else.

It was just so hard to control the situation so far from home. It was even harder when every insecurity I'd ever had was trying so hard to spiral out of control.

From: Em (emkatsaros@dmail.com)

To: Wilhelm (wmeyer@dmail.de)

Subject: Boston is SO great

Hi!

I don't know if you tried calling me—I've been in Boston and they have us in meetings or sightseeing all the time, so I'm never logged in. Boston is really nice—have you thought about what I emailed the other day? It would be amazing at Christmastime. And you'd love the historical dinner place we went to last night—I can explain the whole history part. The house was from the seventeen-hundreds and they had a working colonial farm on the grounds. I know it's not as cool as the stuff from the Middle Ages you have around there, but it was like I stepped back in time and it's so much fun.

Kris is being his usual Kris self. We're stuck together all the time and he always picks the opposite side on anything I say, just to argue. He argued against me about volunteering, if you'd believe that. And don't get me started on NGOs (non-governmental organizations, in case it's not the same in German). I wish you were here, instead—it would have been so nice to walk around the farm with you in the moonlight, talking about history. Maybe if you come here, we'll do a road trip to Massachusetts and you can see what I mean.

A road trip up here in the winter, with snow everywhere,

would be so pretty and romantic and wonderful. We'll skip the stewed pumpkin, though. It was kind of gross.

I have my phone on me, so text or email, okay?

XOXOXOXO

Em

From: Em (emkatsaros@dmail.com)

To: Alec (Alec247@dmail.com)

Subject: Wil

Hey, have you heard from Wil lately?

From: Alec (Alec247@dmail.com)

To: Em (emkatsaros@dmail.com)

Subject: Re: Wil

Yup. We MMORPG'd yesterday. What's up? Aren't you two still fighting?

23

The conference room in the inn, which took up the entire first floor of the house on the row, was surprisingly comfortable for a conference room. While the walls were decorated with antiques and the windows still had their window seats and wavy glass, modern tables filled the room, little touchscreens set into the tables showing what was being projected on the screen in front of us. Signs with our state flags hung in front of our seats, so I couldn't avoid sitting next to Kris.

He looked way too good that early in the morning as he walked in, his hair still wet from the shower and wearing a button-down shirt over jeans that would have looked too formal on anyone else but just seemed to work with him. Take the boy out of Lambertfield, take away his hair gel and student council lackeys, and this was apparently what you got.

Kris took his seat with a nod and a smile and a flush of heat ran through me as I realized I was staring. *He's only being nice to throw you off,* I reminded myself. I'd seen that smile in action for seven years, coming out like clockwork in student council election season against his opponents right before moving in for the kill. He handed me a coffee cup from the fancy coffee shop next to the inn, his fingers brushing mine for the barest of seconds. "Coffee? I didn't see you at breakfast, so I figured you might want something." I opened the lid and sniffed. Mocha hazelnut, no sugar or cream—exactly what I had ordered when we got back from dinner the night before and all the MidAtlantics snuck over to the shop to get coffee. He really had an insanely good memory. I raised my eyebrows and looked at him over the cup.

"It's not poisoned, promise."

I took a sip and let the warmth and yumminess flow through me. "Thanks, but you didn't have to."

He held up another cup that let a stream of vanilla-scented steam into the air. "It wasn't out of my way. I went in for another white hot chocolate. It's like drinking melted sugar, which is awesome."

"Until you crash from the sugar high. Thanks, anyway, for thinking of me."

He took a long sip, then said nonchalantly, "I'll need the sugar. I stayed up late last night watching the movie you suggested."

Shock resonated through me and I felt my eyebrows rise. "Really?"

"Pretty good for something made almost eighty years ago."

I pursed my lips. "'Pretty good?' I think the Academy would disagree with you on that. You're talking about two cinematic legends."

He laughed, a wide, genuine smile stretching across his face. "It's really easy to get you worked up, isn't it? I'll have to try insulting some oldie musical next."

"Touch *West Side Story* and I won't be responsible for my actions."

"Theatre people," he said, shaking his head.

Ms. Shawnee walked into the room and we quickly went silent. Today, she was dressed a little more casually—for her—in a blouse and slacks, her hair so perfect it looked like she'd just come from a salon. For someone who worked with people our age, she was pretty formal all the time. "Good morning, representatives." Our responses spanned the range from extra perky from kiss-ups like Kris to mumbles from the half of the group that probably stayed up all night talking. I just raised my coffee in a semi-salute. At least Ms. Shawnee wasn't the lame type who'd keep saying "Good morning" until we yelled it back. I liked that about her.

"Today will be a full conference day. We have some great speakers for you this morning. In the afternoon, we will be pulling you out individually to work on your speeches with mentors. Wednesday and Friday, you'll meet with them again to put the final shine on your words and presentation, just in time for the competition on Saturday. I promise you'll walk away from your sessions with even stronger speeches than the ones that won in your states."

"I heard they have some radio and TV people and maybe even a presidential speech writer," the guy from New Mexico, Adrien, whispered to me.

"So cool." Forget the speechwriter. I wanted to make contact with someone who had connections in the arts. That would look awesome on my application.

"If you look at the schedules you were given, you'll see that today, we're talking about far-reaching and global impacts of our local actions. Let's get started."

We were supposed to head to the dining room, our rooms, or the common areas of the inn. Anywhere but this conference room. Everyone else had filed out except for Ms. Shawnee and the inn staff coming through to straighten up the tables.

And her patient smile was starting to look tight and tense as her eyes went from Kris to me and back. I threw my notebooks into my bag with a little more force than necessary and started towards the door, but didn't miss a beat in my argument. "What we need to do is figure out how to take our grassroots effort and spread it to the world stage. Not everything has to start big." She must have thought New Jersey-ans were insane. I definitely wasn't helping to clear out any "ready for a fight" stereotypes.

Kris followed, picking up pace until he was right alongside me. Out of the corner of my eye, I could see Ms. Shawnee slump to a chair and breathe a sigh of what had to be relief. "You've got to be kidding me. Do you actually believe anyone in war-torn countries has time to think about things like bake sales and book drives when they're just trying to keep from being blown up or starving to death?" We made it about ten feet outside the room before stopping next to an overfilled curio cabinet.

I leaned against the wall, propping one foot behind me.

These shoes might have made Grace's cut for fashion, but they weren't made for standing for more than a few minutes. Or stomping out of conference rooms. "Little things can make a difference. You don't always need big, showy gestures. And I wasn't talking about bake sales." My hand and arm gestures always got bigger the deeper I got into arguments and I mistakenly tagged him on the arm at "wasn't."

Kris caught my hand and held it for a second longer than I expected. He stepped closer, brown eyes meeting mine in a way that I couldn't look away. "Yes, you were. You just said that about thirty seconds ago." He was close enough that I could feel his breath on my skin.

I found it hard to focus for a second, as if the soap or shampoo he used was making me heady. I exhaled and tried to put as much force as possible into my next words. "It was an example of what we've done in the past. Fundraisers, you know?"

"And, what, earned a hundred dollars towards new pom-poms for the cheerleaders? If you want to make a big impact, you need to think big. And to think big, you need to go bigger than grassroots." Kris looked like he was about to put his hand on my shoulder, but it instead landed flat on the wall right above it. I was blocked in between his arm and the curio cabinet.

"And come in with imperialistic ideas that don't let the people decide how *they* want to handle things? *Right*. Besides, plenty of small efforts grow to make big impacts." I crossed my arms to keep from gesturing or accidentally touching him again. This wasn't the time for plan 'Flirt Kris Into the Losers Circle.' "Mother Teresa based her entire life work off of small actions."

"You're not Mother Teresa."

No, I'm not. The evil little part of me that was dying to turn the flirt on wanted me to say, but I choked it back. I wasn't attracted to him, I reminded myself, even though the tightness in my throat was trying to tell me otherwise. I just wanted to get on with my plan of messing with him as much as he was messing with me. The electricity between us was so strong, though, I was surprised a lightning bolt hadn't formed in those millimeters between our lips.

And I was not thinking about his lips. Damn, this whole getting into character thing was messing with me.

"To start, you're agnostic." He cracked a smile.

That broke the tension. A laugh bubbled up my throat and I gave in, doubling over until my sides hurt. I almost didn't notice that he stepped back slightly to give me room. "True." Two of the maids passed us and gave us weird looks. I straightened up and caught my breath.

He pulled away from the wall and started walking. "At least your name would sound official enough. Mother Ephemie."

I cringed. It was an automatic, natural reaction. "Stop calling me that. I hate my name."

Kris winked at me over his shoulder. "You could have been named after an actor in a movie about immortals who kill each other with swords."

"Seriously?" Now I knew why Alec kept making sci-fi jokes about Kris' name.

"Seriously. My dad loved *Highlander*. He was dying for a son so he could use the name Kristopher." A little bit of red came into his cheeks and he shrugged. "'There can be only one,'" he said weakly, making a slashing gesture as if he was holding a sword.

I choked back another laugh. "That should be the motto for this competition."

"Does it make me the default winner?"

"Doubtful." I gave him a playful shove. "C'mon. We're going to miss the best food. I hear there's chow-dah."

"You might be a good actress, but never, ever try to do a Boston accent again, okay?"

"So long as you stop doing those bad imitations of the North Jersey accent to impress the Southern girls. Deal?"

"You're taking away my best material, Katsaros."

"Tough, Lambert." But I smiled, and, with my eyelashes lowered just enough to give him the flirtiest look in my repertoire, reached out and squeezed his arm before jogging ahead towards the dining room. I could feel his eyes on my back and was glad I wore those butt-hugging designer jeans.

I knocked on the conference room door and crossed my fingers before walking in. The bio said my mentor was some political speechwriter, but hopefully there was a change. Maybe they mixed things up and I was really supposed to be with one of the two directors that were supposed to be mentoring.

The second I saw the wavy black ponytail and teal blouse, my hopes sunk into my stomach and melted through my feet into the patterned rug.

"Hi," I said tentatively. Yay to feeling disappointed and, at the same time, idiotic for hoping there'd be a special change just for me.

My mentor stood and held out her hand to shake mine. "Ephemie, hi. I'm Lauren Shepard. Feel free to call me Lauren." She wore one of those really expensive silk scarves Grace's mom wore all the time, except on her it looked trendy and not stuffy.

Calling an adult by her first name felt weird, ditto shaking her hand, but I shrugged it off and tried to look like I did this every day. "And you can call me Em."

"Nice to meet you, Em." Lauren sat down and shuffled

through her folders. When she looked up again with her dark-rimmed light-blue eyes and smiled, it hit me how much she looked like a young Lynda Carter, back in her *Wonder Woman* days. The thought "I am being mentored by Diana Prince" ran through my head and I had to stifle a laugh. "Let me start by telling you my qualifications. I was actually a Change Council student ages ago and after I graduated from BU with a double major in journalism and political science, I worked with a few political campaigns here in the city. I've written speeches for mayoral and gubernatorial candidates. Currently, I write for Governor Bennett." She flipped the top folder open and laid her hands flat on the pages, which were full of red marks and comment boxes. "I had such a wonderful experience as a student that I volunteer every year as a mentor. This year, I've been assigned to ten of the students in this competition, including you. Do you have any questions for me?"

"No," I said slowly. My eyes were still on the pages under her hands, dread bubbling up in my stomach. This was supposed to be the easy part. The speech was done and I could say it in my sleep. Having someone take control and tear things up only days before the competition terrified me.

"Great. Then, let's get started. I read through and listened to your speech and we have a lot of work to get this up to podium quality." Lauren tapped her fingers on the paper, her perfect, shiny manicure reflecting the markups.

I blinked at her, nausea taking over, every insecurity I'd ever had about my speech threatening to pop up and make an appearance. "I'm sorry, but are you sure it's a good idea to change it now?" My voice started getting smaller but, hard as I tried to up the volume, I couldn't control it. "I won state with the speech the way it is."

Lauren's expression remained patient and almost annoyingly tolerant. "And so did everyone else here. You need to be spectacular to stand out in this group. Your opening and closing are great, but the middle loses focus. You have a great hook, but it doesn't quite play out as well as it promises"

"Hook?" The first thing that came to mind was the pirate. Then guyliner, which the incredibly hot actor in the fairytale TV show wore to make him look even more hot and evil. Neither of which had anything to do with my speech. "What's a hook?"

"It's that part in the beginning of a speech that captures the audience's attention, like a fishing hook. But a good hook is like a promise to your listeners. Right now you catch my interest with your opening, I hear in your speech that you have a role model and you want to create change in the world, but it doesn't carry through the entire piece in a recognizable fashion. We're going to fix that." I couldn't help the frown tugging at my lips and she must have noticed it because she added, "You don't have to change anything you don't want to—"

"Okay." It took both Phoebe and Grace to help wrangle my words into something good last time. I couldn't do it alone.

Her red lipsticked lips twisted up in a wry smile. "—but

you don't have to win, either."

"You're harsh," I said, and didn't even bother to say it under my breath.

"Well, you might not believe it," her eyes met mine, like she could pierce past them and into my brain, "but you're *good*. Better than some adult speechwriters I've met. So I'm not going to baby you. I'm treating your speech like I'd treat one of my own. It has a lot of weaknesses, but I also heard your tape and, because you have such a brilliant delivery, you managed to hide a lot of the weak spots from the judges. Let me guess—you act?"

Dismay turned my insides into a bundle of knots. *Of course.* Even my mentor thought my speech was nothing more than "weak" fluff without a hook. I didn't trust myself to say anything, so I just nodded.

"I thought so. You have a way of putting emotions into your words that people would kill for. It makes you very powerful speaker, but imagine if those words were stronger and had real depth to them. It'll take a lot of work, but I think you can do it." She pulled out a pair of reading glasses and handed me one of the marked-up copies, challenge in her eyes as she looked over the top of the glasses. "The entire competition and organization revolves around change. Are you ready to change?"

The red marks were terrifying, but I sucked in a deep breath and nodded. Anything for the win. "Yes."

Lia waved her fork around in the air as she spoke. "I felt like he was tearing my entire speech apart. I get that he does this for a living, but I'm not one of his corporate clients. It was insane." The dining room was packed for dinner, but her voice carried clearly over the din. Our table wasn't made up of quiet people. "I mean, I read the speeches and I get that some people really need help because theirs are just weak, but most of ours are great."

I noticed everyone at the table nodding and nodded along with them, shoving a forkful of lettuce into my mouth so I wouldn't have to speak, though Lia's words suddenly crashed my appetite. Lia's glance my way when she mentioned "some people" was unmistakable, and I didn't blame her. My mentoring session had been a disaster. Lauren had been so critical of every single word and phase and even the way I said words that, by the time I left the session, my speech was in shambles and I was about ready to strangle her with her perfect silk scarf.

The guy from Louisiana dropped his elbows on the table and our salad plates all rattled. "These speeches got us here. Why should I mess with something that was good enough to beat the hundreds of other speeches in my state? And, honestly, if someone's speech isn't good enough at this point, they really shouldn't be here, anyway. It's not our fault some states dialed it in."

"Exactly. I feel like it's a waste of time that we can spend in the summit or seeing the city. Right?" Lia looked around our table and most of us were definitely in agreement.

Ann didn't nod, instead quietly picking at her salad. "Actually, I had a really good critique. She had a lot of advice about how to change my volume and emphasis to make more of an impact. It's really not too different from a music teacher making corrections." She spoke in a low voice, and like the perfect saint of a roommate she was, turned a soft, comforting smile my way. "Plus, they know more than we do about this stuff. They wouldn't be doing their jobs if they didn't push us to be our best."

That smile made a lump rise up in my throat, and pressure formed behind my eyes. I stuck my fork into my lettuce, skillfully spearing some feta and a crouton at the same time, keeping my attention on my salad so I wouldn't have to say anything. I couldn't help the part of me that wondered if Kris also had a decent critique session and how my gaze went straight to his table across the room. His eyes met mine and, after a moment where time stopped and I realized I was caught looking, I forced my attention to Ann, who was still talking. The sawdust in my throat had been replaced with another kind of feeling, an impatient buzz that made me want to get up and do something, anything.

"…let everything they said to you soak in. I bet after actually listening, it might spark some ideas on how you can make your speech better."

Louisiana shook his head at Ann. "I bet you're in the honor society."

"How did you know?" But Ann's lips were curling up, too.

"Because you're too serious for your own good. You never seem to take a break from anything."

I looked from Ann to Louisiana and a gleeful little shiver ran up my spine. My bat senses were never wrong about potential matches and it was the major distraction I needed, both from my mess of a speech and from my urge to look at Kris. "Could be worse. Nevada brought her homework. Ann's a little less nerdy than that."

Ann's brows drew together. "But I—"

She was so clueless about the potential awesomeness I was about to bring into her life, I couldn't help but smile. I kicked her under the table. "I know, you brought your flute, but that's okay. When you're as talented a musician as you are, you can't slack when it comes to practicing like the rest of us." I wracked my brain to try to remember Louisiana's name, managing to pull it triumphantly out of the millions of layers of fluff and memorized lines from musicals that normally filled it. "Geoff, did you know Ann is in her state orchestra? She's first chair. You said you're in a band, too, right?" I was like Sailor Venus, swooping in with my love-chain attack. Subtly, of course.

Geoff looked as confused as Ann at the change in subject, but still answered. "Folk rock. I play guitar."

"Good. Talk about music instead of arguing over speech stuff we can't control," I said in my most commanding tone. Ann kicked me back, but she turned a polite smile on Geoff. Those two would be together by the end of the week if I had anything to say about it. Good deed done for the day.

I could sense Kris' gaze on me like a magnetic pulse that ran along my skin and my eyes flickered up, catching his again. This time, he looked away, turning to say something to New York girl. It was the weirdest feeling in the world, like there was this rope that kept trying to draw us together even though we were on opposite sides of the dining room. I was definitely getting to him, but it didn't explain the flush that ran through my own body.

Natural reaction to attention that wasn't creepy? Because creepy stares gave me a crawly feeling, which this totally wasn't.

Lia's snort brought my attention back to our table. "Speaking of stuff we can't control, what was up with that talk from the one guy who kept bringing up latrines? I thought he was supposed to inspire us to volunteer for charities like his."

"'Sanitized poo is the future!'" I quoted, dropping my voice and upping my energy to imitate the speaker. It was almost like I was playing a part at this table, too, while my brain waded through the white noise that seemed to have set in. Thankfully, years of acting made improvisation automatic.

"Don't sound too excited about it," the girl from Oregon chimed in, trying to keep a straight face. "Next thing you know, you'll be elbow deep in poo bacteria testing."

Geoff tried to make his brows draw together in a serious look and failed. "Let's make a rule. Engineers should be banned from making presentations. They get way too detailed when they describe stuff like 'fecal containment units.'"

"Oh, guys, I'm trying to eat," Ann said between giggles. She waved her napkin like a little flag.

I looked up mid-laugh and there was Kris watching me again. This time, we locked gazes, and then both looked away at the same time. I didn't know why, but those few seconds left me breathless.

The one constant in Boston I could take comfort in was the seemingly bottomless platter of cookies they kept at the front desk in the inn lobby. The cookie of the day was chocolate chunk and exactly what I needed after that morning. Everyone else was still pouring through the lobby and towards their rooms or the meeting room, so I leaned against the wall to keep out of the way.

Arkansas and Hawaii were headed my way—I flashed them a smile as they passed, but they didn't seem to notice. "...maybe their states didn't have a lot of competition. You would think they'd set minimum standards instead of letting just anything in," the guy from Arkansas said. Suddenly, his accent and longish blonde hair didn't sound or look as cute as they had a few minutes ago.

The girl from Connecticut joined them, slipping between Arkansas and Hawaii. "You mean like the ones that are lists of what he or she wants to do someday?" she asked, poking him in the arm.

"When I grow up, I want to make a difference in people's lives," one of them said in a falsetto voice. A cold lump formed in my chest and my legs turned to lead. They had to be talking about my speech—compared to their serious speech themes, mine had to be as weak as glittery tissue paper.

Connecticut snorted. "All I want is world peace, and we'll skip through the garden of life together as one big, happy family."

"Right." I could hear Arkansas' eye-roll from where I was standing.

"Whatever. At least it's less competition for us, right?" Their voices faded as they left the lobby and I slumped against the wall. I hadn't realized how tense I'd become.

I was an idiot to think I could compete in something like this. Part of me wanted to turn around and confront them and another part of me just wanted to hide until the end of the competition.

I couldn't go up to our room because Ann was bound to start prying and I wasn't in the mood to expose my insecurities to her Midwestern sympathies. Taking a deep breath, I pressed back the tears that threatened to choke and blind me. I wouldn't cry. I couldn't cry. I curled onto one of the overstuffed chairs in the inn lobby, trying to make myself as small and inconspicuous as possible.

A very homesick part of me wished I was back in Lambertfield, with Phoebe comforting me with homemade cupcakes and Grace spouting off some sort of wisdom about people projecting their insecurities onto me. Instead, I was hundreds of miles away in a cold lobby, surrounded by strangers.

"Hey, Em, are you okay?" A hand lightly touched my arm.

Correction: almost all strangers.

I tilted my head just enough to squint at him and give my best "I'm fine, leave me alone" vibe. "Just a headache," I forced out through my tight throat.

Kris' brow furrowed and he pointed towards the front desk. "Do you want me to get you an aspirin or water or something?"

"How about silence?"

"Aspirin it is. I'll be right back."

Just as he turned away, the part of me that needed someone to talk to blurted out in the tiniest voice ever, "Is my speech really empty fluff? Do *you* think I only got here because of my delivery?" My stomach turned at how raw and open I was being in front of my biggest competitor.

Kris stopped mid-turn and studied me for a second, confusion all over his face. "This might not be your world and I really don't understand why you're doing it, but you have an amazing way of making words come to life and a great voice. Probably better than anyone here. You could probably read the water ice menu at Marranos and beat half of them. You don't have anything to worry about." He then finished turning, waving over his shoulder. "I'll be right back with the aspirin."

My heart sped up at how he complimented me followed by a massive crash when I realized that was the most politically nice way of saying yes I'd ever heard. I buried my head into my knees and tried to block everything out. When Kris came back with the aspirin and a bottled water, I took them, even though I didn't need them. And when he perched on the chair's arm and gently rubbed my back without saying a word, I didn't protest. It might have been fake comfort, but at least I didn't have to feel alone for a little while.

25

"We make change," Ann reminded me of the Change Council theme in a tone that was way too perky as she passed me with a box full of peanut butter sandwiches in individual zipper bags. In her quest to force me to get up at an ungodly hour each morning, Ann had come up with the idea that all of us would volunteer at a local soup kitchen before breakfast at least one day of the week, and the organizers loved it. Thanks to her, all of us from the L through "New" states were either lined up behind tables set up in the soup kitchen parking lot or inside helping with lunch preparation.

"Yes, we do," I said back to her, pushing away the voice in the back of my head that said it would rather still be in a warm bed. I filled another cup almost to the top with coffee and, careful not to spill it, handed it to the man in front of me with a smile, then moved onto the next cup. I had probably already handed out almost one hundred coffees by that point and the parts of me not in direct contact with the giant coffee urn were starting to freeze in the early morning cold, but I wouldn't let my smile fade. The middle and last people in the line snaking around the soup kitchen parking lot deserved as much of my attention as the first people.

"Hey." Kris slipped into the space next to me, grabbed a styrofoam cup, and started filling it while I was busy talking to the woman who had just taken my cup. "We finished making the pasta for lunch, so they sent me out here to help."

I took the full cup from him, assembly-line-style and said, under my breath, "Why aren't you handing out sandwiches? I'm good here. We don't need more than one person to hand out coffee." I was too sleepy to waste any of my small reserve of nice energy on him.

"Peanut allergy. That's why I couldn't help make the sandwiches earlier."

"Oh." I passed out two more cups of coffee before adding, "So, the high and mighty Kris isn't perfect, after all."

We started falling into a rhythm of him filling up cups and me handing them out. Kris' eyes scrunched in amusement as he looked over at me. "I think I can survive perfectly well without eating peanuts."

"I don't know about that. The soup kitchen guy," I nodded over at the older man who had been guiding us all morning as we made sandwiches, "said peanut butter is full of protein, so you're totally missing out." I poked him in the bicep, which was decidedly not soft, but I wasn't going to give him the pleasure of knowing that.

He rubbed his arm but otherwise ignored my dig. "That explains why it's always peanut butter and jelly sandwiches in the morning here. I thought it was just because nobody ate peanut butter anymore and the extra jars had to go somewhere." His face was hidden behind the coffee urn and I couldn't tell if he was teasing me or serious.

"Yup, protein and all the good fat. If it's going to be the only thing someone eats all day, it has to…" I tried to remember what soup kitchen organizer guy said while Kris was outside setting up the tables, "'pack a nutritional punch.'"

"Two sandwiches and a cup of coffee isn't a lot," Kris said, his eyes focused on the cup he was filling.

"I know," I said, just as softly. "It sucks, doesn't it?" I forced my most brilliant smile for an older man in a worn puffy coat, "Good morning."

"Yeah." Kris looked up at me as he handed me another cup, but then his focus went past me to somewhere near the end of the line. His brow furrowed. "There's a guy in a suit on line," he said, and his eyes narrowed. "What's up with that?"

I didn't even have to look—I knew exactly who he was talking about. "What do you mean by 'what's up?'" It took everything in me to keep my rapidly growing annoyance out of my voice.

"I mean, he's in a suit," he said, like it explained everything.

"And?" I prodded, pushing back the tiniest bit of glee that was bubbling up at his discomfort at my questions.

"And he has a pretty decent cell phone for a soup kitchen line. It doesn't seem right," he said, not realizing how spoiled and tone-deaf he sounded.

I took the next cup from him with a little more force

than necessary. "So you're saying he looks like he doesn't deserve to be in line?"

"It just seems wrong that he's in line for a free sandwich when everyone else here needs it more."

"Let me guess, you think he's just a moocher."

Kris' hand slipped while filling a cup and he let out a quiet curse as hot coffee spilled on his hand before saying, "Well, yes."

"Don't assume stuff about people."

"I know you love to debate, but c'mon. What else can I assume about some guy with a nice suit and a briefcase waiting on line for free sandwiches?"

"How about the truth?" I narrowed my eyes at him and hoped the people on line weren't watching us. "That guy you think is 'mooching' is a professor at the college we passed on the way here. He," I gestured with my free hand in the direction of the guy who ran the soup kitchen, "told us that, about a month ago, the college converted him from tenure to adjunct—you know, basically fired him and rehired him—with less than forty hours so they didn't have to pay his benefits and he had to choose between having a place to live and eating. That 'moocher' has a doctorate, by the way."

Kris had the decency to look abashed. "Oh."

My cheeks grew warm partly with anger and partly with embarrassment over how much his comment bothered me. "You really don't know anything about the real world, do you?" I said, my words filled with more venom that I thought they could be. This argument hit way too close to home.

"I—"

I nearly dropped the coffee I'd been holding, but forced myself to carefully set it down on the table without showing how much my hand was shaking. "Excuse me." My voice was low and cold, like the time I'd played the Snow Queen, and I pushed past him and into the building behind us.

As soon as I was out of sight, I stopped trying to hide how my hands, and soon my whole body, were shaking. I dropped onto a bench on the side of the big soup kitchen dining area, crossed my arms tightly around myself, and started doing breathing exercises Mr. Landry had taught us to work out stage fright. I needed a minute to compose myself before I could go back out there and pretend that nothing happened.

Kris came into my line of sight, his own arms crossed and his brow even more furrowed than before. "Hey, what just happened out there?"

"You didn't leave the coffee, did you?" Of course he did. Why care about helping people when he could come inside and rub in some more about how his family was so rich they didn't have to know or care about other people's problems?

"Ann took over," he said, calmly, then added in a more annoyed tone, "What the hell was that all about? I get that I made a stupid assumption, but you didn't have to blow up at me like I'd just said the soup kitchen needed to be shut down or something."

I looked him straight in the eye, ready to say everything

was okay, but after less than I second, I dropped my gaze to my knees. "My mom's a professor. You know that," I said so quietly I almost couldn't hear myself.

"Oh." The bench creaked as he sat next to me, keeping a decent amount of space between us. He dropped his elbows onto his knees so our faces were at the same level. "Yeah, but your mom's at a big university and she's pretty high up, isn't she? Like, doesn't she head the history department at Schuylkill U? She's safe from stuff like that."

I side-eyed him hard. "Don't you think crap like this can happen everywhere? And not just universities and colleges, but companies, too." Dad telling us about the layoffs popped into my head and I swallowed hard. "That professor has a freaking doctorate. He probably busted his ass to get it and probably has a ton of student loans. And then he got the rug pulled out from under him."

Kris put up his hands in an "I surrender" motion. "Sorry. You're right, I was being a total jerk out there."

"Yup, you were."

"Wow, it must suck to be that guy."

My side-eye turned into a stink eye. He really *didn't* get it. "You know, people don't want you to feel bad for them. People in bad situations still have their pride, and it's really hard for most of them to ask for help. They don't need your holier-than-thou privileged ass 'feeling sorry' for them." I was on a roll, and Kris wasn't pushing back, so I kept going, pouring out everything that had been building in me all morning from what I'd been hearing from him and all the other clueless people around me as we set up. "And that whole 'there but for the grace of God' crap? That's even more privileged, like the people saying it are shoving other people's problems onto a deity because they think their God is so awful or tiny or limited that he or she would help some people but not others. You," I pointed my finger at him sharply, "have no freaking idea what got those people in line this morning, and that political shit-show you support creates policies that probably shoved some of these people under the poverty line."

That comment made Kris' entire body stiffen. "You have no idea what you're talking about. The same politics you hate have, for decades, focused on creating job growth so people could get themselves out of poverty and made good change in our country. This—" he gestured towards the door and the line of people, "doesn't do anything but stick a Band-Aid on the problem. It's small scale and it's good that we're doing it, but it doesn't fix the reasons people are going hungry. If people are under the poverty line, maybe it's because people like *you* keep pushing the government to help them out instead of giving them a way to do it themselves."

"Really? Tell that to the individuals going hungry. Because without us helping out today, a lot of the people out there weren't going to eat anything. And other people lose their houses or get sick and don't have the money to pay for the medicines they need because of those policies you love that help big companies instead of the little person. And while your precious policymakers fight, those people depend on this…what did you call it? Band-Aid." I straightened up like I wasn't going to give an inch, and so did he. "Your policies don't care about the individual, damnit."

"If you want to make real change, you need to look past the immediate now. Good policy creates economic tides that raise everyone up. You care about the person and so do I. Except where you want safety nets, I want to empower them. We both care about the individual," and then, in direct imitation of me, he added, "damnit."

Ann poked her head around the corner and she froze in place, eyes wide, like she was afraid to venture any closer. "Um, can you two come out here and help us carry in the coffee urns and tables?"

Kris' eyes didn't leave mine as he stood up. "Sure. Be right there." And, without letting me get in another word, he turned and walked out.

From: AKatsaros (katsarosA@dmail.com)

To: Em (emkatsaros@dmail.com)

Subject: How is Boston?

Dear Ephemie,

Call us. Your mom is worried because you haven't called in two days. She also says to tell you texting does not count and that kidnappers know how to text, too.

How are the conference and competition going? Make sure you take it seriously. Your teacher told us you can make good connections for college recommendation letters while you are there.

There was mail for you from Schuylkill University admissions department. Mom and I think you should look at the International Studies for Business. It might be interesting to you because it has lots of travel, which you will like, and you're good with people, and it has a 97% job placement rate. Think about it.

Chloe says hi.

Love,

Dad

26

"Calling home?" Ann asked as she stepped into the room. "Sorry to interrupt, I just need a new notebook and pen."

I picked at the edge of the skin on my tablet. The corner of the yellow swirly was starting to curl up slightly from all my worrying at it. "Yeah. I just wanted to check in with one of my friends."

"I know things were tough for you this morning. I'm glad you have friends to talk to about it," Ann said. She pulled a notebook out of her suitcase, picked up one of the inn pens out of the desk, then inched towards the door. "Remember, we start up again in five minutes."

Damnit, now my roommate felt even sorrier for me. My life had disintegrated into worrying, working on my speech, and waiting for e-mails and video chats. Oh, and mock-flirting with the one guy in my school I'd rather strangle than date.

"Thanks." My phone started playing Alec's signature ringtone of video game sounds and I picked up. "Good morning, sunshine. Thanks for calling."

"With the freaked out text you sent, how could I say no?"

"I didn't send a freaked out text."

Alec made a scoffing sound. "It was ninety percent emoji. You only use that many emojis when you're really happy or really panicked."

That wasn't true. I used emojis all the time. "I just wanted to hear a familiar voice."

"You mean a familiar voice that isn't Kris."

"No."

"And not Phoebe or Grace because the two of them would lecture you about your stupid plan instead of listening to your problems?" I could hear slamming lockers and people talking in the background. Alec made an "oof" sound, followed by a muttered, "sorry."

I made a face at my phone, wishing I could switch to video so I could stick my tongue out at him or flip my middle finger at him. "Aren't you supposed to be in class?"

"I'm on my way to physics lab. Park doesn't care if I'm late by a few minutes." Right. Alec was a physics genius who took science tests for fun. Of course he could get away with things the rest of us delinquents couldn't. "Anyway, what's freaking you out this time?"

"Just… we were at a soup kitchen and Kris pissed me off and…" I shook my head, as if trying to shake away the cloud that still clung to my skin from the morning. "How are things with Mom and Dad? I know you don't have an excuse to go over there, but, I thought that maybe you'd hear something over the fence?" I picked a little more at my tablet skin until another edge started curling up.

"You're not the only connection between your family

and mine, you know. Mom invited them over for dinner the other night and your dad had an interview, so they asked me to babysit Chloe. Who, by the way, is going to be a kick-ass artist. You should see the mini-manga she made." There were a few shuffling sounds on the other end of the phone and then my tablet beeped with a new email. He'd sent me a picture of a few sheets of his manga storyboard paper laid out in a row, filled with colorful sketches and a familiar block-lettered "Chloe" at the bottom of each. One of the recurring figures was in a short yellow dress with corkscrew curls, which made me grin.

"That's adorable."

"She destroyed my acid yellow and cadmium yellow Copics drawing those. It's going to cost more to replace then than what I got for actually babysitting her."

"You gave a six-year-old really expensive markers. What did you expect?" I enlarged and shrunk the picture, smiling at my sister's drawings, which looked like, well, something a six-year-old would make. But Alec had a better eye than me for these things, so if he said she was good, he was probably right. "How did the interview go?"

"Okay, I guess." His tone shifted from amused to cagey.

"Alec," I drew out his name in an almost—but not quite—whiny tone.

"What?"

"What aren't you telling me?"

He made a "No way in hell are you getting anything from me" grunting sound. "You're going to freak out and that's not good for your competition."

"Alec Noah Kohen." I sifted through my memory for something recent I could use to blackmail him if he didn't cave soon.

He didn't say anything for a second, then seemed to heave a big sigh on his end of the phone. "He didn't get it. Something about being too skilled for the position." He continued, pushing on before I could get a word in, "Would you quit freaking out about your family going broke? Even without your dad's job, you're fine. It's not like they even have a mortgage to worry about, like my mom." He was right about that. Dad, especially, hated being in debt to anyone, so he and Mom made a point of paying off the house even before I was born. "Your mom's tenured. She's had, like, a million offers from universities all over to teach. The worst that can happen if, in the really unlikely event Schuylkill U shuts down and she loses her job is that your family has to move to, like, Stockholm or something."

"Stockholm?" Now that added another, new, possibility I hadn't thought of freaking out about.

"Or Kenya, right? Your mom was mentioning how they were interested in having her lead the group on site identifying stuff from the dig?" The only sound on the other end was the rapidly emptying hallway. Another locker clanged, but the sound was distant.

"My family can't move all the way to Africa."

"My uncle's in New Zealand and we see him all the time." Alec's voice had an amused lilt to it and I knew he was teasing me, but it still didn't make the panic go away. The late bell went off in the background and Alec sounded like he was scrambling.

"My family can't move to another continent," I repeated, firmly. "No way. Chloe needs her big sister."

"So look for acting schools in Kenya?"

I stood, unsteadily, and knocked over my competition binder, all the loose papers flying everywhere. "This isn't funny, Alec."

"No, it's hilarious. Please tell me you're not freaking out right now."

I'd clean up the papers later. "I'm not freaking out right now."

"Yes, you are. Honest to God, Em, you're so over-dramatic all the time." I made a little growing sound of disapproval and he added, "I'm serious. You always blow everything out of proportion. Your dad's job, Kris, Rutgers, this competition. Everything is a million times worse in your head because I think you secretly love the drama of it all."

"I do not overdramatize things and I'm fine." I needed to get out of the room and be somewhere where I didn't have to think, but I also needed to be at the conference. With one hand, I pat at my hair to make sure it was still okay, and then grabbed my notebook and room key.

"You're lying. You know I would let you know if you really needed to worry about anything."

"I'm okay, and we're both late. I'll talk to you later. Bye." Halfway through his own "'bye," I hung up, shoved my phone into the pocket of the cute eighties babydoll-style suspender dress I'd found in a shop in Collingswood and sprinted for the conference room.

I slid into my seat next to Kris and tried to catch my breath just as the next speaker walked up to the podium. Kris took one look at my practically asthmatic breathing and handed me a glass of water. "What did you do, run the Boston Marathon?" he whispered, leaning in so I could hear him.

Normal Em would have told him to shut up, but after flipping out on him earlier and to prove to myself that I definitely *wasn't* overdramatic, I was even more resolved to keep to my plan. I took a few deep breaths, putting one hand to my chest while taking the water with my other hand. "Just seeing your smiling face makes me breathless," I said with perfect comedic timing.

He laugh-cringed, "Sorry, by the way, about earlier. I didn't mean to upset you."

"That's okay," I whispered back stiffly.

"Peace offering? Let me buy you a coffee or cocoa after lunch?"

I really needed to work on my speech during our down-time from the conference and figure out what to do about Mom and Dad, and I really didn't feel like exposing myself to more concentrated Kris time, but a good actor always put aside her own feelings to make her character come to life. "Sure."

Game. On.

27

I crossed out another line in my speech and added a note to replace it with something stronger. The entire thing was an illegible mess, with cross-outs and notes in Lauren's and my handwriting, and it sucked beyond belief. The more I touched it, the more it fell apart, like one of the antique chemises the interpretation costumer tried to save this summer. I'd grabbed an empty table in the corner of the coffee shop during lunch, popped in earbuds to block out the lunch noise, but the right words just weren't coming to me. I dropped my pen and buried my head in my hands. I was going to lose. I was going to lose and Dr. Lladros would see how much of a fail I was and my parents would—

"Hey, are you okay?"

I peeked through my fingers at Kris, then dropped my hands and nodded. "Yes. Just—" I quickly pulled out my earbuds, gathered up all my papers into my folder, and shoved them into my bag as my face heated up at being found in that position, "working on speech stuff."

When I didn't elaborate, he said, "Got it, that was me last night. My mentor tore mine apart." Then, with a wave at the shop's menu, he added, "So, what's your peace offering of choice?"

I didn't even need to look at the menu. After only a few days, I already had the thing memorized. We weren't really allowed to leave the inn without permission, but since the café was technically physically attached to the inn even though it wasn't part of it, we were kind of bending the rules instead of breaking them. "You know what? I really want to try the spiced hot chocolate."

"Okay, I'll be right back." Kris walked up to the counter and I could see his reflection as he turned his charm on the barista. The girl's cheeks turned pink and I couldn't help the burst of nausea at the sight of her practically tripping over herself to make our drinks. When he paid for the drinks, she wrote something on a napkin and handed it to him.

"You know, she would have made the cocoa without you flirting with her," I pointed out when he came back and handed me one of the two mugs he was carrying. "It's her job." One glance at the napkin and it was the girl's number, already smudged from where Kris had used it to wipe up a little bit of cocoa he'd spilled on our table.

"What are you talking about?" Kris frowned as he mixed a packet of sugar into what looked like an already over-sweetened white hot chocolate. He genuinely looked confused.

"I—" I stopped myself and instead poked at the cin-namon-dusted whipped cream topping my own mug. I wasn't in the mood to enlighten him and start another fight. "Never mind." Familiar pink and blue hair entering the shop caught the corner of my eye and I subtly gestured with my spoon in that direction. "Check it out."

Kris didn't look in the right direction. "What?"

My lips curled up in a tiny smile and I much less subtly eye-gestured over to where the pink-haired advisor had grabbed a table. "Rosie's here."

"So? I saw her here the other day, too. I guess she really likes caffeine."

"No, she's here all the time. I think she's babysitting us. Coffee shop duty." A giggle bubbled up and I shook my head. "I bet this happens every year." We all thought we were being a little rebellious, but it looked like they knew about us all along.

Kris looked at me for a moment, amusement flowing over his features, then turned to wave to Rosie, who waved back. "She's probably sick of coffee by now. I'll have to thank her later for letting us do this."

I took a sip of my cocoa, my eyes opening in surprise as the kick from the chili powder hit my tongue unexpectedly. It took another two sips before I decided I liked it. "You're such a politician. Always on, always talking to people like you're in the middle of a campaign or something."

"You say that like it's a bad thing."

Instead of arching my eyebrow at him like I usually would, I wrapped my hands around the hot mug and said, "Okay, I bite. Why are you so into politics?"

Kris dumped another packet of sugar into his cocoa then stirred it with the little biscotti that had been balanced on his saucer. "You *do* remember my dad was mayor for, like, eight years, right? And that he's a senator now?"

"Yeah. My parents voted against him in all three elections." I winked to show I was teasing him, even though it was true.

"And he still won," Kris said with a smirk. "The thing is, I loved it."

Of course he would. His dad always had pictures of Kris and his brothers playing soccer on an immaculately manicured lawn or smiling perfectly posed magazine-worthy smiles in his campaign posters. "What, being the center of attention?

"Actually, no, that part kind of sucked, even though our town media is only, like, four people and Mrs. Millstone's gossip blog." He finally took a sip of his cocoa and I was surprised he didn't fall over from sugar overdose.

"Wait, let's pause for a second. She's blogging now?" Mrs. Millstone had been the neighborhood gossip since I was a baby, the person you could go to if you wanted to know anything about anyone in the development where Kris, Alec, and I lived. Mom always reminded us that we couldn't get away with anything, like sneaking out or parties, thanks to our one-person neighborhood watch.

"Yup, you can even get breaking news sent to your phone."

I sat back, imitating his posture, and tried to imagine the older woman typing away into a smartphone. My side hurt from the suppressed laughter and I had to put down my mug before I could spill anything. "Wow."

"Anyway, politics. It was so cool watching democracy in process, and seeing how powerful each of our votes can be. Dad always had people from both sides over for dinner and I'd hang out with him at the town hall when we were off from school. I really liked seeing how hard he worked to listen to all sides and come up with solutions that would make everyone happy."

"Well, I don't know about everyone—"

"You know what I mean," he said, cutting me off. "I saw how much good someone can do as the voice of the people, and I wanted to do the same. And then I really got hooked after joining the student council."

I tapped the table with my fingernail. "Right. You started strong in seventh grade when you won the tech club vote by saying we needed to stop wasting school funds and class time on band concerts because 'they hurt your ears and nobody actually wants to sit through those anyway.'" That may have been the first time in my memory Kris had gone from being that annoyingly perfect kid down the street to despicable.

He rubbed the back of his head and his smile turned sheepish. "Yeah…not the brightest moment of my political career, but in my defense, they really hated having to do the lighting for your concerts."

I waved my hand dismissively at that comment. "Oh, please. The tech club was lucky to have a front row seat to some of Lambertfield's rising talent."

"We're talking about the same middle school band, right?"

Kris leaned forward onto his elbows, a massive, teasing grin on his face. "With the really squeaky clarinets and flutes coming in all the wrong times and Alec massacring the trombone all while playing a *Dirty Dancing* medley?" I opened my mouth to protest, and he added, "By the way, the school got a few of complaints from parents who didn't think it was appropriate for you guys to play that."

I forgot what I was going to say and snorted involuntarily. "Wow."

"'Hungry Eyes' was apparently super offensive. The student council had to weigh in and I got to point out that no one was actually going to see the lyrics." He laughed, too, then shook his head and said, "You got to grill me about politics, so now it's my turn. Why acting?"

I thought about it for a second, breaking up my biscotti into crumbs as I tried to find a way to put something into words that was ephemeral. "I've wanted to be an actress for as long as I can remember. It's a part of me, like breathing. I don't think I could give it up if I tried. There's something..." I dug around for the right word again—"magical" was overused, "amazing" was weak, "...powerful about getting to become another person. I need to breathe and walk and talk like them, and it's a little like getting to play dress up and pretend all the time. And it's so wonderful to finish a scene and see the audience laughing or crying, knowing I made that reaction happen. Not only did I get to inhabit someone else, but I was able to transport the audience into that world, too. It makes all the sweat and makeup and rehearsal worth it, you know?" Kris had stopped drinking and was watching me intently with a small smile, and I felt warmth creep over my cheeks again. "Or something like that," I finished, drowning my mumble with cocoa.

"That sounds pretty amazing. Is that what Mr. Landry said he wants you to do for the fall play? Become the character? You're the lead, right?"

"How…" Oh, right, Kris had been at that rehearsal. "Right. I need to get into Nora's head so that I can inhabit the role. The whole play revolves around her character and her growth, so if I don't get it right…" I brought my hands down in a crashing motion, mouthing "Boom" as I did so. "Nora's hard, though. She has this transformation throughout the play that basically puts her against everything she was taught and expected to be and has her deceiving people through the whole thing. I really need to understand the nineteenth-century way she was raised to think and behave so I can go from this perfect domestic Victorian doll to a woman willing to break society's rules if I want to make this work." I didn't tell him that I had to hide backstage in the prop closet for a little bit to calm down after Mr. Landry had told me the news, how I had to bite back the urge to panic, and curled into a little ball next to the box overflowing with petticoats from our production of Oklahoma. He'd probably find my simultaneous excitement and stressing over messing up a role just another example of me being overdramatic.

"It's a good thing you like history, then." His tone

sounded like he was teasing me, but not maliciously. More like something I'd expect from Alec or Grace.

I raised my mug in mock-salute acknowledgement of his point. "Touché."

"You know, it's impressive you and Matt are both as normal as you are, considering."

And…Kris was back, full force. "Considering what?" I asked, my voice flat and low.

"Considering, you know, the acting thing. Seriously, I have no idea how you put up with some of the crazy I see in your theatre rehearsals."

I pushed my chair back slightly and flattened my hands on the table. "Crazy? First, who said you had to come to them, anyway?"

He didn't react beyond looking over his mug and arching his eyebrows. "My best friend?"

"And second, please. I've heard about some of the fights you guys had in student council meetings. We're the picture of sanity compared to that."

"We don't fight. We debate." He twisted his lips and tilted his head, then said, "Most of the time," he conceded. "And the last time we had a real fight was over the whole ice cream social thing and whether or not the school had to provide a dairy-free option when no one in our class is lactose intolerant."

My hands relaxed slightly on the table and I scrunched my nose at him. "You political types are weird."

"It's just that I think theatre seems to attract really…" he paused, glanced up at the ceiling for a second, and I could almost see him ticking through all the word options before saying, "extreme personalities. Like Maya."

I blinked at him, absently relaxing back into my chair. "Wait…what? What does Maya have to do with this?" If this had something to do with blowback from playing his flirting-for-stuff games with her, I had no pity for him.

Kris ran both hands through his hair, taking a deep breath like he was trying to shake something off. "That girl is super aggressive. I swear, every time I'm in the theatre, she grabs my phone and puts her number into it. She won't take 'sorry, I'm not into you' as an excuse."

"Maybe because *you* use her for her sound skills?"

He blinked a few times at me, eyebrows drawing together as he seemed to process what I said. "She's one of the only people in the school who can operate the board. Landry asked her to help me with the assemblies we're having for Spirit Week next month," he said slowly, then added, "And if I tell her off for touching my phone, it'll be super awkward."

All of my annoyance evaporated. "Oh." I grabbed a napkin out of the dispenser on the table and dabbed at my lips to hide the smile that was threatening to escape. "You're kidding me. *She's* harassing *you?*"

He hid behind his mug. "It's not funny," he said in the closest thing to a mumble Kris could pull off while apparently still trying to sound dignified.

"Of course not." But, as I said it, a little giggle escaped. "I can't believe you're afraid of Maya." At his dirty look, I added, "I know you can't help it, but you need to learn how to turn down your smolder around her. She's just reading you all wrong. Not every girl can see through your super-smooth natural flirtitude."

"Isn't that victim-shaming?"

"True," I conceded his point, but my smile grew even wider. "I'll see what I can do when I get back next week, you poor little innocent Cinderella-boy." I knew for a fact that one of the guys on the stage crew had a crush on Maya and I'd seen her check him out during our shorts festival, so maybe I could work some magic there and take the pressure off Kris.

"Thanks, Prince Charming," he teased back.

"Actually," I said, with a laugh, "Forget Prince Charming or Cinderella, I prefer the Witch."

He seemed to be thinking through that before shaking his head and putting his hands up in an "I surrender" pose. "Okay, not getting that reference. Remember, I'm not into acting and fairy tales and stuff like you."

"Sorry, I thought you were talking about the spring musical." I arched my brow and tilted up my chin ever-so-slightly. "We're doing *Into the Woods* and I'm already a shoo-in for the Witch."

He gestured his mug at me. "I would have thought you'd want to play Cinderella."

"Shows how little you actually know me. I've been dying to play the Witch from the minute I saw the Broadway version with Bernadette Peters." Younger me would wear out the DVD player, looping it to all of Peters' scenes so I could sing along with "Stay With Me" and try to copy the emotions she poured into the song. My smile widened, becoming genuine. "The best roles are the complex characters," I said, archly.

"I'd never have pegged you as someone who would want to play bad guys."

"You know, nobody's one-dimensional and characters aren't all bad or all good. Most antagonists think they're doing the right thing, which makes them really hard but really interesting characters to play."

"Unless they're psychopaths."

"Well, those can be fun to play, too. Scarier getting into their heads, but I like the challenge."

"Why doesn't that surprise me?" He polished off his drink and, as soon as he set down his mug, said, "Before I forget, I'm sorry again about this morning. You were upset and it shouldn't have turned into a debate between us."

"It's okay. I was the one who kept biting your head off every time you tried to talk. It just…it really affected me today."

His eyes met mine and I couldn't look away as he said, gently, "You really care a lot about people. That's nothing to be sorry about."

My heart jumped in my chest and I broke the gaze, focusing on finishing my cocoa. "Thanks." I stood up, swinging my bag onto my shoulder. "I'll probably go again before the week's over."

"If you want a coffee partner, let me know when you're going, I wouldn't mind going back. I like helping individuals." That was probably the closest he'd get to saying my point had stuck with him, but I'd take it. Then, he added, "While working to fix policy so they're empowered to make better lives for themselves."

"You're always on, aren't you?" We headed for the door and Kris nodded another thanks at Rosie.

He nodded, trying to look completely serious. "Always."

"You want to risk potential death by peanut butter again?" I asked in my most dry tone of voice, arching one of my eyebrows.

Kris laughed like I'd caught him by surprise, stopping to hold the coffee shop door for me. "You'll keep me safe, right?" He flashed me the same flirty smile he'd used on the barista.

I passed by him so closely our bodies were barely an inch apart and paused, trapping him against the doorframe as I stepped the tiniest bit closer. If he was going to play that game, so would I. "I don't know. You're my competition, you know. Just one tiny drop of peanut butter on an apple and you'll be out of my way," I said in my coyest, evilest tone. The air grew thick between us and I could hear his heartbeat picking up pace to match my own racing heart.

His eyes locked with mine and he didn't move an inch. "I think I'm safe. You might play bad guys, but you're not one of them." He echoed Grace's latest lecture, except his words were delivered with a serious smile. We stood like that for what seemed like forever until Kris started slowly moving forward, like he was about to close the electric-charged distance between us. His hand barely whispered against my arm.

I arched my eyebrows at him and pursed my lips, breaking away into the cool October air, which felt wonderful against my suddenly way-too-hot skin. "Oh ye of too much faith." I twiddled my fingers and cackled my best evil-queen cackle.

He hung against the doorframe a second longer than necessary, looking like he was trying to catch his breath. Point for me. "In you? Yup. If I can't trust a fellow Lamberfield-ian, who can I trust?"

I just winked at him and cackled again.

From: Em (emkatsaros@dmail.com)

To: Wilhelm (wmeyer@dmail.de)

Subject: Haven't heard from you and Boston update

Hi!

My mentor is really great, and she looks a lot like the actress who played Wonder Woman in the 70's, which makes it really fun to be in her mentoring sessions. She's making me change a lot of my speech to try and make it better. I'd really love to get your thoughts on it. When I'm done, maybe I'll record it and send it to you? Let me know.

Everyone here is so amazing and talented and sometimes I wonder if my stuff is good enough to be here, but...you don't want to hear my worries, right? I know you'd just tell me my speech is perfect, anyway ☺

We helped out at a soup kitchen this morning and I'm now an expert at pouring coffee and making peanut butter sandwiches. It was a really great experience and I'll probably do it again later this week.

Remember when you told me about your favorite café in Freiburg? I'd love to check it out someday. Do they have hot chocolate? It would be amazing to just cuddle the window, like you said you like to do, and watch people walk by while being all cozy and drinking hot chocolate.

I miss you, XOXOXOXO

-em

28

I dropped onto the little couch at the entrance to the inn's lobby bathroom, counting the rings coming through my phone. I had a few minutes before we were supposed to board the bus to Breed's Hill and I needed my best friend.

"Come on, be there. Please." When Phoebe finally picked up, there was the distant sound of some blustery music with a lot of brass—right, she was probably watching early morning marching band practice. "Feebs, my life is falling apart," I said, digging behind my back with one arm to save the stupid oversized doily that had slipped its way off the back of the seat. "Everything sucks," I added before giving up on fixing the doily and dumping it on the embroidered cushion next to me.

"Wait a minute, I can't really hear you." There was some shuffling on her end and the music grew fainter. "Okay. The bleachers kind-of block the drumline."

"If you keep hanging out there, you're going to become a marcher by osmosis." I could picture her leaning against one of the bleacher supports, wearing Dev's marching band letter jacket. "Osoba's probably hoping Dev will be a good influence and you'll want to wear matching uniforms and freeze your asses off in the middle of a football field together."

She laughed and the sound untied a few of the knots that had twisted inside me. "Sure, and when I trip over the fifty-yard line and break my arm, you can take my place."

"I'll be right on it as soon as I'm done fighting with this stupid lace couch thing." I poked at the stiff cotton. "You'd love it here. Even the bathrooms in this place think they're from the nineteen-hundreds and have lacy yarn stuff everywhere."

"Antimacassar," Phoebe said, absently.

"Excuse me?" Coming from her that could have been a character or a place or just a big vocabulary insult for all I knew.

"Victorians used antimacassars to protect their couches from the macassar oil guys used in their hair back then. You asked me to crochet a few for the historical society, remember?" When I didn't answer her little yarn-loving trivia factoid right away, Phoebe said, "Hmm. Okay, I should have at least gotten some sort of word-nerd comment from you for that. What's wrong?"

The twisting came back full-force, complete with a little bit of nausea. I pushed the words out quickly, my fingers tangling in the *antimacassar*. "What's wrong is that I'm going to lose this competition, my life sucks, my family might move to Kenya or Sweden, and I shouldn't have even bothered to come here. My speech is the worst one and everyone knows it."

Another *hmm*, though it was one of her knowing hmms.

"First: You're being ridiculous about the moving thing because I know for a fact from Alec that's not real, just some wild guess of yours. And I wish you had told me you were worrying about this stuff earlier. Second: The part about your speech being the worst is not true, and third: What do you mean 'Everyone knows it?'"

I didn't bother to answer the "wild guess" thing but moved straight onto the speech. "It *is* true. Everyone else here is serious and I'm just," I fluttered my hand around, whacking one of the chair arm antimacassars onto the floor, "only here because you and Grace basically wrote my speech."

There was a huffing noise on the other side of the phone. "No, we didn't. You wrote your speech—"

"I said it out loud and you guys wrote it down better," I corrected her.

"Actually, the voice to text software wrote it down and you cleaned it up. *Your* words won state, Em. Grace and I made suggestions in a few spots to smooth it out, but that's all your hard work."

There wasn't any use in arguing with her. "Anyway, even with all your help, it's still not good enough. They got these mentors to come in and help us make our speeches better. I've seen everyone else's critiques and all of them just have a few red lines here and there on the paper, but my mentor tore mine apart. According to her, *everything's* wrong with it. I can't write and I still haven't found my hook and—"

"That's really mean if she's telling you that. Why would they let someone like that mentor at this competition? You should definitely ask for another mentor."

"No, she's right, my speech totally sucks. I hear people talking about how some of us are only here because of delivery, and I know they're talking about me. It's obvious."

"Oh, Em." There was a metallic sound in the background, like she'd just slid down the metal column holding up the bleachers and the zipper on her jacket whacked the rivets a few times. There was a good chance Phoebe was now sitting on the ground, a concerned look on her face. I held tight to that picture in my head. "I'm so sorry people are all being awful. I believe in you."

My fingers curled around the edge of the sofa's wooden trim, squeezing tight at the ache that just kept growing as my words came out. "They're not being awful. It's so much worse because they're actually nice people. At least, most of them. And all of these people can't be wrong about my speech, either." The best thing about Phoebe was that she just listened, unlike Grace, who, thanks to her super logical brain, always tried to figure out ways to fix things. Or Alec, who always told me I was blowing things out of proportion. The way I was feeling at the moment, I needed a listener, not a fixer. I took a deep breath. "I miss you guys."

"This is going to sound a little weird, but I think it's really good you're doing this without us. It's like you've created a character description for yourself of a talented actress who is outgoing and flirty, but you don't think things like speechwriting and debating belong in that description without us around to help you, and that's so not true. Maybe your mentor sees that, too. You're so freak-ishly talented, Em, and maybe being away from us will let you see that."

That speech was something I'd expect from Grace or Leia, not Phoebe, and it felt weird to have her dissect my fears so perfectly. Weird enough that I couldn't brush it off like I could one of Grace's "you're awesome" speeches. "Still, it's lonely here."

"You have Kris." I snorted at that, and Phoebe added, "And Ann and some of the others you mentioned before. And it's not like you can't call or text me whenever you want."

"I know. You're the best. I just wish…" I thought about the unanswered emails and texts I'd sent over the past few days, "I was hoping Wil would have tried to fix this by now," I said in a whisper, as if the softer I said it, the less real it would be. "I don't know what he's waiting for."

Phoebe was silent for a second, before saying, just as softly, "Oh, Em. The way you've been talking, I thought you two fixed things."

"There wasn't anything to fix. It wasn't even a real fight, but he won't answer any of his texts. What if Grace is right? What if he really is ghosting me?" I swung my legs over the sofa arm and lay on my back, draping my free arm over my eyes, the antimacassar-thing a giant lump in the middle of my back. "Maybe he met a five-foot-nine Veronica Lake wannabe supermodel named Katja and they're too busy making out in front of the pillar in Freiburg for him to bother with me." I could practically see the girl. Gorgeous, completely sure of herself, and not thousands of miles away. The exact opposite of me.

"Wow, that's specific." Phoebe picked a perfect time to develop a dry sense of humor.

I uncovered my eyes and glared at my phone. "You *do* realize I'm emotionally fragile right now, right?"

"Sorry. Honestly, though," she said really slowly, drawing out the word, "Is this really the time to worry about Wil? You're only away for a week, and I know it's hard, but a week really isn't a long time. You can worry about fixing this when you get back, if you still want to."

Her last few words stung, but her comments actually made some sense, even though it was weird to hear Phoebe give me relationship advice. "He *could* just be giving me space so I can focus on the competition."

Phoebe made her skeptical humming sound, the same one she always made whenever I tried to convince her to watch *Vampire Teens*. "Maybe, but whatever it is, it's not worth overreacting about. And where the frack did you come up with Katja?"

"Please, it's totally possible. Have you seen some of those German supermodels?"

She definitely was choking back a laugh. "Stop worrying about it," she said, raising her voice as the sound of crescendoing horns came closer. "Everything's going to be fine."

"You're starting to sound like me."

"Mmmhmm. Speaking of sounding like you, aren't you supposed to be doing some conference stuff right now?"

I rolled my eyes up to the ceiling and took a deep breath. "It's okay, the less continuous exposure I have to Kris, the better for everyone around us. Honest to God, when he's not trying to mess with my head, he's arguing with me about everything. If I say it's Tuesday, he'll come up with some argument about how it's Wednesday in Japan or something ridiculous like that."

"You're overreacting about him, too."

"Whatever. You don't have to play nice with him twenty-four/seven." I almost went in to how he was starting to really make me question my own feelings in moments like the coffee shop, but then the door banged open, breaking that train of thought. New York waved as she passed me but if she thought being fake-nice to me would get her inside information about Kris, she was so wrong. "Besides, he'll be fine. He's getting enough attention already," I said in an almost-whisper. I didn't need Miss Empire State going back to Kris, saying I was talking about him. I glanced over towards the stalls and realized it would probably be a good idea to stop before she did hear something. "You're right, though, I have to go. Our bus is probably already here."

"Have fun. You're awesome, your speech is awesome, and you really, really deserve to focus on just you right now. You earned it." Phoebe's voice wrapped around me like a hug.

A little moisture sprang up at the corners of my eyes and I rubbed my sleeve across my face. "Thanks. I'll call you tomorrow."

29

"So, this is what happens when you let them loose on the site of the first battle of the American Revolution," Ann commented as we watched about ten of the guys from our group mock-battle on the wide green field of Breed's Hill. The guy from Alaska war-whooped as Michigan fell over from an imaginary rifle shot by New Hampshire.

I snorted as Kris joined the "battle" and pretended to stab Michigan with a bayonet. "Boys."

"Do you think we should take a video of this?" Lia casually pulled out her phone. "For posterity and scientific research reasons, of course." The guy from North Dakota dove for cover behind a tree before Alaska could "get" him.

"Of course. It would be really remiss of us not to." The girl from New York clapped as Kris fell over in the worst acted death scene I'd ever seen. "Oooh, maybe I should go over and try to nurse him back to life."

My brows drew together and I side-eyed her. Was she serious? "Sure. Maybe you'll get 'shot,' too." Ann nudged me in the side and I shrugged. There was a good chance everyone else was thinking the same thing at such a dumb comment.

"I'd totally give Kris mouth-to-mouth," Colorado-girl said to New York with a wink.

Apparently not.

Ann pulled me away from the group before I could even open my mouth. "I'm saving you from your own snark," she said with the tiniest smile.

Over her shoulder, I could see some of the girls from our group swarming the "battlefield" to join in the chaos. New York and a few of the other girls were all over Kris. "It's ridiculous. They're all acting like preschoolers." The back of my neck warmed up in perfect time with my annoyance.

Ann turned and finally let out her suppressed laugh as the rag-tag bunch of "zombie soldiers" chased the other girls. "We've all been working really hard. I think everyone's just letting off a little steam." Kris grabbed New York around the waist from behind and twirled her around before dropping her and zombie-stumbling after the girl from Arizona. "And that's a new twist on the Revolutionary War." She glanced back over at me, tilting her head and frowning. "Are you okay?"

"I'm fine. It's just…" Why was the whole zombie battle bothering me so much? I turned my back on the chaos and Kris getting tackled by the girl from Vermont, who supposedly played rugby. My annoyance at the whole group went up a notch. "…they have no respect for historical landmarks."

Ann managed to look skeptical and amused at the same time. "Sure."

"Zombies," I muttered under my breath, then added, "It's really hot out here. I'm going to find some shade." The morning was clear and sunny, making it unusually warm for October. Most of us had left our jackets on the bus and now even my miniskirt, long sleeved t-shirt, and Keds were starting to feel too heavy.

A breeze blew over the hill and Ann pulled her sleeves over her hands. "Right. It doesn't have anything to do with—"

I cut her off with an arched eyebrow and a circular hand gesture just like Osoba used for her cutoff in band. "Zombies? No. I'm going over there," I waved vaguely in the museum's direction, "before I die of heat exhaustion," I said before taking off. As I got closer to some of the people who weren't "battling," I slowed down as their words carried over on the wind.

Illinois lounged on the lawn, twirling a blade of grass between his fingers. "…expected more serious competition."

The girl from Kansas laughed as she dropped onto the grass next to him. "You mean super-positive 'ohmigosh, I'm going to make a difference!' fluff isn't serious to you?"

"Good one," he said, giving her a fist-bump. "This isn't elementary school, it's the real world. The one from New Jersey was the worst, too. Almost like a cheerleader wrote it. Rah-rah, change!"

"Right? I mean, you hear her during the conference, right? Like, she has absolutely no clue about the political process, it's all bleeding heart and social justice stuff for her with no real action, like she's some sort of Internet meme.

She really doesn't deserve to be here. At least the guy from her state has some sense."

I couldn't take it anymore—a cold breeze clenched my lungs and pushed me to move again. I shook my head, picked up my pace, and swept past them, forcing my expression to neutral.

"Oh, hey Em." Illinois looked up with surprise, but shot me a smile like he hadn't just been trashing me two seconds before.

Without saying a word, I waved and kept moving, trying to ignore the nausea that replaced the annoyance rolling through me from a few seconds before. It was hard enough to feel like I wasn't faking that I belonged in the summit, but I didn't need to be reminded of it when I was supposed to be having fun. Maybe my speech wasn't anything like their deep analyses of global policies, but it wasn't their right to decide whether or not I "deserved" to be a part of this. Before I could get my breathing back to normal, though, our tour guide called us all together to hear her speech about the obelisk and the history of the site, and I kept to the back to get a minute for myself.

"Hey, you okay?" The girl from Puerto Rico whispered to me, touching my arm gently.

I nodded. The last thing I needed was to break down in front of everyone just to prove to them even more that I didn't belong in their polished change-making elite. Like Puerto Rico, who had her gap year already set up to help at a local charity instead of going straight to college for some complicated science degree I couldn't even pronounce. "I'm just a little tired," I finally squeezed out, forcing my spine out of its slump and smoothing my expression into something super perky that would have made Shirley Temple proud.

Everyone grew quiet when the guide started speaking and her practiced spiel was what I needed to refocus. I couldn't let what I'd heard from Illinois and Kansas get to me. Of course my friends were right, and of course, Kris wasn't my only competitor, but in that moment, the only thing I could control was my plan. Plus, a little part of me had to admit it was a fun way to take my mind off everyone else. So when the guide said some of the funds for building the obelisk came from a fair and bake sale, I grabbed that opening. I craned my neck to find Kris on the other side of the semi-circle and, the second I caught his attention, stuck my tongue out at him. His head shake was worth the annoyance that crossed New York's face as she clutched at his shirt sleeve.

Afterwards, when we were given free rein to explore the museums and obelisk, Kris came up and poked me in the shoulder. "That was really mature."

A little satisfied feeling rose up in me when I noticed he'd ditched New York and the rest of his groupies, but I didn't let him see it.

"Says the guy who was pretending to be a Revolutionary war zombie," I countered. "Just in case you missed the point, Sarah Hale raised funds for this," I gestured at the giant white obelisk looking over the site, "with a *bake sale*. Now, what were you saying about little things not making an impact?" At least teasing Kris helped push away some of the low-level nausea that had washed over me.

"She was a famous author with a ton of fans and she auctioned off letters from Revolutionary War heroes during the sale. I doubt your bake sales raise enough for monuments."

"Not the point. Do you concede that I'm right?"

"No."

"Stubborn." I couldn't explain the kindergarten impulse that came over me, making me tap him on the shoulder and say, "Catch me before I get to the top of the obelisk and maybe I won't hold this over your head the whole rest of this trip," before taking off towards the obelisk entrance. I didn't look back to see if he was following.

Luckily, the prospect of almost three hundred steps scared off most of our group and I easily dodged around the few who were on the first ten steps of the stairway. By step thirty, my legs were burning and I started slowing down. This was stupid and childish and…

"I can hear you slowing down," Kris' voice echoed through the curving stairwell and I upped my pace, exhaustion be damned. I knew how hard it was for him to turn down a good challenge. Usually, it wasn't so literal, but maybe he would get so tired he'd drop out of the competition out of exhaustion. I ignored the fact that my own body thrilled at this game, giving me a burst of energy I didn't have seconds before.

By step one hundred, I slowed down again and hoped that Kris wasn't some sort of superhuman. I also wished I hadn't been so lazy in gym glass when Coach Rentz was trying to build our endurance and hoped Kris was as much of a slacker as me. *Not with a body like that*, my oxygen-deprived brain pointed out, and I shoved logic aside as I powered up the stairway, taking the barest second to peek out the window and freak out a little bit over how high we already were. Then, it was back to focusing on the endless curve of stairs.

I felt something brush at my waist just as I took my last step into the top floor of the obelisk and immediately hunched over to catch my breath.

"Caught you," Kris' voice reached my ears, sounding as out of breath as me. His hand caught my wrist and suddenly my throat tightened a little bit more. I was so hot at the moment; I regretted my long sleeves.

"No way," I choked out, and leaned on what looked like some sort of cannon with a hole in it, clutching at the stitch in my side. He still didn't let go of my arm. "I said catch me before I reach the top." We were the only ones at the top of the obelisk and my voice echoed in the round room. At least I could focus without Kris' usual entourage around.

"And I touched your back when you were still on the steps." Kris leaned flat against the wall next to me and tilted his head to look at me. "Which means no more bake sale talk."

"Really? Because I bet my grandmom's mini tea cake recipe could get us a monument just as tall as this one…" I said teasingly. My lungs still felt like a giant had played hopscotch on them, but the feeling had died down to a small giant instead of King Kong. My heart still tried to escape out of my chest.

"Breaking your end of the bargain already. I should know never to trust the competition." Kris squeezed my wrist and pulled us over to one of the windows. Boston lay before us, the harbor beautiful and sparkling. "Whoa. This might be worth not being able to walk for the rest of the week."

"I may never climb a staircase again, but yeah." I took the opportunity to stick my head right next to Kris' and pointed at one of the white spires, my finger pressing against the window pane. "That's Faneuil hall, I think."

"I think you're right."

"This is the second time this week you've said that." I pretended to check my phone. "And darn, I wasn't recording. Want to say it again for posterity?"

"You really like egging people on, don't you?"

"It's fun with certain people. I like seeing how they react." I smiled and stared out at the city below us, remembering a similar conversation I had with Wil right before Junior Prom. "Wil would agree with you on that." He never took the bait, no matter how hard I tried. Unlike Kris, Wil was perfect that way, never getting ruffled over anything, even though it killed any possible fun flirt-fights.

Kris copied my posture, and made a noise that was half laugh-half exhale. "I can't even imagine what it must be like to date you."

I turned my head and said, archly, "I'll have you know that it's a truly amazing experience. I'm the perfect girlfriend."

But, as I said it, my lips curled up and I scrunched my nose. I was secure enough to find humor in my imperfections, even around my arch-enemy.

"I believe you," he said, playing along, but his grin matched mine. "Speaking of, are you guys still dating? I saw through the social media grapevine that you and foreign exchange student are no more."

My smile disappeared as quickly as it had come. I turned back to looking out the window so he couldn't see my face. "Well, you saw wrong. He knows how important this competition is to me and he's just giving me space."

"Oh, come on. I can't believe Em Katsaros, self-proclaimed relationship expert, is in denial about a break-up."

And, it began. I was surprised he hadn't waited until closer to the judging to start showing his real self. I forced myself to keep my voice level. "'Self-proclaimed?' You're just annoyed that, because of my expert help, Phoebe ended up dating Dev instead of you."

"Actually, no." His totally non-combative, conversational tone made me look back at him in surprise. "I got to spend a lot of time with her when we set up the reading in the schools week. She's definitely one of the nicest people at our school," he paused, then added, "at least, she's a lot nicer than any of her friends," at that, he looked pointedly at me, "but it was like last year she was trying to be someone else. It's really weird. The real her is kind of better than the fake her, but not really my type, if you know what I mean."

"Oh, you don't know the half of it." Last year, Phoebe

had tried to turn herself into her favorite book characters to get both Dev's and Kris' attention, but thankfully ended up realizing she liked Dev better. I was surprised Kris was perceptive enough to notice

"I'm not putting down your friend, by the way. I still like her a lot—" at my side-eye, he quickly added, "—as a friend, but her and Jacobs are perfect for each other."

"You can thank the relationship expert for that one."

Kris gave me a 'Yeah, sure' look, and said, "Anyway, you completely changed the subject away from your ex-boyfriend and your denial."

He wasn't going to let it go and it was grating on my nerves. "Wil and I are fine. Better than fine. In fact, he's coming here during winter break to visit me," I said, tilting up my chin in a "Don't challenge me" fashion.

Kris shook his head at that comment, and cleared his throat in a way that made it sound like he was trying not to laugh. "I'd check to see if he bothers to follow you back again on Photogram before you make any plans."

"You *obviously* don't understand the nuances of our mature relationship." I pulled up one of Wil's latest Photogram posts of a late-blooming yellow rose and hit the translate button for the text. "See? 'Thinking of a beautiful—' okay, whatever that word is didn't translate, but whatever— 'girl.'" I popped my phone back into my pocket. "He's talking about me."

"He could be talking about another girl."

"No, yellow's my favorite color. Everyone knows that.

Hell, *you* even know that. And stop being a jerk just to prove some wrong point you're trying to make." I drew myself up even straighter and stuck my nose up in the air. As if he thought he had a right to comment on my relationship with Wil. "Profound and abiding love like what Wil and I have won't get hurt by a little time not talking online."

"Please, it's not like you two could have had a really deep relationship. Did you ever even talk?"

It was so weird how his jab made it sound like he'd been listening in on me, Ann, and Lia at the colonial dinner. Or listening in on any of my conversations with Phoebe or Grace and Leia. The thought dropped to the pit of my stomach like a rock, but I decided not to let him get to me. Wil and I talked enough, especially considering our language barrier. Time to change the subject before I decided to shove him down the stairs. "Enough about my personal life. I didn't climb almost three hundred steps to hear your wrong theories." I bumped him with my shoulder. "Pretty nice view for something built thanks to a bake sale, huh?"

He turned to look at me and shook his head, but his lips were pressed together as if he was trying not to smile. "You're really not going to let that go, are you?"

I leaned in closer as if I was about to share a secret. "I'm stubborn. You should know that by now."

He didn't move back or break eye contact. "So I ran up here and tagged you on the top step for nothing?"

"I was already at the top. And you got a great view, some exercise, and amazing company."

"Well, if you were smarter you wouldn't have worn a skirt that short to run up stairs in front of someone…" he started, then laughed as I whacked him in the arm. "Just kidding. I was too busy trying not to trip and break my neck on the stairs."

Luckily, my skin tone meant a blush just looked like I was wearing a little more makeup, but I could feel the heat creeping up my neck and over my cheeks. "You better not have seen anything." I was thankful I had worn thick tights even with the warm weather. "Perv."

"Uh-uh. I'm a perfect gentleman. Momma Lambert would kill me otherwise. That's why I'm also going to ignore the fact that you cheated and broke your own rules."

"Right. Smooth answer." Looking straight into his eyes made my guard slip the tiniest bit. "How do you do it?"

His brows furrowed together. "Do what? Ignore your Em-rule-breaking?"

I tilted one of my shoulders up in a weak shrug before folding my arms in that tiny space between us. "Give these perfectly scripted answers. Never let stuff faze you." I glanced out the window again and added, "Just…this place. It's, like, how much tinier can we be? People fought and died and so many of them were around our age. And what have we done, really?" Kansas' words echoed back at me and I wanted to kick her and myself for making me so weak in front of my adversary.

"It's not as if I'm confident all the time," he said. I looked back up at him, thrown off by that whisper, but his focus was completely on the city below. "And just because we're not ambushing redcoats doesn't mean we're not making a difference." We were so close, and when he tilted his chin towards the stairway again, it nearly grazed my cheek, bringing my pulse back up to its running-up-stairs pace. "Ready to head back down? No racing this time, because we need to be in one piece to compete on Saturday."

I met his gaze again and forced a "confident" smile. "No winning through forfeit?"

"I never forfeit. And I always win." Kris broke away and headed towards the stairs, leaving me even more breathless than the stupid race. I leaned against the window and he stopped on the top step. "You coming?"

"Yeah." I broke out of my reverie and hurried towards the stairs, brushing past him on the way down. "See you at the bottom."

From: Change Council Scholarship Team (ccscholar-shipteam@uschangecouncil.org)

To: Undisclosed Recipients

Subject: Expected Behavior for Change Council Conference Attendees

Dear Students,

It was brought to our attention from US Park Service employees and tourists that some of you were exhibiting behavior unbecoming of US Change Council state representatives while visiting the Breed's Hill historic site the other night. Remember that, while you are attending the conference, you are representing both the US Change Council and your respective states and that we expect professional behavior at all times. Please respect your national monuments.

The following behaviors will not be tolerated and may result in either reprimands or removal from the competition:

1.Excessive roughhousing

2.Pretending to be secret service agents protecting a foreign diplomat (note: the Boston police did not appreciate this behavior)

3.Excessive use of vulgar language at a national park (no, we don't care if you're recreating a historic battle. And for historical accuracy, our revolutionary war soldiers did not become zombies)

4.Mooning

You have put in a lot of hard work to get this far in the competition, and are proud of all of you. We know that you are all very conscientious citizens and likely did not mean to disrupt public peace or disrespect our country's historical sites, and that this behavior will cease. Your chaperones are present to reinforce proper behavior. Please listen to them.

Final note: Remember that students are not allowed off inn grounds without Change Council supervision. This includes the coffee shop next to the inn.

Sincerely,

The US Change Council Scholarship team

 WilOfHyrule: @HokageAlec I cannot believe you still are talking about the last game. I demand a rematch.

 HokageAlec: @WilOfHyrule Bring it on. I tackled you and won fair and square last time.

 WilOfHyrule: @HokageAlec I'll be around soon. We can rematch then.

30

By Wednesday morning, I still couldn't get the roller-coaster conversation I had with Kris in the obelisk out of my head. I hated feeling out of control, and those few minutes had thrown me off-balance the rest of the day. Even breakfast was filled with this uncomfortable tension that kept both of us from really speaking up or arguing. It drove me crazy because I couldn't tell who had the upper hand in this weird mind game going on between us.

It was also exhausting to deal with Ann's optimism or the soul-sucking reminders from some of the others that I wasn't Change Council material. I was usually the "hang out with people as much as possible"-type, but needed to regain my balance and a quiet afternoon on my own would be perfect for that.

As we got on line to get into the Museum of Fine Arts, a shadow fell over me and I looked up to find Kris practically breathing over my shoulder. I took a deep breath and turned on flirty-Em mode, looking up at him through my eyelashes.

"I'm surprised you picked the museum over Fenway. Isn't baseball a rite of passage for the American male?" Letting a teasing smile curve up my lips, I added, "Oh, wait,

I forgot. You hate athletes."

Kris laughed. He stood close enough I could feel his chest shaking in tiny almost-touches against my shoulder. "First, I don't hate athletes. I happen to be a fencer, in case you didn't know. It's just not a school team. And you and your friends are really good at taking things out of context."

"You've campaigned on cutting funding to sports teams every year since, like, sixth grade."

"Guilty. But that's because they were usually the last to see cuts in our school. The hockey team got their ice time paid for the year because two of the parents are on the school board, but your precious theatre club got denied funding for the spring musical scripts. Mr. Landry and I had to do some creative alumni networking to make that happen."

I didn't know about the scripts, which were freakishly expensive and the reason why we had a few years of doing cheaper, older musicals my freshman and sophomore year, and why our fall plays were sometimes written by one of the seniors in creative writing class. But I wasn't going to let him off that easily. "And, you were the one who used the term 'football rejects' in a conversation with my best friend. In front of a lot of people who have friends on the football team."

"I was nervous and trying to sound cool in front of her," he said, looking a little sheepish as he said it, which made me stop in minor shock right before I could drop another example. Kris, admitting he didn't have game? Before I could tease him about it, though, he added, "You'll never let me live that down, will you?"

"Grace is still demanding a formal apology." The line moved and I stepped diagonally so he could come up alongside me. I looked him up and down out of the corner of my eye. The fencing thing explained why he was so toned for a political geek, even though his choice of a snobby sport wasn't surprising.

"And you?"

"I'm reserving judgment until I hear why you're here instead of visiting one of the icons of baseball history."

"Honestly, I have better things to do than look at the dugouts for a team that isn't even from Philly." He bumped my arm as we moved forward and I was glad for my jacket because of all the little shivers that ran through me in that second. "Is that a good enough answer?"

"Let's see. Supporting Philly teams and commonsense about what's interesting. Works for me." Red handed us both tickets and reminded us to be back at the entrance in three hours.

As we entered the hall, our group stated breaking into smaller groups, but I noticed that Kris kept pace beside me, not joining anyone else. He turned the museum map around in his hands like he was trying to get his bearings. "So, where are we headed?"

"We? Now you're hanging with the competition?"

"Um, everyone here is my competition."

"True. So why aren't you bothering the rest of them?" I jutted my chin at the girl from New York, who didn't seem to have seen us yet.

Kris didn't even bother to look. "It's nice to be around a familiar face for a little while, even if it's yours." There was that smile again, and another shiver ran from the base of my neck and down my spine. This was an act. I was just getting into character so much that feeling attracted to him only made sense. It was like when I wore floofy fifties dresses while we worked on *West Side Story* or lots of dance clothes when I was in *A Chorus Line*. I was inhabiting my role a little too well.

I narrowed my eyes at him, but opted for tossing back my hair and opening my own map. "Fine, but if you don't like ancient cultures, you're out of luck." Mom and Dad would both kill me if I didn't visit the Ancient Greek collection and I couldn't miss Egypt and Africa. "That's Mom's specialty." Without waiting for a response, I walked towards the stairs. Plan "Mess with Kris' mind" would only work if I wasn't constantly fawning over him—making them chase me a little bit always worked with the guys I liked. I had to make Kris keep following me.

He tugged at my jacket's sleeve so we were back to walking side-by side. He leaned in close enough that his breath tickled my cheek and sent another shock through me. "Love them." He then pulled ahead while I was frozen for a second so I was the one following him.

So, he was going to ratchet up the game? My worry faded to the back of my brain and a grin spread across my face, so wide it almost hurt. Sometimes love and war were the same thing, and, if he was going to try to mess with me, anything was fair.

I leaned closer to the glass to get a better look at the vase with a bunch of training athletes. "Mmm, look at the muscle definition on that javelin thrower."

The disgust on Kris' face was pretty obvious, even in his reflection. "So…if it's ancient, it's okay to just have naked people running around on stuff? Because nowadays we'd call it porn." He poked me in the shoulder, but I purposely ignored him.

"You're just prejudiced towards athletic people. Besides, this is history and art. Think of it: Someone in 430 BC painted this. Two thousand, four hundred years ago." I glanced back at him for only a second, then moved around to see the other side of the vase. "And, damn, they were hot even back then. Like this discus thrower's butt. Nice."

"You're making me rethink this ancient world thing." He put his hands on my shoulders and I let him pull me away from the vase. "What would your parents think of you staring at a discus thrower's butt?"

I waved my free hand dismissively. One problem at a time. "That I have good taste in art?"

"You're…" He shook his head, so obviously trying not to laugh that it made me laugh, and slid one hand down my arm so he now pulled on my wrist, right at my jacket cuff. A part of me wondered what it would feel like if his hand slipped a little lower and touched my skin. "I don't even know what you are."

"A history genius."

"I'm getting you out of here and into Ancient Egypt

before they kick you out for molesting the statues or something."

I faux-pouted, then something caught my attention out of the corner of my eye and I rotated my wrist so now I held his. I pulled him over to another display case. "Wait." A delicate gold wreath made to look like olive leaves sat in the case. It was so amazing, down to the little veins detailed into the leaves, I could stare at it forever. "What do you think? I could totally rock this at school." I let my fingers linger on his arm for an extra second before letting go, but his grip on my wrist didn't change.

"If anyone could make it work, it would probably be you." He sounded sincere, but this was Kris. He was as good at looking like he cared as I was at becoming another person onstage.

"I'll take that as a compliment."

He pulled again, but a little gentler this time. "Now, c'mon, Ancient Egypt. Maybe the mummies will give you nightmares and you'll be too tired to give a decent speech."

"Diabolical plan. But I thought everyone was your competition?"

"Well, some people are tougher competition than others. We're products of the same school system. I expect you to make me work for first place."

The challenge warmed me instead of the annoyance I expected. Maybe I really was becoming immune to his ego. "I'll take that as a compliment, too." I let him keep a constant pull on my arm as we walked, especially since his thumb kept rubbing over my cuff and sliding closer and closer to my skin. "But I bet it'll backfire on you, especially when I tell you about the hooks they used to take out the mummies' brains through their noses."

"That's disgusting."

"Who's going to have nightmares now?" When he turned his head to look at me, I winked. "Just call me the queen of diabolical. I receive tributes in the form of chocolate, golden wreaths, and first-place scholarships."

He tugged my arm so we were nose to nose and, looking into those gold-flecked eyes, my lungs stopped working. "Chocolate I can do. Golden wreaths might be a little *Mission Impossible* for me, but not totally impossible. But we'll see who gets the scholarship." Before I could respond, he pulled ahead of me and I had to focus on breathing and moving my legs to keep from being dragged across the museum floor.

One point to Kris. Crap.

31

"Oh. My. God." I craned my neck back and stopped mid-step, grabbing the staircase bannister. The skylight above us almost blinded me until my eyes adjusted to take in the paintings and columns surrounding it.

I tilted back a little too far and Kris reached an arm around my back to steady me. "Whoa, careful. I want to get you up to the rotunda in one piece."

"This is so seriously amazing. Look, that's Apollo," I pointed at the mural above us, "and Atlas holding up the world, and Perseus killing Medusa. On Pegasus." I couldn't help but grin at the familiar winged horse. My eyes dropped to the mural directly in front of us. "And those are the Danaïdes. See how they're trying to fill a bowl but the water keeps pouring out of the bottom?"

Kris followed my finger with his head, eventually turning his attention back to me with a surprised look on his face. "How do you know all this?"

"Like I said, my mom is a history professor—I was practically born knowing about ancient Greece, Rome, Egypt, and Western and Southern African civilizations. If you didn't notice this whole time," I nudged him in the side, bringing myself a little closer. "Also, my dad's from Greece, so I couldn't get away from all this growing up."

"That explains your name." His smile was weak, almost sheepish. "Meanwhile, my family's been in Lambertfield as long as anyone can remember. I think my great-grand-mother was a Quaker from Philly, but that's about as foreign as we get."

"You know, even though they were a small group, lots of Quakers were really active in abolition and suffrage. I even got to see the actual Germantown petition against slavery from 1688 where they argued for equal rights for everyone." I said, starting up the stairs again. "Not a bad background to have."

"Huh." Other than that, Kris kept silent and kept pace with me, his head also tilted up to take in the awesomeness above us.

We reached the rotunda and I leaned against one of the pillars, purposely trapping Kris' arm behind me. I may have been stunned by the beauty of the place, but I was still on a mission.

"Okay, you're right. I'm glad I survived to see this." The rotunda was stunning, skylights illuminating the John Singer Sargent murals and plaster reliefs on the ceiling. It took my breath away, and I couldn't help but lower my voice to a whisper, like we had stepped into a cathedral.

Kris pulled out his phone to take a video of the scene and it was cute seeing him fumbling with it one-handed. "Definitely better than a dugout," he said under his breath.

Trying to keep from smiling, I focused instead on

the murals above us, my eyes drawn to one of a boy with wings. "That's Eros and Psyche." My standing-in-a-church behavior slipped for a second and I pressed my lips together in embarrassment as my voice carried across the rotunda. I toned myself down to an indoor volume. "It's one of my favorite stories," I said, tilting my head so I could get a better view of the painting meets sculpture-like raised plaster. Eros was flying down to embrace Psyche, both forever frozen in an almost-kiss.

"Eros?" Kris asked. Out of the corner of my eye, I noticed his head tilt toward mine in what had to be an attempt to copy my angle.

"Cupid, but not the baby version. Aphrodite's son?" I turned my attention back to Kris and noticed how incredibly close we were, partly because I'd sort of trapped him in that position. Not like he had tried to move or free his arm or anything. I pushed through the tight feeling of my breath catching in my throat and tried to sound as normal as possible. "His mom got jealous of Psyche's beauty, so she sent Eros to go make Psyche fall in love with some really ugly guy so she'd be miserable. Instead, Eros ended up stabbing himself with his own arrow and falling in love with her." The heat from his arm and shoulder seeped through my shoulder and into my back.

Kris snorted. "Talk about a massive screwup. Let me guess, they lived happily ever after anyway?"

"Eventually. First, she was sent to the top of a mountain and the winds carried her to this garden, where she thought she was married to some sort of monster. Then Eros had sex with her in the dark for a whole bunch of nights until she got curious and found out his identity. After that, he banished her back to earth, where she was tortured by her mother-in-law, before he forgave her and they lived happily ever after."

"And this is one of your favorite stories?"

"What can I say? I'm a romantic."

"Sounds like it. Pornographic pottery and stories about anonymous sex. Kinky, Katsaros."

I tried to give him the stink eye, but one look at his face made me laugh instead. "You've blown my cover, Lambert. Just don't tell the teachers or it'll ruin their image of me as an innocent little flower."

"You trust me with this information? I could use it as blackmail material, you know." The rest of his face betrayed the smile he was definitely trying to hold back. "Judges, Em was trying to corrupt me with her wanton ways." The smile finally broke through, developing slowly across his lips, like he was sharing a secret with me.

That smile combined with him standing so close did things to my stomach and skin, fire and ice alternating though me in mini-shocks. I stepped a fraction of an inch closer to him, freeing his arm, but he just moved it with me so his hand now touched my waist. "Wanton ways? Judges, Kris has absolutely no proof. I think he's just trying to besmirch my pristine reputation."

"I think you're trying to influence the jury with SAT

words." His voice became softer and it was like the rotunda grew smaller around us, the other people fading away.

The pressure of his hand on my back made me lean forward the tiniest bit more. I rested my fingers on his other arm for balance. "We did decide that I am the queen of diabolical plans, remember?" That fire and ice swirled together, starting with the spot where his hand touched my waist and shooting to where my hand touched his sleeve. Damned character acting made my heart speed up to hummingbird pace. His exhale danced across my cheek, then chin, raising goosebumps on my whole body.

"I can be just as diabolical," he whispered, and leaned his head down.

My reflexes took over and I closed my eyes and tilted up my chin. Every piece of me wanted to reach up and seal the space between us where we stood in a frozen millisecond, like Psyche and Cupid. His arm pulled me even closer, fingers tightening into my side, and his body heat filled the air between us, warming me until my jacket felt too hot. His hand brushed a stray curl from my forehead and rested oh-so-lightly on my cheek.

"It's nice seeing the real you, Em." His words brushed over my lips and I caught my breath.

Just as our lips whispered against each other, my eyes shot open and the ice took over, reminding me I wasn't supposed to want this. I wasn't supposed to let the game get this far. I stepped sideways, breaking contact with Kris' arms. Shocks ran through my whole body and I resisted the urge to jump him. *Crap, crap, crap.* "I...I need to go take care of something. My mom wanted me to see...something..." I waved vaguely at one of the hallways leading from the rotunda and backed away.

Kris blinked at me, confusion and concern written all over his face. "I'll come with you."

"No, I'll be right back. I just have to take care of this one thing." Before he could protest, the guys from California, Colorado, and Arizona wandered into the rotunda. They headed toward us and I said a silent thanks to whatever greater being might be out there. "You guys all go ahead, I'll meet up with you at the bus." I then rushed off, ignoring Kris' voice behind me and totally unaware of where I was headed.

He said he was also diabolical. I already knew he was trying to mess with me by not acting like himself. Was this almost-kiss another part of the act? His last whisper echoed in my brain and it was like I had my own heart and organs torn out to put in the mummy jars. Painful and empty and nauseating. "*The real you...*" It was one thing to play mind games with Kris, but kissing him was different. I'd almost crossed a boundary I couldn't. But I couldn't ignore that there was something about how I felt when he was that close that had nothing to do with acting.

Our sort of, maybe, almost-kiss still tingled on my lips, even though it was the barest brush, like the flutter of Psyche's wings. I brought my fingers up to my mouth, trying to remember and press the feeling away at the same time. A statue blocked my path. I froze and looked up into a face composed of pure sympathy. The placard said she was Guanyin, the goddess of compassion. Even though she was made for a temple in ancient China, she looked like she was reaching across the centuries just to comfort me.

"Help," I whispered to the statue. I had to stop lying to myself. This was more than getting into character, and I didn't know how to stop wishing all this was real. Fear and a suffocating helplessness broke me at that moment and I just sat where I stood, dropping my head onto my knees and drawing solace from a piece of stone.

32

By the time Kris found me heading back to the museum entrance, I was already back to my usual composed self. We avoided talking about what happened in the rotunda and I was happy to latch on to Ann the second we found the others. Kris kept throwing me weird sideways looks, but I was just too tired to care.

Ann narrowed her eyes at me and pulled me over to the side. "What happened?"

I composed my features into a blank, happy slate. That was one thing I was good at, unlike, oh, not almost kissing the guy I was supposed to be crushing. "I think we just fought over whether an Egyptian soldier would beat a Navy seal or something stupid like that." I added an unconcerned shake of my head, like the answer was obvious.

"If you two didn't fight every second, I'd be worried. School has to be a nightmare for both of you."

"It's a really big school." I looked over her shoulder, noticed Louisiana looking our way, and quickly changed the subject. "So, why is Geoff looking at us like he's been stranded in an all-boy's school for years and just saw a girl for the first time? Is there anything you want to tell me?"

Ann's cheeks turned a pretty pink and she pulled her hair forward to play with it. For the first time today, I noticed she had it loose instead of in the usual bun or braid she wore outside of our room. "We just checked out the Textile collection. He wasn't even bored while I talked about sewing and how the clothes were constructed."

"I bet," I said, teasingly. I turned slightly so I didn't have to see Kris out of the corner of my eye. At least matchmaking was something I did really well. Grace would probably say I was trying to deal with my own out-of-control life by trying to control someone else, and this time, she'd be right.

"There's a jacket from the sixteen-hundreds, and you should see this one dress from the seventeen-hundreds. The embroidery is amazing." Apparently, sewing was Ann's passion in addition to music. I needed to introduce her to Phoebe's sister. "And then we went to the musical instrument wing and you should see the flutes they have here. They're gorgeous."

"Did you invite Geoff to our room later so he can hear you play?" I asked.

Her cheeks turned pinker. At the rate we were going, she'd never need blush again. "I...no." Her voice came out in a hiss and she lowered it even more. "The boys aren't even allowed in our side of the inn."

I shrugged and pulled myself into the bus, picking a seat that kept me as far as possible from Kris and guaranteed Ann would have to sit next to Geoff if she wanted to finish our conversation. Unfortunately, that meant sitting next to

Red and his endless mountain of checklists. "It's not like you're going to *do* anything, Saint Ann. But if you want to keep being perfect, do a mini-concert in the sitting room. He's allowed there." I pointed at the empty seat next to Mr. Louisiana of the gorgeous eyes and accent. I gauged her reaction, trying to figure out how much to push without going anywhere that would *really* upset her. "If you don't do it, I can't be responsible for anything I might say during breakfast tomorrow."

Kris passed as he walked down the aisle and gave me a confused once-over before continuing to the back of the bus.

Geoff looked across the aisle at me, but addressed his question to Ann. "What is Jersey talking about?"

"I don't know. People from the Mid-Atlantic are insane." Ann tossed her hair over her shoulder so it fell waterfall-like into her lap.

"Now that's the truth."

As the two of them fell into adorably awkward conversation, I sat back, leaned my head against the back of my seat and closed my eyes. I was transported back to the rotunda and the look on Kris' face before he leaned in and we almost, sort-of kissed. The fire that ran across my skin whenever I thought of that moment wasn't like anything I'd ever felt before. Thrill and dread mixed in my blood again and all I wanted to do was bolt back to Guanyin and hide for the rest of the competition. If he was trying to mess with my mind enough to throw me off, he was winning.

When the bus stopped in front of the restaurant where

we were eating lunch, I rushed to the bathroom the second I got off the bus and locked myself in one of the stalls. I needed a minute to myself before going back to the crowd, like being in the green room or breathing behind the curtain before a show.

Stupid hormones and stupid museums with romantic paintings. Stupid, manipulative boys who knew how to play to people's emotions to get what they wanted. Stupid me, for thinking I could stoop to his level. My chest tightened and I bent over to try to catch my breath. I sucked in a lungful of air and tried to think of Wil and Germany and the Freiburg Christmas market thing he had been telling me about for weeks.

Crap. I'd forgotten all about Wil at the museum. I forced in another breath before guilt could pull me back under. It was going to be okay. I was going to fix all of this. I thought of Wil's dark-blue eyes until the memory of golden-brown ones faded into the background.

Anxiety squashed as much as I could, I pushed the stall door open and straightened my top and jacket. All I needed to do was avoid Kris the rest of the night and, tomorrow morning, I'd be ready to tackle him again. "Just breathe," I said and stepped into the restaurant.

Hi Wil!

How are you? I haven't gotten any emails from you, so I wonder if you're okay. But if you're busy, I understand.

Things are wonderful here in Boston. We went to the art museum and all I could think about was you. It's impossible to forget you; we're so much a part of each other. There's this really awesome statue of Guanyin that I just sat in front of for a while—if we ever do that road trip here, I'll show you that statue. Do you remember when we went to the art museum in Philly and I showed you Tanner's The Annunciation and told you it was my favorite painting because of the expression on Mary's face? Well, this might be in the running for my favorite statue because the compassion on Guanyin's features is…well, it was like a real person was looking down at me and offering her comfort, you know?

I wish you were here to support me like you always do. The judging is soon and I'm scared because I really want this scholarship and I'd love to know you're cheering me on. I'm trying to avoid Kris because he's a pain, but they keep sticking us together. Ugh. But at least I have thoughts of you to make it all bearable.

Anyway, love you, talk to you soon.

XOXOXOXO

Em

From: Wilhelm (wmeyer@dmail.de)

To: Em (emkatsaros@dmail.com)

Subject: Re: Museum of Fine Art in Boston

Em, we are not dating right now. We should not be emailing.

I am glad Boston is nice and good luck in the competition.

-Wil

33

"You're distracted today." Lauren's words were a statement, not a question, as she pulled the battered and marked-up copy of my speech out of my hands.

I stopped mid-word and took a beat to look up from the now-empty space between my hands. Part of me wanted to say something like, "Yeah, I'm just a giant eff-ed up ball of emotion right now with the suckiest speech in this place, so can we skip to the part where I fall apart and lose this competition?" Instead, I calmly said, "Distracted? What do you mean?"

She didn't even bother to hide her frown. "I work with politicians, who are incredibly good at hiding their emotions when they have to. You're not that good an actress."

I flinched. "That's a little harsh."

"It's my job. If I don't call you out when I think you're at risk of endangering your performance in the competition, I won't be much use as a mentor." Lauren set her elbows on the table and dropped her chin into her hands. "So, what's wrong?"

"I'm fine. I just can't be on for twenty-four hours a day," I said, trying my hardest not to sound peevish. Let her try being so composed when the boy she loved was ghosting her and when she's being emotionally manipulated by the guy she's trying to emotionally manipulate.

Lauren studied me for a long moment, then reached into her purse and pulled something small out of the front pocket. Without saying a word, she dropped a worn patch into my hand, its frayed edges tickling my palm. I studied the patch, my fingers brushing lightly over the raised image of the planet Earth, the loose blue threads of the ocean waving as I passed over them. It looked like some sort of planetary merit badge.

"Okay, I give. What does this have to do with being on and making speeches?"

"It's a reminder." She just swung us into weird Zen-mentor territory and I was getting whiplash. One minute, she pulled the speech out of my hands and covered it in red pen and highlighter, the next, she handed me merit badges. "Right now, you have the whole world in the palm of your hand. You have so much potential. It's so easy to get distracted and drop it." She leaned forward on her elbows again, her face lit up like a stage light. "But here's the thing—boys, problems, so many other distractions—you have time for those later. Right now, what you need to do is focus on making the best speech possible to win the scholarship. Have fun out there," she waved towards the door, "but don't let all that affect this." Her finger jammed straight down onto my speech like a perfectly manicured missile.

If only it were as easy as she made it sound. She probably

didn't have her nemesis competing against her way back in the days of *Clueless*-style plaid shorts and the *Backstreet Boys*. "Right." We'd taken a left turn from Zen to inspirational self-help.

I tried to hand back the patch, but she shook her head. "It's yours. I want you to keep it as a reminder of where you need to focus." Her ponytail bounced with her eager words. "This entire conference and competition are about change. To help change the world, you'll need focus and determination. To make it in the world, you need the same. I believe you can do it. Don't sabotage your chances by dropping this amazing opportunity you've been given."

"Do you have ten of these in your bag?" If she handed a patch out to every person she mentored every year, she probably had stock in a patch-making factory.

Lauren's smile was bright and she looked like she was about to launch into some long reminiscence. "No, that's one of a kind. My mentor gave me the same lecture when I was in your chair. It's helped me a lot when I had to make choices in my life. Right now, I have a feeling you need it more than I do."

"Just..." I was about to say 'you have no idea,' but bit it back and instead said, "...thanks."

She nodded, then looked at her wristwatch and quickly closed a folder on my speech. "Almost lost track of the time. My next student will be here in a minute." She passed the folder over to me. "Go work on this and I'll see you Friday."

I shoved the patch in my pocket and stood. "But we

didn't really talk about what I needed to fix."

"The text looks fine. I need you to focus on the delivery for our next session. You need to make the audience believe you."

Great. Instead of a coaching session, I got an old patch. Helpful. "Okay. Thanks."

"Remember, don't lose your focus."

"Right. Got it." Between my emotional mess and rollercoaster mentor, I definitely wasn't going to get anywhere near the top ten if I couldn't.

Between avoiding Ann's endless flute practice sessions and trying not to bother her while working on my speech, the inn sitting room practically became my second room. While Ann and probably most of the other competitors were asleep, I set myself up at the old writing desk in a corner of the room with Lauren's notes. On her way out, one of the inn employees had dropped off a cup of herbal tea for me and its spicy smell filled the room. For some reason I couldn't completely explain, I sat the stupid patch in my line of sight, its edges defined in the low light.

It struck me as hilarious that I was doing exactly what Alec and the others had told me not to with my entry. Thanks to Lauren, I tore the speech apart word by word, trying to understand her critiques from our first session. Too much emotion, not enough emotion, too much showing, too much doing. She said the text on my latest draft was okay, but I needed it to be perfect. It had to be perfect.

I needed to place high enough to impress Dr. Lladros, prove that I deserved to compete for this as much as anyone else, take Kris down a peg, and get enough scholarship money to keep my parents from telling me I was throwing away a perfectly good free education. And the competitive part of me just wanted to win.

Phoebe and Alec always said that I either overreacted or turned into a control freak when things got tough. This was the only thing in my life at the moment I could control.

A little note penciled in the margin of the speech jumped out at me: *What does Em believe and want?"*

I looked at the patch again. Life had been so wonderfully black-and-white back home, like a classic movie. Old Em wasn't caught up playing mind games and instead dreamt of a good scholarship and a winter wonderland reunion with Wil, who called and texted all the time like the perfect boyfriend in an epic romance. Kris was a self-centered jerk. I'd caught the attention of one of the professors at my dream school and she'd remembered my name. Pre-Boston me just wanted to blow the New Jersey judges away with my awesome speech.

Now, everything spiraled out of my control and it scared the hell out of me. So, I wrote and rewrote, picking apart every paragraph and sentence. I needed to block out the memories that kept flooding back from the museum and hold tight to the one thing that was separate from Kris's games and my swirling mess of emotions.

"Damnit." A cramp ran through my palm, forcing me

to shake my hand and take a second's break to sip at the tea. My fingers weren't used to holding a pen this long and I ran through a mental litany of curses at Lauren and her old-fashioned way of critiquing things.

What did I want? I wanted to win the competition. I wanted the scholarship. I wanted everything to be simple and straightforward so I could just have fun in Boston before competing. I wanted—I pushed away the last thought and picked up the patch, turning it over and over in my hands. I needed to focus on winning. If that meant I had to forget every second of the romance-scene perfect moment in the museum, that's what I had to do.

No boy, especially a hot but pain-in-the-assedly self-centered boy, would keep me from making my real dreams come true. I flexed my fingers one more time and dove back into the critiques.

When the words started blurring together on the page and, more than once, I woke up with my face pressed against the desktop, I dragged myself up to bed. I'd focus more in the morning. And tomorrow, I'd raid the kitchen for coffee.

34

"Welcome to the Old South Meeting House." A man in colonial costume stood on a raised platform as we milled around the floor of the meeting house, checking out rows of seats that looked like a cross between church pews and pens, down to their hinged doors. I couldn't help but pay more attention to the giant arched windows that surrounded us than him. "On December 16, 1773, a meeting was held here to debate the tax on tea that was waiting to be unloaded from a ship called the *Dartmouth*, docked in Boston Harbor. Today, you will be given the chance to recreate the debate. Some of you have been given roles, but the rest of you will be divided into either Loyalists or Patriots."

Red and the other advisors were handing out cards already marked with our names and roles. My heart sunk a little bit when my card didn't have anything but my name and "Loyalist" printed on the front. "Seriously, a Loyalist?"

One of the actors in colonial costume squinted at my card, then smiled up at me. "New Jersey had many disaffected Tories and Loyalists before and during the war. If you are up in Boston at this time, you are likely the daughter of landowners who are thankful for the crown's protection."

I shook my head. "That sounds more like Kris' family."

"And that's why I'm a Loyalist, too. Hail King George," Kris said as he came up beside me, waving his own paper.

"Okay, now I definitely need to be a Patriot." I dug my nails into my palm and tried to force away the museum-emotions that threatened to overwhelm me again. I was an actress. This was a game where winning was my only goal. End of story. Although a tiny part of me did do a happy dance when I saw New York point to her paper and mouth "Patriot?" to Kris, then frown when he shook his head.

"Perhaps you're a Loyalist because your parents are merchants with many Loyalist customers, like your friend's family," the man suggested patiently. I could tell he wanted to move on to someone who didn't care what role they got.

"You don't know her very well," Kris retorted, which earned him an elbow in the side from me. "Ow. You know, your elbows are freakishly pointy."

"The better to maim you with." At least my words didn't come out tight. I could totally make it through this.

"I'm sure you'll enjoy the debate regardless." The man nodded at nothing in particular, then moved on to the guy from South Carolina, who had apparently gotten an actual part in the recreation.

I looked from the actor to Kris, who shrugged. "I think we scared him away."

That earned him a major eye-roll. "Maybe it was your whole 'Hail King George' thing."

"My father's lands have benefitted from our relationship

with England. Besides, our governor, who happens to be Benjamin Franklin's son, supports the king, so why shouldn't I?" His expression was a mixture of amused and superior. He tilted up his chin proudly. "I need to think of Lambert's fields first."

I watched him with amusement. This was a side of Kris I'd never seen before and, even though most of me wanted to bolt away, another part of me wanted to keep as close as possible to see if he could keep it up. "Now who's getting into character?" Around us, everyone else found their seats. Weighing the option of sitting up on the second level against being closer to the action by sitting in one of the pens down on the main floor, I finally slid in to the row closest to us and Kris followed. His leg pressed against mine and, as a constant static hum of energy took over every inch of me that touched him, I regretted my decision. I shifted slightly to break the contact, pretending to fix the skirt on my awesome vintage nineteen-sixties dress. I needed to tug it down, anyway, because the short skirt rode up to show more leg than he needed to see.

"I saw we were coming here and did some research last night. You know that's where our town got its name, right? Lambert's fields? I probably had a few Loyalists in the family, but maybe they ended up becoming my Canadian cousins when England lost the war and Loyalists moved north."

He really did look like a kid who had just been offered a pony and a treehouse full of candy. I tilted my head and tried to reconcile this Kris with all the other versions of him

I knew. "I didn't know about the Lambertfield thing. That's funny. Still, I know I would have been a Patriot back then. Down with the king and all that."

"Well, you're a Loyalist now." Kris moved slightly to flick the card in my hand, his leg back to pressing against mine. Now his hip touched my hip, too. "I thought you liked acting. Act."

I thought about my own ancestors, none of whom were anywhere near Lambertfield during the Revolution. Dad's family was back in Greece, where Yiayia joked we could trace everything back to Adam and Eve immigrating to Larissa. Mom's family was either somewhere down South or still back in Africa. Even with Dad's family history, it was weird to imagine being able to talk about somewhere your entire family was from. Kris didn't even have to think of a character, but me—"I'll take the merchant thing, then. Or maybe I'm just trying to impress a Loyalist boy." If I was going to get into character, I might as well kill two birds with one stone. I bat my eyelashes at him like Mary Pickford in one of her silent films, all big eyes and overdramatic gestures.

He laughed, earning us a dirty look from one of our advisors, since it was perfectly timed with the moment the person on the podium had finished giving the statistics of the total dead and wounded from the Revolutionary War. He cringed slightly, and then leaned in to whisper in a low voice that ran straight to my bones, "Perfect. We're going to kick Patriot butt."

35

Weirdly enough, Kris and I made an awesome team. When it came to debating, he had no trouble getting into character, perfectly outlining logical reasons to support his side while deflecting any cons shot our way, while I brought passion and insightful jabs that tore down their arguments. And all the energy we normally put into fighting each other in the summit was now focused on taking down the debaters on the Patriot side, even though we knew this wasn't real and history told us we were going to lose in the long run.

As we stood to leave the meeting room, Kris looked flushed but happy, like he was coming down from a debating high. "That was fun."

I followed him, still trying to break character and come back to the twenty-first century. "I bet they regret putting the two of us on the same side. Damn, we're loud."

"Nah. Connor and Vero were louder."

"Who?"

"Oklahoma and DC? The advisors are probably happy that, for once, it wasn't the Em and Kris Argue Show." He turned his head to look back at me and seemed to light up even brighter. "It was nice. And see, I acted, without having to get into tight pants."

As he made his way out the door in front of me, I glanced down at his jeans, and, despite the non-tightness of those jeans, I couldn't help but notice his toned butt. "Mmmhmm." And then, I wanted to kick myself. What was wrong with me? Stupid hormones and character acting were bringing me right back to thinking of him in ways I really shouldn't. I'd already promised myself to focus on really throwing him off—play hot and cold until he was just as confused as I felt, but so far today I was failing miserably. Yesterday, Kris had thrown quizzical and almost apologetic looks all through dinner while I hid from him, and he seemed off his game a little bit in the summit this morning. If I didn't eff this whole thing up, I might beat him at his own game.

But, instead, I spent most of my time trying to keep from jumping him and breaking this weird tension that had built up between us, at least on my side. When we reached the bus, Kris let me go in front of him and sort-of helped me up by putting his hand on the small of my back, sending sparks shooting straight up and down my spine. I was so screwed.

The cold from the stone bench outside the inn seeped through my dress and tights, but I didn't care. Thanks to the chill, there wasn't much chance Kris, New York girl, or any other sane person would come out here and hear me. "You were right."

"Since I'm always right, you have to be a little clearer

about what," Grace said, and I could tell she was trying her hardest not to sound gloat-y.

"About messing with Kris' mind. This whole plan is back-firing on me." A couple passed, looking like something out of a movie as they walked arm-in-arm along the brick sidewalk, and my stomach twisted even more. This part of Boston was really pretty at dusk with its old-fashioned streetlights but I couldn't enjoy it while agonizing over my life choices.

"Oh, Em. You didn't actually do it, did you?" Not-gloat-y turned to disappointed really quickly and I braced myself for the lecture she was bound to dive into.

I didn't bother to state the obvious. "He's better at this than me. I should have known, but, crap…"

The movie or video game or whatever in the background suddenly stopped. "Who are you two talking about?" Alec asked, his voice as clear as Grace's. I stifled a groan. Of course she'd have her phone on speaker.

"Kris," Grace said, matter of factly. "And Em's ridiculous emotional manipulation plan."

"The way you said that makes it sound so much worse than it really is," I shot back.

A lifetime of living next door to him meant I could recognize Alec's "Here she goes again" snort, even over the phone line. "I told you it was a dumb-ass idea, Em."

"I didn't ask for your opinion, oh he-who-internet-stalked-the-girl-he-liked." I narrowed my eyes at the tourist who stopped and stared at me after that comment until she hurried away from my glare of death.

"It wasn't stalking, I just followed her on Photogram under a different name," he said in an annoyed mumble. "And we're not talking about Laura. We're talking about you doing something stupid to mess with Kris, even if he's a jerk and deserves it."

He was right and the twisty-choking feeling just got worse. I might be able to lie to myself, but not to someone who was practically my brother. "Thank you for making me feel like an idiot. Now, go away, Alec. I need to have a girl-to-girl talk with Grace."

"Please. Girl-to-girl with Grace is about the same as girl-to-girl with me."

"Wrong answer, Kohen." I had this image of Grace reaching over, pinching the sensitive part of his ear, and dragging Alec out of her room. There was a lot of shuffling, scrambling, and an "ouch" in the background before the speakerphone turned off. "Okay, I kicked him out. What's so huge you didn't want him to hear?"

A deep breath did absolutely nothing to loosen the vice-grip on my lungs. "I need to make sure this stays between you and me." I shook my head and added, "And Leia, because I know you're probably going to tell her, anyway."

"What about Phoebe?"

"No way. She'd go all fairytale dreamy-eyed on me and I don't need that."

There was a plopping sound in the background, like Grace had dropped into her butterfly chair. "Now you're scaring me."

I stood up and started pacing. Maybe moving would break up the nervous energy squeezing the life out of me. "It's backfiring. Kris is just too damned good at this manipulation thing."

"So? What you need to do is stop the ridiculousness and focus on your speech. Repeat after me: Kris isn't my only competitor."

Of course she didn't understand that it was more than just the competition. "I almost kissed him," I said in the softest whisper I could manage.

The choking sound on the other side of the phone would have been funny if my life wasn't turning into a bad made-for-TV movie. "Oh. Wow. I didn't see that coming."

I leaned against the inn's brick wall. The fingers of my free hand automatically started digging into the grout. "It's just…he throws me off. I expect him to act a certain way and then he pretends to be nice to me, and I don't know how much of that is pretending or just a side of him I've never seen before." The choking feeling lessened the more I dumped my problems on Grace. "Maybe I'm just getting too much into character."

"Maybe. Or maybe it's Stockholm syndrome. You are kind of trapped with him. His ego's probably blocking all the oxygen in a five-foot radius."

My nail chipped off a little piece of grout and brick. Great, now I was an emotionally distraught vandal. "Right. God, this sucks."

"So stop that stupid plan of yours," I could almost hear

Grace's shrug and her mental gears turning. "While you're at it, I'm sure there are plenty of other guys there you can terrorize. Just avoid Kris."

I let that thought hang for one beat, two beats… Damn, she was always so *practical*. "I can try."

"You're not going to take my advice, are you?"

"Maybe?" I bit the nail that I'd broken in my unintentional vandalism of the brick wall.

"You do this to yourself, you know," she said, but her tone wasn't harsh or annoyed, just matter-of-fact.

"Thanks for the nonjudgmental support."

She laughed and fear's awful grip on my insides loosened a little bit at the familiar sound. "If you wanted to cry on someone's shoulder, you should have called Phoebe or Leia, you know."

"I love you, too," I said, sticking my tongue out at my phone and wishing I'd turned on the video chat.

I could just picture Grace sticking her tongue out on her end of the call, too. The long *pfft* sound coming through the phone confirmed it. "Just don't do anything I wouldn't do. Which means you'd be totally safe when it comes to kissing boys, especially majorly jerky boys."

"Yeah. I'll think about that," I said, the laugh that bubbled up on that comment pushing away a tiny bit more of my stress. "Thanks."

"You're welcome," she said, her voice still laced with concern. Grace might be the annoyingly sensible one, but I knew she cared. "Anything else?"

"Sure. Can you get Alec back on?"

She hesitated. "He's a little pissed at you right now."

"He'll deal."

"Okay…" In the background, I could hear Grace calling Alec back into the room again.

"Pick up the phone," random threats of violence, and "emotionally vulnerable," floated back to me before Alec heaved a big sigh and said into the phone, "Oh, *now* you want to talk to me."

Insulted nerds were the worst. "Alec…"

Another overly dramatic "You are wasting my precious time" sigh. "No, that's okay. I'm taking the high road and ignoring your blatantly sexist behavior. What do you need?"

"Do you still e-mail with Wil?" I asked in a rush, forcing the words out in one breath before I could second-guess myself.

"Yeah, got one from him the other day."

So my theories about him being too busy to email anyone didn't pan out. All the unease from before came roaring back up. "Did he mention another girl? Like a supermodel named Katja or something?"

"No." Suddenly his disinterested tone shifted straight to eager, like I had just brought up a new Star Trek series or something. "Damn, I need to move to Freiburg if Wil's hanging out with supermodels."

If I wasn't so nauseated from Wil-stress, I would have offered to kick Alec's butt all the way to Germany. "Funny. Can you let me know if he does? I'm trying to figure something out."

"Sure, because I'm a good friend who helps everyone and yet, gets left out of the loop all the time," Alec said, blowing the needle off my sarcasm meter.

"You know the guilt angle only really works with Phoebe."

"Are we done? I have zombies to massacre."

I broke off another tiny chunk of mortar. If I was going down for vandalism along with everything else, might as well go big. "Yeah, thanks."

Before I could hang up though, he added, "Hey Em?"

"What?"

"Just…what Grace said. Focus on the competition, okay?" All of his sarcasm and annoyance were gone.

I wanted to jump through the phone and either strangle or hug him. "You stinkin' eavesdropper."

"You politician-kisser."

Forget the hug, I'd strangle him if he weren't a six-hour drive away. "Ew, it wasn't like that. I just—"

He made static-y sounds on the other side. "Sorry, I think our connection is getting messed up." More static-y sounds. "You lost your chance to tell me the whole story."

"Bye, Alec."

"Bye, Em." He stopped the sounds and grew serious. "Kick ass. I know you can do it."

I pocketed my phone and headed back to the bench, sat, propped my elbows on my knees and dropped my head into my hands. It was hard to tell whether I wanted to laugh or cry.

36

The conference might have catered to the political and history geeks, but that night's event was one hundred percent for the performing arts nerds. This theater was famous for its acoustics and layout, and somehow the conference organizers had managed to get us into a practice session—like a dress rehearsal without the dress part. It was funny to see Kris and the rest of his kind hiding out in the back rows of the lecture hall-like theater while us artsy types clumped in the front, close enough to feel the vibrations from the drum set as the classical-pop fusion songs zinged straight through my body. Let him have his groupies hanging all over him and feeding his ego. I had my music. I could easily take Grace's advice in a place like this. The fact that New York was practically sitting in his lap didn't bother me. At all. I barely noticed it.

Even though the performers were students from a local musical conservatory and only a year or two older than us, they were amazing. Strings and woodwinds mixed with the voices of two lead singers who definitely had opera training but didn't sound like Sarah Brightman trying to sing a pop song, which, as much as I admired her musical pedigree, was just a huge no. The songs were organic and powerful and it was impossible not to let them seep through my skin to break away anything that wasn't music.

The concert was a break from all the crazy in my life, at least. Lost in the music and the presence of the performers, it was easy to forget the stress from the night before. It only took a few seconds of music to unravel the knot that suffocated me and tangled around my stomach. I let it soak through my skin and straight to my bones.

"I don't know how they do it," I said to Alaska in a loud whisper.

Alaska nodded back so forcefully, I thought she might hurt her neck. "I know. Listen to her vibrato. It's almost not human." She never took her eyes off the stage.

"I want that sheet music," Ann said, staring wide-eyed and covetously at the flutes.

I smiled at my roommate. "Agreed. If we played more of this and less of those John Williams medleys, I'd actually practice more often." That earned a laugh from Ann, which she tried to muffle with her sleeve. Oregon-girl turned around and narrowed her eyes at me, putting her finger in front of her lips. I straightened up and tried to be the perfect model of a concert audience member while Ann shook in silent laughter next to me.

When the musicians took their bows and headed off-stage, Red made an announcement that we had a few minutes to explore the theater before the bus came to pick us up. I walked up to the edge of the stage, staring up at the gorgeous swirly chandelier, my fingers rubbing against the worn edge of the floorboards. It even smelled just right, the perfect mix of floor wax and dust. I needed another minute of this place before crashing back to reality. A flash of motion to my right made me look up just as some of the guys hauled themselves onto the stage. The boy from North Dakota grinned down at me, holding out his hand in invitation. "You sing, don't you?"

I let him help me up and latched onto Alaska, pulling her with me. "A little bit," I said with a laugh. "Aren't we going to get in trouble?"

"For a song or two? No way. They said we could explore the theater, didn't they? Aren't you dying to check out these acoustics?" North Dakota was apparently worse than me when it came to rule bending.

Mr. Arizona passed in front of us, striking the cheesiest musical theatre pose I'd ever seen, jazz hands and all. "You know," Arizona grabbed Alaska's hand and twirled her so her skirt fluttered around her. "I think tonight is *grand* for singing.'" With barely a pause, he broke into the chorus of the song from *State Fair* and sang directly at Alaska, tilting up her chin with a flick of his finger when she started giggling.

In the rest of the theater, everyone else seemed to pause, their attention finally landing on all of us who had taken over the stage. To my surprise, Red and the other advisors made no move to stop us, just smiled and watched. They were apparently cooler than I thought. Virginia ran up from one of the side aisles, vaulted onto the stage, and pulled Arizona into a waltz. Even though it looked like only Arizona and I knew the lyrics from this song, everyone chimed in when they realized we were repeating the chorus, our voices mixing perfectly.

When it came time for the next verse, North Dakota pointed at me and I launched into the solo, twirling starry-eyed around the stage with an imaginary partner in a way that would make Mr. Landry proud. When I got to the part about feeling like I was falling in love because of "you," my twirl landed me squarely facing the audience. One face in particular came into focus and a funny thrill rushed through me when Kris' eyes met mine on that line. I became Nora reaching her emotional breaking point in *A Doll's House* whirling wildly in the tarantella, trying to distract Torvald from the letters and herself from her own emotions.

I shook off the feeling as fast as I could and let an impulsive idea take over, jumping off the stage as the chorus started again. I caught Kris' hand, pulling him down the aisle and away from miss-prissy-Empire-State and skipped around him until his ears and the back of his neck turned red. "C'mon, sing," I said between breaths. Maybe silliness would shake the painful, unsettling feeling tickling at my lungs and heart. Plus, Kris hated attention when he was out of his element. It was all a part of the plan, I told myself.

He shook his head and tried to pull free. "I'm tone deaf."

"Kris." I dragged out his name, a pleading whine in my voice. "Live a little."

I didn't expect him to cave, but after twisting his face

into a grimace, he surprised me by joining in on the last line of the chorus, completely off-key but still at the top of his lungs. Once the song ended, the people left on stage dissolved into laughter and the advisors finally tried to get us organized again.

Kris narrowed his eyes at me. "Happy? You better not have been recording that."

"You really are tone deaf." The stern set of his jaw seemed to grow sterner and I poked him in the shoulder. "Remind me not to ask you to try out for the spring musical."

"I never said I was perfect. Just really good at almost everything but singing."

I gave him one of my scrunched-nose grins. "It's healthy to step out of your comfort zone. I'm glad you did."

Arizona and North Dakota passed at that moment, pulling me away from Kris. Each linked arms with mine and walked towards the exit like Dorothy and her friends in the *Wizard of Oz.*

"Told you it would be awesome." North Dakota said, waving at two of the other states who held the doors open for us so we could keep up our ridiculous formation.

I didn't even look back at Kris, instead putting a Dorothy-like bounce in my steps. "It was fun. I so needed that."

Arizona nodded, his green eyes bright. "Hell, yes. Maybe we should plan a flash mob at Faneuil Hall during the awards ceremony. Break up the tension?"

Red chose that moment to pass us, pausing mid-cell call to our bus driver to say, "Don't even try, Garrett," before hurrying ahead without another look at us.

I winked dramatic stage-winks at the boys on either side of me. "Sounds like fun."

It was nice to just forget about focus and Kris and live in the moment again.

EmmieBear: Sang on stage for the first time in ages tonight and I'm on such a music high. Love ya, Boston!

EmmieBear: I could sing all night, I could sing all night! (but I have a roommate)

KLambert: @Emmiebear Focus! Competition soon!

EmmieBear: @KLambert Whatever. Really creative screen-name, btw.

KLambert: @EmmieBear I was going to go with "Not that actor from Highlander" but it took up too many characters

EmmieBear: @KLambert How did you find me, anyway? Are you Internet stalking me?

KLambert: @EmmieBear What? No.

KLambert: @EmmieBear I saw you chatting with @BookishArcher on her feed.

EmmieBear: @KLambert Are you Internet stalking my bff? @BookishArcher

KLambert: @EmmieBear No. Go to sleep. We've got one more day of conference to get through tomorrow. No yawning!

EmmieBear: @KLambert I'll have you know I look my most adorable when yawning.

KLambert: @EmmieBear Not when a diplomat is talking

EmmieBear: @KLambert Poo, she didn't notice. She was too busy messing with the laser pointer.

KLambert: @EmmieBear I can't believe *you're* representing our state

EmmieBear: @KLambert Admit it, I'm fun. Wanna sneak down to the lobby and sing stuff from classic musicals?

KLambert: @EmmieBear Logging off now. Good night.

EmmieBear: @KLambert Don't forget my latte tomorrow. I'll need it AFTER SINGING ALL NIGHT

KLambert: @EmmieBear *puts in earplugs* Good. Night.

37

"Focus, Em." Lauren tapped the table with her pen, stopping me mid-speech. "I know you can read better than that."

I took a deep breath and tried to keep from balling up the speech and throwing it at her head. I'd read my poor, butchered speech aloud three times already in our session, and each time, she stopped me part of the way through. I closed my eyes and started again, the speech already burned into my memory. "I am a vital component in the fight to 'make the world better.' I—"

"Stop." Lauren pulled my speech from my hands and lay it face down on the table. "Do you really believe what you're saying?" I blinked at her and was about to answer when she continued, "Because, right now you don't sound like you do."

"I'm sorry," I said, hoping I looked tired enough that she'd just let me go. Not even Mr. Landry, who was pretty tough for a theatre advisor, ever pushed me this hard over five minutes of dialogue. Lauren, though, was relentless.

"Did Katie—Ms. Shawnee—tell you I actually requested you?" That caught my attention and she seemed to know it. "When I heard your speech, I was impressed by the passion in your delivery, and I loved how you wove Pierre- Saint Ruffin's—"

"Josephine Saint Pierre Ruffin," I corrected her, adding, "Only an amazing civil rights leader and social worker from Boston, that's all."

Maybe the sarcasm was lost on her, because Lauren just kept barreling on. "Weaving stories from her history throughout your speech as examples really bound your speech together with a common narrative, which made it incredibly powerful. I wanted to work with you because I knew I could make your passion shine."

"Thank you?" Fear mixed with doubt in my veins. She was probably about to tell me I sucked and should give up. Or maybe she'd suggest I needed another four hours of reading my speech until my delivery became less automatic and more human.

"So, where is that passion?" At my blank look, she pushed some more. "Why did you choose to write your speech this way? A lot of the other speeches are about things your competitors are doing right now. Why did you decide to talk about who you want to grow into?"

"I don't know." I shrugged, trying to remember the minute the idea for the speech came into my head. "When I told my friend, Alec, about the competition and how the nationals were here in Boston, he pulled up all these trivia facts about Boston, because he's weird that way. When he told me about this person, I just felt like she was someone worth learning from." Lauren nodded at me to go on, and it was like a giant river of words filled with all the feelings from that first burst of speechwriting just came flying out. "I loved how, even with everything going against her because of her race and her gender, she still believed she was—and we are—an important part of fighting for equal rights for everyone. And she did that while editing a newspaper, serving on boards, and doing social work. She did a lot of little things, too, that became big things. I just think if she was able to do so much even though black women back then didn't have a lot of rights, what's my excuse now for not trying to make the world a better place?" For some reason I couldn't explain, the back of my throat tightened and my eyes teared up. I wasn't like Phoebe, who cried at puppies in toilet paper commercials. It had to be because of exhaustion from the roller coaster of emotions I'd been feeling all week.

Lauren handed me a tissue and tapped the table with her pen, her expression smug. "That's the passion I was talking about."

"Are you a speechwriter or a psychotherapist in disguise?" I pushed back the teary feeling and tilted my head to regard her. "And do you beat up the governor to get her to sound more passionate in her speeches, too? Or give her patches?"

That smug expression turned even more annoyingly smug with a bunch of amusement thrown in. "Not exactly, but she's had years of practice. Plus, I think you just needed to reconnect with the you who wrote the original speech." She flipped my speech back over and shoved it in front of me. "Now, hold on to that feeling and try again."

"I am a …" My voice curved around the words, speeding, slowing, stretching, flying. Crescendoing and decrescendoing at just the right moments, like playing my flute or when I'd sing. For five minutes, I lived my speech, the tiniest vibrations from my voice resonating throughout my entire body. I became a character, but the character was actually me. I'd been so busy pigeonholing myself into characters everyone else believed I was this week that I almost let go of full, three-dimensional Em who had dreams and potential. The Em who could be pretty amazing, in her own way.

I finished, then inhaled and exhaled once before slowly looking back up at Lauren, who just nodded. "I think you're going to do great tomorrow."

EmmyBear: *Direct Message @WilOfHyrule* Hey, can we talk?

EmmyBear: *Direct Message @WilOfHyrule* Nothing about us, promise, just really nervous about tomorrow and it's so important

EmmyBear: *Direct Message @WilOfHyrule* I just need a friend.

EmmyBear: *Direct Message @WilOfHyrule* Call me, please? I could use one of your pep talks right now.

38

"I'm not looking forward to tomorrow," Ann said, her heels clicking on the shiny inlaid wood floor. She was wearing a floor-length gown made out of white-blue lace layered over white-green satin, and had pinned tiny blue-green flowers in her loose hair. It was like she had taken her usual elven princess look and amped it up on steroids. I was amazed she hadn't started glowing like Galadriel.

I followed, trying to keep my balance in Grace's mom's shoes. Considering how super-expensive the designer heels were, I would have expected them to be easier to walk in. Still, they looked awesome with my black dress, the lace inset running from my toes to my ankle coming pretty close to matching the lace on my dress' neckline. "Forget about the speech and at least have some fun tonight." My own stomach played Twister with itself, but I tried not to let it show in my face. I really had to take my own advice. Just because my entire future depended on me doing great in a five minute speech tomorrow morning didn't mean I had to go into freak-out mode. "Missing out on a chance to wear a gown and eat fancy food won't help your speech tomorrow."

I tried a little twirl straight out of a forties musical and, even though I wasn't a dancer like Grace, my short skirt flared out delicately in cute layers of lace, satin, and tulle and my straightened hair fluttered around my face. I liked my curls—they were wild and unpredictable sometimes, just like me. Tonight, though, I'd straightened my hair so it sat a little below my shoulders. It was fun to have a serious whoosh instead of a bounce.

"Still, I think I'm cutting out early tonight." Ann looked back at me before opening the dining room door. "I wish I was as good at not worrying as you."

"We're alphabetically in the middle. That will give us plenty of time to freak out tomorrow morning." The room where we normally ate our meals had been transformed by twinkling lights and crystals the staff had hung from the normally bare chandeliers. Little bowls of floating flowers and candles sat in the middle of each table. Combined with all the mirrors in antique frames that normally lined the walls, they didn't need the big overhead lights. "Besides, look at all the pretty," I added, my stomach untwisting just the tiniest bit. I studied the room and found Mr. Louisiana hanging with a bunch of other guys by the appetizers. Grabbing Ann by the shoulders, I pointed her in his direction. "Speaking of, that's what you are, especially right now. Go show off your gorgeous self."

"Are you always this pushy?"

"This is nothing. You should see what she did to her best friend," Kris' voice came from behind us and I waited a count before turning around with a tolerant smile plastered on my face. I had to work to keep that smile in place and to keep from gaping, because he looked better than I expected. The last time I saw Kris dressed up was at the junior prom, and even though his ultra-conservative suit jacket and slacks were pretty much the same style, this time they looked really good on him instead of stuffy.

Like, "force my brain cells to work enough to come up with a snarky response" good. "Says the guy who hit on her."

Ann's voice pulled my attention away from Kris and back to the rest of the room. "Wow." Her eyes had widened just enough to give her a Lucille Ball-comedic look. "I don't like drama, so I'm going to go…" she waved her hand vaguely towards Louisiana and the other guys, "… over there." She moved so fast, some of her hair whacked me in the arm.

I looked over my shoulder to smile wryly at Kris. "See, you scared my roommate away."

"I think that was just an excuse," he pointed his thumb to where she was already tapping Geoff on the shoulder. When I turned back to Kris, his gaze was drifting slowly down my body, taking in my outfit, and fire traced its way across my skin down the same path. After what felt like a lifetime, he focused on my shoes. "Those are really high heels."

With the five-inch heel, I was eye-to-eye with him. Forcing myself to be as bold as I normally was even though my skin was still burning, I stepped closer so he had to look back up at my face again. "Grace lent them to me. They're Jimmy Shoos." His brow wrinkled and I laughed, even though laughter felt so alien at that moment. "What, you don't keep up with fashion? I'm surprised. Don't you try to know everything?"

He ignored my dig and poked at my shoulder, just where the illusion lace that travelled up from my dress' sweetheart neckline ended. "Aren't you afraid you're going to fall over?"

"If you keep poking at me like that, I might." The fact that his hand lingered on my shoulder wasn't lost on me, and I reached out to grab his arm, pretending to catch my balance. Two could play this game.

"Then maybe we should sit down. That way, you won't fall over, die of embarrassment, and just hand first place to me."

"That's really altruistic of you," Ooh, look, an SAT word. I preened. "But 'we?' You keep hanging with the competition, don't you?"

"Maybe I'm trying to psych you out." At that, my skin chilled, even though I already knew this was Kris' strategy. His one comment completely killed any possibility that lurked in the back of my mind he was actually being human and nice and not-Kris-like. He sat at the nearest table and I followed robotically. "Or maybe for some crazy reason I'm actually starting to enjoy hanging out with Pine Central's drama queen."

"They didn't give us much choice here, did they?" I put on my perkiest voice. "We're going to be such bffs when we get back home." I clapped my hands together and made a face with a saccharine smile and starry eyes, tilting my head towards him.

Kris draped an arm around the back of my chair. "Yeah, we'll make friendship bracelets and have sleepovers." He stopped, blinked, and realized what he said, red creeping up his neck and tinging his ears and cheeks. "Um…"

I couldn't help but laugh, and couldn't help how warmth replaced the chill on that comment. "I know what you meant." I pushed back any memory of our museum sort-of kiss, but my whole body felt overheated.

"Smooth, Jersey." Saved by Louisiana. Geoff and Ann dropped into the empty chairs next to me, the guy and girl from Florida following them.

Kris seemed to have recovered quickly. "I guess you mean Em, right? Because I never say anything stupid."

Geoff laughed. "Whatever makes you feel better."

"Just don't have the sleepover in our room, okay?" Ann added, and I threw her a dirty look. Perfect timing for her to get a sense of humor.

My phone beeped and I dove for an excuse to pull myself out of the conversation and check it, dropping my pink feather covered clutch onto the table. I felt my brows starting to furrow together as I stared at the screen and my Photogram notification icon. *WilOfHyrule tagged you in a photopost.* What was Wil doing up this late?

"Is that a bag or did you kill a flamingo?" Kris poked at the clutch tentatively with one finger, like he was afraid the pink awesomeness was going to bite him.

Florida craned his neck to look around the way-too-high centerpiece. "I vote dead flamingo."

"Cute, guys." I swiped at my screen and cursed the spotty reception in this room. "I'm going over there—" I gestured towards the wall of window seats, where there had to be better reception, "—so don't do anything to my purse that you'd regret."

As I walked closer to the window, I watched the little hourglass on my phone flip over until it finally disappeared and Wil's latest Photogram of him kissing a drop-dead gorgeous girl appeared on my screen. An ivy-covered stone house by a sparkling canal framed them, the girl's light-blonde hair and white dress picked up the colors of the sunset as it blew in the wind, and Wil... Wil was dipping her slim form in a perfect curve. The kind of picture I'd always said I wanted to take with him whenever he showed me pictures of his city. With his photography skills, it looked like something straight out of a magazine, perfect and obviously planned—probably with his stupid tripod and remote. As I read over the English translation he'd put under the German text, "One *month with my one true love*," the blood rushed away from my face and the room suddenly grew cold.

I looked up, saw Kris and Ann watching me from our table, and forced a deep breath. I needed to get out of there and to somewhere I could call Wil without giving a room full of people a show. Taking the deepest breath in the world, I drew my back straight and glided out of the room as fast as my Jimmy Shoos could carry me. I was Audrey Hepburn as Eliza Doolittle, confronting Henry Higgins at his mother's house, not letting the hurt or anger show on my face. Only when I got out the door did I realize my purse, with my room keycard, was still back on the table.

I couldn't go outside and I didn't want to be the cliché girl chewing out her ex in the bathroom, so the sitting room was my only choice. Luckily, it was empty and I grabbed the closest chair to the fireplace so I could blame my reddened face on the heat.

I looked at my phone again and the stupid Photogram was still there—it hadn't been a hallucination or a mistake. I started typing in his number, but then Grace's practical voice popped into my head—why would I want any guy who didn't want me one hundred percent?

Because I love—loved—maybe loved him? I dropped my phone into my lap and wrapped my hands under the edge of the chair, my fingernails digging into the soft wood. Without even wanting to, the images popped into my head from our first kiss at the Harvest Fling to our last kiss in the airport, him murmuring "*Ich libe dich*" in my ear on our last hug.

The world shattered around me, like the time I dropped mom's favorite vase onto the kitchen floor. Except this time, the pain was much worse than getting hit by broken glass and radiated from deep in my lungs instead of from outside cuts zigzagging my skin. "Crap," I whispered, swallowing back the real curses threatening to come out.

"Em? Is everything okay?"

My eyes shot open. Kris was right in front of me, a concerned look on his face. I waved him away, wishing my nose hadn't already started to fill and that my eyes didn't feel wet. "I'm fine," I said, mentally cursing how my stuffed nose totally contradicted my words. "You don't have to worry about me, I'll be right back. I just need to finish this." I pointed at my phone.

Instead of leaving, Kris dragged over one of the other armchairs and put it facing me so that, when he sat down, our knees touched. "Don't pull that 'I'm fine' stuff with me. We've known each other too long. Seriously, what's wrong?" He wasn't wearing his jacket and I couldn't help but notice how his shirt color combined with the firelight brought out the gold in his eyes.

I shook my head, partly to focus, partly to contradict him. "Well, first, you don't know me that well." At his patient look, I blew air through my lips. "You don't." When he still didn't move, I shook my head. "What the hell, you're going to find out the second you get online, anyway." I pulled the Photogram post back up and handed Kris the phone, my hand shaking as much as my voice. "I texted Wil this morning saying I wanted to talk because I was nervous about the competition tomorrow and how I missed talking to him and he tagged me in this, instead."

Kris squinted at the screen for a moment. I couldn't look away as he read and could see him doing the math in his head. Talk about something with the perfect timing to screw me up for the competition. Instead of either pity or a grin, though, his lips went from frown to straight line and his jaw clenched the tiniest bit. "Wait, didn't you two only break up the other day?" I nodded. "So, you said you just needed someone to talk to and he sent you this?"

He handed me the phone and I shook my head, wishing I could drop my eyes or at least go back to my super-calm Audrey Hepburn impression. "Yes...No...I get that he was ignoring my texts and emails all week, but this time I told him I just needed someone who wasn't my friends or my parents. And I thought Wil could..."

"What. A. Bastard."

The same weak part of me that had hoped to get back together with Wil was dying to defend his actions, but I bit the inside of my cheek and waited, instead. In stage directions, I'd never understood the whole "His eyes held hers" thing, but suddenly, I couldn't look away from Kris'.

"He's lucky he's on another continent," he continued.

"You'd kick his ass for me?" I asked, not even bothering to hide my surprise. I pictured Kris swooping with his fencing sword in like a hero in a fantasy film, knocking Wil out before grabbing my hand and—

"Um, actually, I think you'd do a pretty good job, yourself. Especially in those heels." At my tiny, tortured laugh, he added, "Wil's an idiot."

"That, he is."

"...for letting someone like you get away."

"Someone like you" made me pause, but I shrugged and

was finally able to drop my eyes down to my lap, my fingers playing with the tulle peeking out from under my skirt. "I should have known. Everyone else saw the signs, even you, but I was too stupid to accept it." Oh, God. I was starting to sound like something out of a predictable rom-com, like I was fishing for compliments or something. "But, whatever. You were right," I said quickly, shutting my eyes and bracing myself. "Go ahead, gloat."

"You'll have to say it again so I can record it," he said, but his joking tone was balanced by a still-furrowed brow. "Seriously, are you okay? Do you need anything?" He reached for my hand but I pulled it back, pretending I needed to readjust my belt.

I shook my head and tried to look flippant. "I'll be fine." My voice took on a biting edge, like I'd swallowed shards of broken ice. "Besides, this helps you in the competition, right? Because I'm such a mess?"

Kris sat back, his lips growing even straighter than before. "You realize I've been joking about beating you, right? There are over a hundred good speeches here. You have to think I'm a pretty awful person to single you out and hope you crash and burn."

"But you said, back in homeroom—"

He cut me off. "That I wanted us to take first and second place. Of course I want first—the scholarship money would be great, but I play fair. Always." On "always," he leaned forward until we were nose-to-nose. His hands gripped the armrests and I was trapped between him and the back of my chair. My focus dropped straight to his mouth and the ghost of those few seconds in the rotunda wrapped around my entire body with an electric hum. After too long a beat, I sucked in a breath and forced my eyes back up to his, a little heady with proximity and his unique Kris-smell of lemon-verbena soap. He reminded me of sunshine and summer, especially with the warmth rolling off his body and those gold-brown eyes burning into mine.

"Now, you're going to compete tomorrow and give a speech that makes me work a million times harder than I've ever worked if I want to beat you. And forget that asshole." His voice was forceful, and he managed to catch my hand and squeezed it, like he was trying to transfer some of his fierceness into me. "Half the guys in this competition, hell, our school, would do anything just to get you to smile at them, so he's the one who's screwed, not you. Got it?" Not knowing what to say, I just nodded. My heartbeat echoed in my ears and pounded in the fingers of the hand he held, so much I couldn't believe he didn't feel it. I held my breath, waiting.

"Good." I expected him to lean closer after saying that, break the tension in our locked gazes, give into the intense pull of the moment, but instead, Kris pulled back and stood up. I fought back the irrational disappointment that washed over me. "I'll let the others know you're okay. Come back to the table when you're feeling better."

He was out the sitting room door by the time I breathed again and unfroze. As much as common sense me wanted to stay in the room, my idiotic heart forced me to stand and run-walk after him, instead of running the other way. I'd been seeing him all wrong this entire time. I dumped all my pride at the door and, hanging on the doorframe, called out, "Kris!"

This was stupid and dangerous. I was confused from Wil's message and Kris' reaction, my emotions were a giant hormone sundae topped with an overwhelming urge to break into tears. But when he stopped in the hallway and turned around, I walked right up to him, grabbed his sleeve, and pulled him in until we were face-to-face again, just like in the sitting room. I couldn't think or breathe, I just had to act. Before he could say anything, I pressed my mouth to his and any doubt or confusion melted away in the heat that jumped up between us, so wrong and so right at the same time.

To his credit, Kris caught on fast, kissing me back with the same fierceness that had been in his voice earlier. His hand slid to the back of my head, fingers burying in my hair and pulling me even closer than I thought was possible. It definitely wasn't one of those tame, awkward first kisses. We were lightning and thunder together, a storm of pure energy wrapping around us. I was convinced if we broke apart, we'd let off a massive shock.

So, we didn't.

Thanks to my low-backed dress, his fingers played against the bare skin right above the small of my back. A charge ran up and down my spine and I wrapped my arms around his neck, trying to melt into him.

Eventually, we had to break for air and Kris dropped another, tiny kiss on my lips before leaning his forehead against mine. His breathing was ragged, matching me exhale for exhale.

"Em," he started, his voice rough and sounding a little tortured. "We shouldn't—"

I didn't let him finish, pulling out of his hold and taking two steps away. I didn't need another crushing moment that night and didn't want to hear him try to reject me. Training my eyes on the toes of my shoes, I said, "Sorry. I'm just so messed up right now with Wil and the competition and I got a little carried away. Pretend that didn't happen."

"But—"

I pasted a smile on my face and forced myself to look up at him. His confused expression nearly broke me. "Because you know that's what I do, right? Just get right back into things. And hot boys are my one weakness. Sorry about jumping you like that. It won't happen again."

Kris ran a hand through his hair, making it even more adorably messy than it was before. He studied my face for a minute, probably trying to figure out what to say, then shook his head. "If that's what you want." He walked towards me, passing so close I first thought he was going to go for another kiss, but he didn't stop. With a wave, he headed in the direction of the dining room. "See you at the table."

As soon as he disappeared around a corner, I dropped onto the hallway fainting couch and buried my face in the dusty upholstery. Crappity, crap, crap. The best kiss I'd ever had in my life was from the one person I'd despised for years on the night my dreams of getting back with my boyfriend crashed and burned. Because my life sucked so much and I was so screwed beyond belief.

Tomorrow was going to be bad. Incredibly bad.

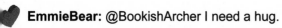 **EmmieBear:** @BookishArcher I need a hug.

39

"What the hell is wrong with you?" I railed at my tablet, which was propped up against the lamp on my nightstand so I could look straight into Wil's eyes. "Decent human beings don't do what you did. Deciding that the perfect time to tell me you cheated on me when we were dating is the night I reached out to you *as a friend* for support so I could build confidence for a really important speech? That's just so, so…" I searched for the word, "scummy." I held back the urge to face-palm for settling on a word straight out of Chloe's arsenal.

To his credit, Wil's complexion had gone grey. "I did not cheat." He had to have felt some guilt because he hadn't shut down the chat, but his whole lack of reaction while I reamed him infuriated me. At least, if he yelled back, I could hate him, but with his calm apologies and quiet explanations, I couldn't get myself beyond deeply despising him.

I tilted my head and dropped my shoulders in a "Do you think I'm stupid?" gesture. "I can do math, you know."

Wil blanched even more—soon, he was going to match his sweater. "We did not kiss until after," he made a breaking apart gesture with his hands. "For respect to you."

"Respect? Oh, wow, aren't you considerate." My voice was dripping with sarcasm, which he was sure to understand even if he didn't get all I was saying. "Was tagging me in that Photogram out of respect, too?"

"Liesel thought—" he said, stopped, then started again, still cowed. "She saw your text and thought, perhaps—"

I narrowed my eyes at him. "Oh, *Liesel* thought?" Great, now he'd ruined *The Sound of Music* for me forever. "Please, tell me what utter genius *Liesel* came up with."

"She thought I was not..." he furrowed his brow, searching for the right word in a way I used to think was cute. Now, it was just annoying. "Obvious to you."

"Obvious that you're a massive a-hole?"

"No, obvious that we are not getting back together," he said, in a tone I knew was meant to be gentle, sympathetic, and calming. Like I was a child who needed things spelled out to her.

That made my blood boil. If Wil was turning white, my cheeks were probably coral. "Oh, you were pretty obvious about that when we broke up. I've moved on, too, but you don't see me posting pics of me kissing the guys I kissed *after* we broke up."

"I am sorry. I thought—"

"You thought wrong." I looked at the clock and posed my finger over the red "close chat" button. "I have to go do way more important things than talking with someone who jerked me around. Have a nice life with Liesel."

"Goodb-" I hung up on him before he could finish.

Exhaustion poured over me as I shut down the chat program and flipped my tablet face-down so I didn't have to see the chat request messages coming through. Missing breakfast to tear into my ex-boyfriend while he tried to look calm on his side of the ocean took every last bit of fight out of me.

I looked up from my lap when a coffee and a scone appeared on my nightstand. "It's pumpkin spice and the white stuff on the scone is clotted cream. Eat it. I know you said you weren't hungry, but I don't want you to be up at the podium with your stomach growling," Ann said, sounding bossier than I'd ever heard her before. She went to grab her speech folder and breezed towards the door again. "I have to go, it's my turn soon."

I pushed the scone aside and took a quick sip of coffee. "Thanks, but I don't have time to eat. You know that. We're in the same group this morning."

"Oh, didn't they tell you? You were moved to the last group right before lunch."

"But it's in alphabetical order," I protested, but Ann opened the door and waved.

"Something about schedule changes. Wisconsin switched with you and Kris. Anyway, see you there."

"Good luck," I said, waving weakly. I picked at the scone, breaking it into crumbly bites. The schedule change was huge, giving me time to pull myself together. After what happened with Kris last night and the morning's call, there was no way I'd be mentally ready in time for a nine a.m.

speech. I was a great actor, but not that great, not yet.

A thought hit me, and I froze mid-scone-bite. Ann had been spending the past week re-reading and studying everyone's speeches, comparing them to hers. What if she wanted me out of the competition and this was her way of disqualifying me? As much as I hated feeling suspicious about someone I liked, I rushed to pull on a pair of shoes and head downstairs to check, just in case.

Right before getting to the lobby, I saw Kris lounging against the wall, flipping through his own bright blue speech folder. I froze, trying to think of another way to get to the lobby without him seeing me, but then he looked up with the tiniest smile I'd ever seen. "Hey, isn't it awesome that they moved our time?"

"So it's true?" I awkwardly tried to imitate his pose against the opposite wall. Last night's kiss came right the front of my mind and I had to fight the urge to recreate it right there in the hallway. "What happened?"

He shrugged. "Some scheduling issue, so they switched us with the guys from Wisconsin. It's weird, but I'm not going to complain about the extra time." He pushed away from the wall and walked close enough to me to be at hover distance but far enough away that he didn't invade my personal space. "I heard from Ann you were on a call with Wil this morning? Are you okay?"

"Yeah. It only took two texts and going through Alec to guilt him into accepting my chat request this time."

"So, are you two...?" Now he was the one who looked

uncomfortable while making a "back together" gesture with his hands.

"After what he did to me?" Why was he curious about our relationship status? I shook my head and reminded myself Kris was still my competition. And probably playing me in a different way than Wil had been. "Hell, no. But I tore him a new one and probably scared him into never dating another American again."

He reached out and I thought he was about to touch my arm or something, but then his arm swung back and he scratched the back of his neck instead. "Way to represent our country, Katsaros."

"All in the name of diplomatic unity, right?" I cringed, my brain going straight for every bit of innuendo he could get from it. "That didn't sound right."

"And this is when I leave before I say something that will get me in trouble." He waved his folder at me. "I'd better go back to my room and practice some more." He turned, then, after a few steps, stopped and looked over his shoulder at me. "Rest up and forget that asshole, because you're going to need all the energy you can get to even get close to my awesomeness." Without a wave or another word, he walked around the corner towards the boys' side of the inn, cocky swagger in every step.

Maybe going over my speech and eating breakfast were both great ideas.

I closed my eyes and began another round of breathing exercises, my belly expanding with every inhale and flattening again under my hands as I exhaled through my mouth. In and out, until the tension in my body slowly released. I slipped Lauren's patch out of my speech folder and worried the edges with my fingers, taking comfort in the now familiar stitches. Next to me, Kris paced up and down the hallway with headphones on, probably trying to drown out the other speeches. The organizers let us stay outside the main hall until our turn, but I could still hear the speeches through the open door. The boy from West Virginia stepped up to the microphone and my nerves came back in a wave. We were next, and since the competition believed in "ladies first," that meant I was up on deck.

I waved Kris down and pointed towards the door. Without turning off his music, he nodded and followed me as I slowly made my way into the hall and towards the front.

Breathe, in and out. I deserved to be here. Another set of breaths. I was going to be amazing. I always was.

West Virginia finished his speech and, as I started up the steps to the stage, Kris slipped off his headphones, reached up, and squeezed my arm. "Be incredible. Make me work for first place."

Just his touch made my breathing speed up again and, as I took my last steps towards the podium, I did another set of breathing exercises to try and get it back to normal. Laying my folder on the podium and the patch right next to it, I adjusted the microphone and looked out on the conference room. It took every ounce of effort in me not to look to the left, where Kris was standing. A tiny thrill ran through my body.

"Be incredible," I said under my breath, before opening my folder and starting my speech.

For five minutes, the world fell away. I became my words and they filled the room, soaring and dipping with feeling. I poured my thoughts and beliefs out to the audience, opened myself up to show the raw, real me. "…I still have a long way to grow. But every day, with every step I take to make myself a better, more educated person about the problems in the world, and every step I take to support those making a difference, that's a step closer to me finding a way to lead change. I want to be like those people who shaped our country, someone who is not afraid to stand up to the conventions to make change happen. And I can do it. We all can do it, if we just stand up for what we believe, pick up our pens, our phones, *use* our voices. I'm a teenager. I can't vote, but I can educate others about voting. I don't have the money to donate, but I can donate my time. I can make a difference and can learn how to keep making a difference as I grow. And I can get there by looking at history and using it to help push me into the future, because I *am* still growing into this person I aspire to be, and I *am* the future." The echo of my voice faded from the room and I found that my hands were still shaking the tiniest amount as little tremors ran through my body. It took all my focus to smile and make my way off the stage without tripping.

Speaking my own words to a room full of people was so much more powerful and emotional than anything I'd ever done before. Not even becoming one of Shakespeare's characters for two hours had this much of an impact on me.

Kris passed me on the stairs and paused to lightly touch my shoulder and nod before continuing over to the podium. I could leave the hall, but a part of me wanted to stay and hear him give his speech. As I took one of the seats near the stage stairs, I was amazed at how confident he looked as he smiled out over all of us. In his slacks and dress shirt, with his hair slicked back for the first time that week and a serious look on his face, he looked like he belonged up there.

Then, he spoke.

I'd read the early version of his speech, the one they included in our packets, but between the changes he must have made with his mentor and actually hearing him read it out loud, it was incredibly different. His voice carried over me and a shiver ran down my spine. His words had presence and weight. In that moment, my own speech felt like crap—light, fluffy "I think I can change the world" stuff when compared to what he talked about—legislation and protests and people our age actually changing the world.

"Words are powerful things, but given a voice, they soar. We are the voices our country and world needs, and I'm proud to be a part of this amazing chorus." His speech ended, breaking his spell over us all. His eyes met mine as he looked over at me, probably gloating because he knew he kicked my butt.

So, I got up and left before he could get back down from the stage. It might have been a little bit of a diva move, but, damnit, I could be a diva if I wanted to. It was probably the only thing I had left.

EmmieBear: @WilOfHyrule I know you don't care, but I kicked ass today. Have a nice life with Liesel

@EmmieBear has blocked @WilOfHyrule

KLambert: @EmmieBear Nice job this morning.

EmmieBear: @KLambert Thanks, you too.

KLambert: @EmmieBear We've got first and second in the bag ☺

EmmieBear: @KLambert I hope the judges agree with you.

KLambert: @EmmieBear Hey, are you okay?

EmmieBear: @KLambert Okay?...?

EmmieBear: @KLambert Oh, Right. I'm fine.

KLambert: @EmmieBear Okay, good. Because if you need one, I'm sure I can bend Change Council rules and get a hot chocolate or something for you.

EmmieBear: @KLambert My knight in a shining fencing suit

KLambert: @EmmieBear ???

EmmieBear: @KLambert I'm okay, thanks. I'm thinking of getting an apple cobbler latte later but I need to call Phoebe and get ready for tonight

KLambert: @EmmieBear They make an apple cobbler latte?

EmmieBear: @KLambert If you weren't too busy hitting on the barista, you'd see it's been on their menu this whole time

KLambert: @EmmieBear If you weren't too busy flirting with anything with a pulse, you'd realize me being polite isn't "hitting on someone"

KLambert: @EmmieBear You'll know when I'm flirting

EmmieBear: @KLambert Well, I—

KLambert: @EmmieBear Speechless? (Pun intended)

EmmieBear: @KLambert Sorry, gotta go. Feebs is calling

40

"I need this so much," I said between sips of the apple cobbler latte that had mysteriously shown up at my room door only a few minutes before. I tried not to think too hard about how it got there, and focused on the person on the other side of the phone. "You are the best best friend I could have ever picked. I still can't believe you're coming up." I was cross-legged on my bed, phone pressed to my ear.

"Whatever. What's the point of having family in Boston if I can't visit the city when you're blowing everyone away with your stage presence? Thank goodness for the Acela."

"I don't know about the blowing everyone away part," I said, picking at the cookie I had swiped from the basket by the front desk after lunch.

"What?" Her question was immediately followed by a hushed, "Sorry, sorry." There were a whole bunch of rustling sounds on the other side of the line. "One sec, they're kicking me out of the quiet car," Phoebe said after a moment, her voice a low whisper.

"Quiet car? Who sits there?"

"People who like to read on trains in peace and quiet?"

"They exist?"

I could picture Phoebe standing in the little space between train cars, blowing air out of her lips like she always did when I got to her teasing limit. "Yes. Anyway, so, what happened?"

"Beyond the fact that I'm terrified I'm going to place absolute last?"

"I doubt that. And I'm sure that professor you wanted to impress will be happy with how you did no matter where you place."

I tugged at a loose thread in the quilt. "I think..." I started slowly, "a lot of this isn't about Dr. Lladros or the scholarship anymore."

She was quiet for a moment, then prompted me with, "Okay, so what *is* it about?"

I pulled at the thread until it bunched up the stitching in that part of the quilt. First the wall, now a quilt. I was becoming a repeat vandal. "I'm just so tired of not being taken seriously. I'm more than fluff, no matter what some of them think." The words that had been building up in me over the past few days bubbled to the surface, tumbling out before I could stop and edit myself. "I wanted to show I'm just as good as Kris or those snotty-ass speechwriting political nerds. I want to kick the hell out of all their asses to prove I belong here as much as they do because being awesome at acting doesn't mean I couldn't and didn't write the best speech anyone ever heard."

"And the scholarship would be nice," Phoebe prompted, with something that sounded a little like pride in her voice.

"True, especially if it lets me show Mom and Dad that I can succeed on my own terms, too." I walked over to the window and stared out at the quiet Boston street in front of the inn that was starting to feel as familiar as my street back home. When I'd walked on that street for the first time a week ago, I had no idea how much things could change in such a short time.

"You did it. I believe in you," she said, sounding just like a Disney princess, and the comfort in her voice was like being wrapped in one of her cozy knit shawls. It was nice knowing my friends always believed in me, no matter what. "I missed your confidence, by the way."

"Well…"

"There's something I'm missing, isn't there?"

"Um… I kind of kissed Kris last night." I closed my eyes and cringed, imagining Phoebe's reaction. It sounded awful even coming out of my own mouth.

She was speechless for a moment. "Oh *frack*, ouch. How do you kind of kiss someone?"

I waved my hand vaguely in the air even though she couldn't see me. "I don't know. It just happened."

"Did you deduct kiss-status points because he's not that great of a kisser? Is that how it became kind of?" Her voice melted into pure sympathy.

"No." Memory of last night's kiss rushed across my skin and suddenly the room felt a little too warm. No kiss had ever done that to me before. "He's amazing, like 'I thought my panties were going to catch on fire' amazing." I had to fan myself as I spoke and my coffee became too hot to drink.

"First, don't say that word. It icks me out."

"Amazing?" I teased.

"No, the p- word. Stupid name. Second, eww. Fiery underpants? Seriously?"

My face split into a wide grin. It was way too easy to tease her. "Doesn't Dev make your—"

"Please don't go there."

"Right. Super holy virgin and all that."

Phoebe made an insulted sound, her voice going a little squeaky. "You're evil."

My grin faded as I leaned my forehead against the window, watching as people passed by in their uncomplicated Saturday afternoon lives. "Thanks for not saying 'I told you so' about the whole flirt-Kris-to-failure thing."

"Oh, don't worry. You'll get enough of that from Grace when you get home on Sunday."

"I'm not looking forward to that." Hiding out in Boston forever sounded like a good idea at the moment. Maybe I could get a job as one of the historical re-enactors, like Historical Hottie.

"So…you kissed Kris? On purpose?"

Sometimes, Phoebe's innocent world-view was beyond ridiculous. "No, I just tripped and happened to fall onto his face," I said sarcastically.

"That actually happened in *Starstruck*." She was probably talking about another book.

"Well, this isn't a book," I pointed out, then got up and

paced the room.

"You never know. Stuff like that happens in real life."

"Well, in 'real life' what's happening is I think I'm falling for Kris and I think he was just playing me as much as I was playing him. You were all right, my plan backfired spectacularly and I'm so screwed."

"Did he…kiss you back?" She sounded a little choked on "kiss," like it was a dirty word or something. "From what I remember, Kris really gets into it."

The mental image of Kris kissing my best friend annoyed the hell out of me, but I knew that tone of voice. She was definitely screwing up her nose in disgust at the memory. "I'm pretty sure he kissed me back, but maybe it was because I kind of threw myself at him last night. He was being so sweet about Wil sending me the Photogram of him and his new girl-toy…"

She cut me off with a, "Holy frack, what?"

"Oh, yeah. The Wil and Em show is officially over. I'm pretty sure I was right about the supermodel thing, too. Except her name's Liesel."

"I'm so sorry, Em." Phoebe's voice was gentle, like a verbal hug.

My shoulders went up and down in a shrug. Talking it out made it feel like it had happened to someone else a long time ago. "At least I was right." There wasn't as much pain wrapping around my heart as I thought would be when talking about Wil.

"He's a jerk."

"That's pretty much what Kris said." I picked at the curtain for a moment before burying my face in its velvet. "But instead of just saying thanks, I tried to set his pants on fire. Because I'm an idiot. And then, we go to do our speeches this morning and he had to give this amazing speech. People were sniffling in the audience, Feebs. Hell, *I* almost cried."

"What's with you and fiery pants? Isn't that what happens to liars?"

I let a frustrated puff of air through my lips. "When you're *five*. What do you and Dev *do* in his room? Macramé?"

"Hey, first, what my boyfriend and I have decided we are comfortable doing or not doing is our business and second, don't take your frustration out on me," she said, her voice a cross between squeaky and insulted.

She was right, I was touchier than usual. "Sorry, I just had a fantastically craptastic few days. I'll try harder to pretend everything's peachy."

"I think this might be a good thing. The competition part is over and maybe now you'll believe Kris isn't as awful as you thought. Maybe you two might get together and, I don't know, set more pants on fire?"

I loved Phoebe, but she was so naïve. "Sure, Feebs. We'll totally forget ten years of despising each other because we got along for less than a week? This isn't one of your books where everything ties up nice and neat at the end. We'll probably just go back to barely tolerating each other when we get home." *Barely tolerating each other from a distance*, I added silently. As far as possible from those eyes and that body and the lemon-verbena soap he used.

"Right." A muffled sound filled the background and she waited for it to finish. "We're almost at the station, so I have to go. We'll talk tonight."

"Go, I don't want to be the reason you end up in Rhode Island or something." Before I hung up, I added, softly, "I'm so glad you're going to be here."

"Of course. I'd never miss this. Forget Wil and Kris, and I'm sure you did great. Did I miss anything?"

"Maybe the part about how I'm just the most amazing person on the planet?"

"Bye, Em."

I laughed as she hung up.

They made us sit in the same order as we had for the entire conference, which meant I was back next to Kris as we filed into Faneuil Hall. It was so hard to believe we'd been there only a week ago—it seemed like forever since he and I had been on the stage, having a showdown. And now, I was thankful I was ahead of him in line. No excuses to even look his way at all, even though I wanted to. He was still in his dress shirt and slacks from the morning and looked like he'd stepped right off a movie screen.

In a sea of mostly black, grey, and blue, my bright yellow drapey jacket stood out. I played with my belt, tying my bow a little neater. I sat down and crossed my legs, smiling at the quirky yellow shoes that Phoebe, Grace, and Alec had gotten together to give me on my birthday. It was like my best friends were right there with me.

"Em!" A tiny, familiar voice squeaked over the crowd and I looked up into the galley to see Chloe hanging over the railing, arms flailing wildly. Just like I was impossible to miss in yellow, her bright green jumper and cowboy boots stood out against the white railing, proof that my impeccable taste in clothes was rubbing off on her. Behind her,

Mom, Dad, and Phoebe were also waving and laughing at the same time. I faked a smile and princess-waved up at my baby sister, who let out a musical giggle and princess-waved right back.

"Is that your little sister? She's cute." Kris whispered from beside me, and I managed a slight nod without actually looking at him. Of course she was adorable—we shared the same genes.

I fidgeted my way through the pledge of allegiance, national anthem, and Ms. Shawnee's long speech about the conference and growth and how we were amazing young people who were going to change the world.

Right. Maybe people like Kris could do that with their charities and grand political plans. Me, I was relegated to a lifetime of bake sales and just talking about change, if the difference between our speeches meant anything.

Finally, she started announcing the top twenty speeches, working backwards. I bounced in my seat impatiently, my fingers crossed and fake-clapping for everyone whose names were called. We had bonded enough over the past week that I was really happy when some of my friends were called, but it was still hard to feel excited when my insides were churning, waiting for the results to be over. When Kris's name was announced for ninth place and he stood to go get his plaque, my entire body slumped. If he got ninth, that meant I didn't even make it in any of the scholarship slots. Probably fiftieth or one hundredth place.

"Congrats," I murmured to him when he got back to

his seat, pasting that same fake smile on my face. Kris was beaming, despite his placement. "Sorry you didn't get first."

"There are some pretty amazing speeches here. Being in the top ten isn't bad."

I tilted my head back, staring at the painting hanging above the stage and willing the whole ceremony to finish as fast as possible so I could go eat something fantastically fattening. I closed my eyes and let Shawnee's voice turn into a drone until something jostled my arm. I turned to give Kris a dirty look, and he pointed to the stage. "That's you, Em." I stared blankly at him and he and the guy from New Hampshire practically shoved me to standing. "Third place? Go."

Shock ran through my system, along with an unholy mix of disappointment for not winning first and the happy realization I didn't suck major suckage. I was like Judy Garland in my yellow-brick-road shoes, blinking at the brightness around me as I made my way up onto the stage, in such shock I couldn't even manage to fake-smile. Ms. Shawnee squeezed my hand tight, handing me a plaque and turning me around for a photo-op where I must have looked like a deer in headlights before I was passed over to the judges, who whispered things like "good job" as they shook my hand. One older man with a smile that stretched across his wrinkled face and touched his dark eyes nodded as he shook my hand and said, "Incredible speech, young lady. I'll be requesting a copy of your competition recording for my school."

I gaped at him for a moment before finding my voice. "Thank you." I was passed on to a few more judges before stumbling off the stage and getting engulfed in a giant ocean-scented hug.

"I told you the speech was fantastic. Congratulations." Lauren pulled back, studying me at arm's length before hugging me again. "Now, breathe. You look a little lost." I started walking back to my seat, but she held on to my arm. "You can stay here for now. They're going to want pictures with you and the first- and second-place winners afterwards."

With all the hugging and handshaking, I'd missed hearing second place, but seeing the girl from Wisconsin stumble down the steps with a dazed expression that reflected what I felt pretty much let me know she was second. We high-fived and shared a grin before she went to stand by her mentor.

Ms. Shawnee went into the usual "drag things out as much as uncomfortably possible" with vague praises about all the speeches and how this winning one blew away the judges, etc, etc, before finally getting to the point. "And this year's US Youth Change Council speech competition first-place winner is Geoff Stirling from Louisiana."

A whoop came up from the crowd, joined by whistles and cheers from my fellow competitors. Geoff was sweet and fun, and it was impossible not to feel happy for him. I picked Ann out of the crowd and she was bouncing up and down, clapping a in a way I never expected my sometimes uptight roommate to act. After all the handshakes, Geoff stepped up to the podium, started his speech, and I had to admit it was awesome. In the span of five minutes, he ran us through a range of emotions, starting and ending with laughter. If I had to lose to anyone, at least it was a speech that unquestionably deserved first place. The little jealousy monster in me picked out any mistakes and places where mine was better, but I squashed back that monster and my disappointment at not making first as hard as I could.

Third place out of over one hundred speeches was huge, and the ten-thousand-dollar scholarship that came with it wasn't bad, either. Which Phoebe and my parents told me over and over again as they swarmed me after the awards ceremony. Chloe had claimed my plaque and was walking around showing everyone how my name was really spelled. If it weren't so cute, I'd strangle her.

I was one of the few people there with family and friends who had come to the ceremony. Even Kris' parents hadn't been able to make the drive, but Mom said Dad had insisted on being there. "I'm so glad we decided to come," he said as he hugged me tight. "A webcast wouldn't have been the same as seeing my baby get an award in person." He pulled back and his dark eyes were shining just as much as mine had to be. "I'm proud of you. I can't wait to hear your award-winning speech."

Mom was next, squeezing me so tight I could barely breathe. "We missed you so much this week. I don't know what we're going to do when you're away at college."

"I don't know either, especially if you're in Stockholm

or Nairobi." My voice wavered on that sentence, but I'd promised myself I'd be strong about it so I wouldn't stress my parents even more.

Mom pulled back for a moment to give me a knowing look. "Let me guess. Alec?" At my nod, she hugged me again and said, "Honestly, you two are worse than Chloe when it comes to wild speculation and blowing things out of proportion. We're not going anywhere." I breathed as much of a sigh of relief as I could while being squished to death.

"You said 'away at college,'" I said into her shoulder.

"Considering how clear you've been that you're not interested in spending time on campus with me, your wonderful and loving mom…"

"Is Dad going to be mad?"

Mom's body shook with laughter, and she reached up to gently pat my hair. "Oh, honey, he's not. You two are so much alike, when things get tough for you, you try to micromanage other peoples' lives." I stiffened at that incredibly untrue assertion and she laughed even harder. "We're both a little disappointed and worried you're not taking our advice, but…we'll talk about that when we get home, okay?" She squeezed me even harder. "Today, we're *both* over the moon for you. Trust me."

The guilty weight that had been sitting on my lungs from the second I saw them in the crowd lifted the littlest bit. "Okay." I peered over her shoulder, trying to find Phoebe or Ann or anyone who could get me out of the constant cycle of hugs. It was starting to get a little embarrassing.

I couldn't see Ann, but Phoebe was on the other side of the hall, smiling and talking with Kris, who, in a *Twilight Zone* moment, was laughing like they were best friends. As soon as I caught her attention, I waved her over with a "help me" look on my face. And bit back a groan as she nodded and dragged Kris over, too.

Mom let go and gave me a confused look. "Are you okay?"

I smiled a wavery smile. "Just hug-suffocating." As soon as Phoebe got close enough, I broke away and threw my arms around her. "Why did you bring him over with you?" I whispered in her ear.

Phoebe gave me a giant, slightly evil-looking grin, which was a new look for her. "Payback."

"Wait until we get home and I pull out pictures from your vampire phase to show Dev."

She raised an eyebrow, but didn't say anything, instead stepping aside to leave a clear shot for Kris. I tried to turn and talk to her some more, but she was already talking with Chloe. Biting back the urge to head over to them, I turned back around and tried to look composed. I hated how his smile had gone from infuriating me less than a week before to making me breathless.

"Maybe we didn't get first and second, but at least you listened to me," Kris said as he stepped a little closer than just friendly.

The lack of preamble threw me off. "What?"

"I told you to be incredible, and you were." His smile

came out full force—developing slowly enough that I just wanted to reach out with my finger and trace his bottom lip as it spread.

I clasped my hands behind my back. "Oh." The retort I had prepared had died on my tongue and I just stood there, unsure of what to say beyond "Thanks."

"Of course, if I had gone first, the judges might have been so blinded by my brilliance that they would have forgotten about you, but you got off easy. This time." After the week we'd had together, I couldn't tell if he was joking or just being his usual egotistic self. Before I could say anything, though, he waved at someone over my shoulder and shrugged apologetically. "Sorry, I promised Marina I'd catch the first bus with her so we could grab a coffee. I figured you'd be busy with your parents."

I tried to see who he had been waving to, but there were way too many people around us. "Marina?"

"New York? You really do suck at names, don't you? Anyway," he looked like he was about to hug me, but then just reached out and awkwardly pat-squeezed my arm, "Congratulations again."

"You, too." I resisted the irrational urge to go over to Marina and shove her into Boston Harbor like a human-shaped teabag and instead waved like an idiot as he walked away. I froze, staring after him and wishing I had some, any, stage directions to make me move again.

"If he's really not into you, you're so screwed," Phoebe said as she came back up alongside me, "because the look on your face just now almost broke my heart."

"That was pain from too much exposure to Kris. Stockholm syndrome, whatever you want to call it." Grace's excuse rolled easily off my tongue. "And since when did you become a relationship expert?"

"I don't need to be a relationship expert to be an Em expert." She gently fixed my jacket and smiled softly. "You won third place, have a scholarship, and I promise we'll get you a happily ever after in everything else, even if it takes a little bit of time. You deserve it."

42

"Your sister is adorable," Ann said as she braided her hair back for the night. Being the responsible type, she already had most of her suitcase packed, unlike me with my over-flowing mess of clothes and shoes.

I nudged a shoe back into my suitcase. "Try living with her. The adorableness wears off really fast." I gave up on trying to fit things in the bag and just sat on the lid. Maybe my weight would compress my clothes enough to fit more. "If you want, I'll let you ride home in the backseat of a car for six hours with her tomorrow while I fly."

Her expression turned the slightest bit sympathetic. "It's still sweet your whole family came up for the awards ceremony."

"Yeah, that was a nice surprise. Feebs is up here all the time because she has family in Boston, but I didn't expect Mom and Dad to make it."

Ann finished her braid and looked up to see me playing a game of twister with my suitcase. With a laugh, she pulled me away from the bag. "Let me help you. If everything came here in that bag, it should be able to go home in the same one."

"I don't know. My friend Grace has magical packing powers."

"So do I. Stand back." I dropped onto the bed and watched as Ann sifted through my clothes, rolling them into tight fabric logs. After a few minutes of silence, she looked up and said idly, "It was really nice of Kris to ask the Council committee to move you to the last group, wasn't it? You might not have done so well if you had to go right after the call with your ex-boyfriend."

My brows knit together. "What? I thought they just needed to shuffle some of us around."

"Just you and Wisconsin?" She shook her head, her eyes focused on her task of finding the perfect spot in my bag for a pair of rolled-up jeans. "No. When you didn't come down for breakfast, he got really worried. When I told him about how you didn't really sleep and that you were on a call with Wolfgang—"

"Wilhelm," I corrected her.

"Wilhelm. He figured you'd need more time to prepare. So, he asked Ms. Shawnee and a few of our competitors if they were willing to switch. Since the two state representatives have to go together because the judging packets are ordered that way, he said it was for him, not you." Ann did some sort of origami with my dress and fit it in a tiny corner next to one of the Jimmy Shoos. She finally looked up, waving the other one by its heel. "You know, he risked his placement by doing that. If they said no, it would have really reflected badly on him. But at least Casey and Mike were willing to switch."

The air seemed to grow thick, like I had stuffed my face into a feather mattress. I dropped my gaze to the comforter and picked at the lace around its edge. "I didn't know." My voice sounded strange, soft and subdued.

She shrugged, then stuffed the shoe in alongside the other one. "I know you two have some sort of messy history, but I think he's a really nice guy."

Even though Ann had no reason to lie, it still all just didn't compute. I looked back up at her and tilted my head. "What about years of being the ego king of Pine Central?"

"Maybe it's like what I told you the first night we got here. Maybe he was just as boxed in as the rest of us with everyone's expectations at home. This might have been the only place where he could be himself. Or maybe you've been seeing him this one way for so long that it took getting you both out of your regular environment to see the real him."

"Or maybe having our time slot moved later gave him an advantage, too?" I said, but my argument was half-hearted.

Ann finished sticking the last shirt into the suitcase and stepped back, regarding me with a patient look. "Right." The bag was perfectly packed, with room for a few extras in the morning. The girl was freakishly good.

I needed time to digest this new information about Kris. Closing my suitcase and pushing it aside, I moved on to a new, temporary distraction. "So, why aren't you out somewhere in the hallways making out with Geoff?"

"Because, unlike you, I'm a rule follower. And you're changing the subject."

"I know. I need time to process. But I also can multi-task, and since matchmaking happens to be a forte of mine, I'm keeping busy while processing." I shifted to sit cross-legged and leaned back. "So, hot Louisiana boy?"

Ann played with the end of her braid, her expression shy. "He's promised to fly out for my winter formal and, if we're still together by then, we're talking about going to each other's proms. Plus, we might meet halfway and rebuild some homes that were destroyed by the tornado in Oklahoma." The braid dropped to her lap along with her hands. "It's a little bit crazy, especially considering what happened with your long-distance relationship…"

"Just because things didn't work out for me and Wil doesn't mean it won't work for you. We're seniors. Even if you started dating someone in your own school, you don't know if you'd be going to the same college. And, anyway, first-place speech winners are hot."

"So are selfless classmates." If eyes could actually twinkle, hers did at that moment.

I swatted the air in front of me like I was pushing away a fly. "Shh, still processing."

Ann laughed. "I'm going to miss you, roomie."

"Ditto. I won't miss your flute practicing and volunteer talk, though. You made me feel like the most inadequate, lazy person on the planet, but that's why you're going to end up on some famous orchestra and flying out to saint-hood ceremonies and I'll keep talking about how I knew you way back when."

"Well, you can get a start on sainthood with this one charity I know about. It's music-based, started in your hometown...I can put in a good word for you with the head of the teen advisory board."

"Yeah, well, like I said, processing. Plus, the teen advisory board guy might be busy driving up the Turnpike to hang out with Miss New York."

"Doubtful. I have it on good sources that last night's coffee ended with Marina getting annoyed because she finally realized he isn't into her." Ann's lips pressed together like she was trying to hold back a laugh or wide grin. "Just in case you were wondering. Which I'm sure you're not because you're still processing."

That last part made me laugh. I rolled onto my back and stared at the canopy above me. "I'm going to have to introduce you to my friend Grace. I didn't realize it until now, but you both have the same sense of humor." I rolled my head over to look at Ann, someone who probably wouldn't have become my friend if we hadn't been put together for a week. "We're staying in touch, right?"

"If you don't, I'll cyber-stalk you anyway to find out what happens when you get back home."

"Boring, I promise you. Kris will go back to being class president, sitting at the student council table and being too good to hang out with the little people, and I'll go back to flirting with the hottest guys in the theatre club. Or band. Whichever comes first." I made a show of tapping my cheek with a pointer finger. "Or maybe I can branch out and date a football player. That might be fun."

She shook her head, a frown replacing the smile that was there moments before. "I'm no psychic, but I think you're wrong."

"And I think you don't know how life in Lambertfield works. Trust me, it's better this way."

43

Leaving Boston was tough. Unlike most of the group who headed for the airport early that morning by bus, all of us whose parents had driven in for the ceremony got to hang in the lobby, waiting.

Rhode Island kept a steady stream of conversation going, but after the emotional rollercoaster from the night before and all the hugs and teary goodbyes from the morning, I was too exhausted to even act interested. When Phoebe walked through the front door, I was convinced I had to be hallucinating my escape. "Feebs?" Rhode Island paused at my confused outburst, looked up, shrugged, and went back to her story.

Phoebe made her way across the lobby to our chairs, eyes wide and taking in the room. Knowing her, this inn was probably looked like something in her book du jour. "I'm bumming a ride home off of your parents. They offered last night." She perched on the arm of my chair, one hand reaching out to touch the wallpaper. "I hope you don't mind being squished with me in the back of a car for six hours."

I cringed at the thought. "Can we take the Acela back, instead?"

She lifted a shopping bag embossed with "The Midnight Read" up off the floor. "Can't. Just spent the ticket money stocking up on bookish goodies."

"Why am I not surprised?"

"If you're nice, I'll share my signed copy of *Northern Light* with you." She reached into the bag and waved a hardcover with the picture of a girl in a rainbow dress on the cover.

"Tempting," I said dryly.

By the time my parents arrived, Phoebe had integrated herself into the remaining group. For someone who was really shy, she hid it pretty well while talking hot book boys with Delaware. Without missing a beat in trading her contact information with Rhode Island, she grabbed my suitcase so I only had to shoulder my Change Council bag. Phoebe waited at the door with my parents as I hugged everyone and went up to Ms. Shawnee.

In a move I couldn't have predicted from her starched appearance, she swept me up in a bear hug, then held me at arm's length and said, "I'm so glad you were a part of this. Don't lose that passion you had in the summit and in your speech."

I cracked a wobbly smile. "Sorry about how Kris and I exploded all your discussions."

"Don't be. I'm glad you both cared enough to put all of yourselves into your debates. Though I feel sorry for your teachers if you're in the same classes," she added with a shake of her head.

"Yeah, it can be fun."

"I'm proud of you," she said, pulling me in for another hug. "I know we're going to hear big things about you."

I didn't know what to say, so when she let go, I just squeaked out a "thank you" and hurried to the door. Adults with high expectations scared me.

Loading my things into the car and answering all of my parents' and Chloe's questions made my head spin. I grew quieter than usual just to save my sanity, like a turtle retreating into its shell. Once we hit the Massachusetts turnpike, Phoebe seemed to sense my mood and kept Chloe busy learning how to knit while my parents argued in the front seat about the best route to get home. It was impossible to be everything they wanted when a whole week of growing came to an end and I hadn't yet had a chance to get used to my new reality.

Reality number one, I counted off as we passed Worcester, I had fallen into something beyond hormonal lust for Kris. Not love, but beyond the "wanting to turn into a puddle under his smile" stage. He had gotten under my skin in ways I hadn't anticipated, paid attention to parts of me other boys ignored, and fired me up like no one else ever had. Everything felt a little…dimmer without that constant spark between us.

Reality number two, Kris probably didn't feel the same way about me, even though some of the things he did, like kissing me back in the hallway or changing our competition time, made me wonder if it wasn't an act. But, in his defense, it was pretty hard not to kiss me back, since I happened to be an amazing kisser. Not as amazing as he was, but, still... the boy had no chance.

Reality number three, no matter what either of us felt, we were going back to a world that expected us to act certain ways. Kris would go back to his ladder climbing and stepping on any hands that got on the rungs, I'd go back to my world of people who thought that kind of behavior was disgusting. We were both actors in this high school drama and our roles were already scripted for us.

Reality number four—I didn't have the energy or strength to upend any of those other realities. Breaking up with Wil might have sucked, but being rejected by Kris would make the rest of my school year unbearable.

Phoebe leaned over somewhere around Hartford and whispered under the sound of Mom and Dad debating whether or not we needed to stop at the next rest stop, "Are you okay?"

I leaned my head onto her shoulder. "Yeah. Just watching my realities crash all around me."

From: S. Lladros (S.Lladros@RUmail.edu)

To: Em (emkatsaros@dmail.com)

Subject: Received Audition sample

Dear Ephemie,

Writing personally to let you know we've received your audition samples for your application. I'm particularly looking forward to seeing how you interpreted the *A Doll's House* monologue.

Again, I want to reiterate my congratulations for winning third place in the Change Council competition. You certainly lived up to all our expectations and I can't wait to hear the recording of your speech. Please note that I cannot use it when considering your application, but that we are all very proud of you.

Kindest Regards,

Sandra Lladros

44

Over the next few weeks, I lost myself in a whirlwind of preparation for the fall play and catching up with all the classwork I'd missed for the competition. Kris and I were back to our old habits in class like nothing had happened. If we didn't have to do interviews together for the class paper or the local TV station, we probably wouldn't ever have to talk to each other.

There were moments—like in US history when Mr. Valla brought up Boston and our eyes met. Or the random inside jokes about Loyalists or peanut butter when we passed in the lunchroom. But, otherwise, it was like the competition didn't happen. Reality number three realized.

It didn't matter. I had my scholarship—maybe not as big as first place would have been, but it was definitely going to help, and in a few more months, I'd be away at school and would never have to see Kris again. Things weren't perfect, but I could make them work, like how I'd slowly started convincing first Mom, then Dad, that applying to theatre programs was not a bad thing.

Opening night of the play, I stared at my reflection in the "vanity" our crew had set up in the hallway by the backstage door—a beat-up long cafeteria table with a full-length mirror propped lengthwise on it and bulb lights glued around the edges of the mirror. My Victorian gown was a dull beige shade that, combined with my minimalist stage makeup, did nothing for my complexion. I twisted my hair into a French twist, tugging at the curls to fake as much Victorian-style volume as I could get with short hair, but, combined with the high neckline of the straight-jacket-like bodice, the whole look was still severe. Nora was supposed to be the domestic ideal of beautiful, a doll, but—I looked over at the sexy, ribbon-y red and black Tarantella outfit hanging on the rack and the vain part of me wished I could wear that the whole time instead of this Victorian straightjacket. Phoebe's sister had made it for me with the wardrobe master's permission, and she had winked as she handed it over, saying something about how it would look extra flirty from the audience.

It was crazy, considering how much I wanted to play Nora and how I usually didn't care how I looked in my costumes as long as it fit my character. But the same part of me also knew that Kris would be in the audience, cheering on his best friend, Matt, and that stupid part wanted to always be heart-stoppingly gorgeous in front of him.

Dev finished gluing on a handlebar moustache and reached over to steal my contour palette. "So, what's up with you and Kris? You two have been acting weird since Boston."

I *ssh*ed him. "Matt might hear." Kris' best friend had already finished his makeup but was pacing and doing breathing exercises only a few feet away from us.

"In character already, *Nora*, and hiding things from your 'husband,' hmm?" Dev twirled his ridiculous moustache and gestured with his eyes towards the curtain. "Here is one enigma, Mrs. Helmer. I peeked into the audience. If nothing's going on with the two of you, why is our class president in the third row?"

I closed my eyes and set my lips in a straight line, breaking out of character so fast that normal people would get whiplash. "Because his VP is Torvald?"

Dev raised an eyebrow but didn't say anything, instead smiling an infuriating smile. He made an annoyingly good Krogstad, with the potential to be as much of thorn in my side as the bank assistant was Nora's.

It wasn't hard to know what he was thinking. Phoebe told us ages ago that Kris never sat in the front during performances so he could sneak out and avoid actually watching the show. "Damnit, is Phoebe getting to you, too?"

Shaking my head, I stomped over to the backstage door and looked back to see if he was following. I wasn't going to start reading into where people sat in an auditorium. Dev should have known better than to screw around with me right before the curtain went up. "I'm gonna have a talk with that girl when we're done here. Just no more about this from you, okay?" I said in a stage whisper that got me a dirty look from Alexis, our stage manager.

Dev winked, and, without saying anything else, slinked off into the backstage shadows. He grabbed a paper off a chair and waved it like it was the blackmail letter in the play before disappearing behind the backdrop. Theatre people could be so weird.

45

The post-show high was always my favorite part. Taking time to wipe off the makeup and become myself again was like a magic trick, like ending the ultimate game of dress-up. My ribs were finally starting to loosen up after so many hours compressed in a corset, and I was finally able to take deep breaths of modern, liberated air. My poor hair was going to need massive amounts of conditioner when I got home to keep from turning into a giant knot from letting it loose during the tarantella scene, then manhandling it back into a twist for the rest of the play. I checked myself in our mirror, tucking my bra strap under the strap of my gauzy top. Tomorrow, I'd leave in jeans and a sweatshirt, but it was tradition to look awesome on opening and closing nights.

"You're both coming to the diner, right?" the girl who played Mrs. Lynde asked as she passed in a black dress, her hair tied up in a tight bun.

Dev answered for both of us. "Yup, we'll be there." He finished wiping his eyes with a cotton ball and cringed at the black film still visible, even in his reflection. "I swear, it's like this stuff embedded itself in my skin."

"Think of it this way, it'll be less work to get into

costume tomorrow. And, in case you haven't figured it out yet, I happen to know that Phoebe has a soft spot for guyliner." I grabbed my makeup tackle box and costume bag. "Let's go, our public is waiting."

Out in the atrium, my family crowded around me, Mom pulling me into a tight hug, Dad saying I did a great job. It was awesome, but I couldn't help but notice the little hollow feeling in the pit of my stomach as I watched Dev swing Phoebe into a kiss. I really missed that, the feeling of knowing someone who wasn't a family member or friend but who cared about me was watching in the audience. I blinked back a tear that threatened to escape thanks to my stupid post-show emotional rollercoaster and gave Grace, Leia, and Alec the biggest, most enthusiastic smile I could muster.

"That massive butt-padding they put into your dress looks good," Alec teased, miming a bustle with his hands. "Maybe you should bring the style back full-time." He tapped me on the shoulder with his rolled up program when I stuck my tongue out at him.

"I didn't even recognize you at first." Leia went to private school, so she hadn't seen the promo posters around the school. "That was fun, but I like your musicals better."

"I agree. You have such a pretty singing voice, it's almost a shame they didn't put it in here." Grace pulled me into a hug, and held me back out at arm's length with a semi-serious expression. "That last scene broke my heart. You're so talented; you know that, right? Don't ever let anyone make you give it up unless you want to."

I dragged her back into a hug, whispering, "Thanks," before letting go.

Dev and Phoebe joined us, Phoebe already pulling on her shawl and looking adorable in a dress I was positive her sister had made for her. She'd come a long way from trying to copy book characters' outfits.

"Sorry to break in," Dev said, "but if we don't leave for the diner soon, we'll be at the outcast table."

Alec snorted. "You're theatre *and* band geeks. Doesn't that already make you outcasts?"

"You should see what the outcast table looks like in geek-land. It's not a pretty sight," Phoebe said, grey eyes wide. "C'mon, Em."

"The rest of you can come, if you want. If they let Phoebe in…" Dev laughed as Phoebe bumped him with her hip.

"That's okay, I was going to watch a movie at Leia's house," Grace said, just as Alec said, "Sorry, I have a science-meet tomorrow at eight. I need to go study." Dev and I shared a *look*, and I could practically read his mind. Still, both of us had enough self-control to keep from making a "Who's a geek now?" comment to Alec.

"Okay, so we'll see you tomorrow. Are you riding with us, Em?"

I shook my head. "Mom let me borrow her car." I caught sight of a familiar head of dark hair near the atrium doors. *Shit.* I thought Kris would be gone by that point. "You guys go ahead. I'm just going to talk to my parents and I'll meet you there."

"Okay, don't get lost."

"Cute, Dev. Real cute." I waved goodbye to my other friends and hurried over to Mom and Dad, who gave me a five-minute lecture about curfew and not driving anyone else—the usual. By the time they were done, I had hoped Kris would be gone, but he was still there, talking with random people. My insides twisted on themselves again, like they were trying desperately to tie a knot.

As I headed out, I stayed close to the atrium wall and tried to pretend I didn't see Kris as I passed him, but his hand snaked out and caught my arm. "Hey, Em, do you have a minute?"

I nodded and leaned against the wall, trying to look casual by crossing my arms. At least it was him and not me who literally reached out. "So, you came to the show."

"I always do. Matt's my friend." Kris leaned against the wall, close, but I couldn't tell if it was because of the crowded atrium or not. I couldn't help but peek over his shoulder to make sure my parents were already out of there. There was no way I wanted them to come over and introduce themselves, or worse, for Dad to jump to conclusions and start his "touch my daughter and I'll kill you" Greek-mafia-style lecture.

"Yeah, but you don't actually watch. What, nothing interesting to read in the library tonight or something?"

He at least had the grace to drop his eyes and look somewhat sheepish. "Phoebe told you about that, huh?"

"I was shocked to see you in your seat the whole show." Every nerve in my body screamed at me to notice how his shoulder barely brushed mine, shivers running through me with every tiny shift in contact.

His eyes grew wide with a cross of what looked like surprise and a little bit of satisfaction, like when Chloe got the last of Grandma's double chocolate s'mores cookies. "You looked for me?"

"Third row center is pretty hard to miss."

"Great seats and a good cast are impossible to resist, you know." That satisfaction was starting to turn ever so slightly into smugness. He pushed his hair back and I noticed he hadn't used even a little bit of gel. A part of me hoped it was because of my comments back in Boston. "I really liked Nora. The actress who played her was incredible."

My lips completely ignored my attempts to act cool and went straight into a goofy smile. After an embarrassingly long second of this grinning and gazing like a freshman gaping at a hot senior, commonsense kicked me back into motion. "Thanks. And thanks for coming," I pushed off from the wall, but since he didn't back up, I was practically chest-to-chest with him. "But right now, I have to go. Cast party at the diner."

He still didn't move, and I had to tilt my head up to look him in the eye. "Can I ask a huge favor?"

"What?"

"Meet me at Marrano's after your cast party? I think we need to talk."

Why? I almost said, but I didn't want to get my hopes up. My heart stopped beating for a second and I had to wait for it to restart before saying, instead, "It'll be late…"

"They're open 'til one; we can get some coffee or something."

I found myself nodding, like I was a puppet and Kris somehow knew which strings to pull to make me say yes. Right now, his smile and proximity were pulling all the right ones. "Okay. Does ten-thirty work?"

I didn't need a midnight rendezvous with Kris, but I could spend half an hour with the cast and crew, and then head over to Marranos. I'd still be coherent at that hour— exhaustion plus a hot guy usually meant mistakes thanks to sleepy judgment I regretted later.

"Ten-thirty's perfect." He pulled back so fast I didn't have the time to adjust to the sudden loss of his body heat. "See you in a few."

The wall was the only thing that kept me upright as I watched him walk away, a little badass in his step like the hero in a disaster film. Despite my natural cynicism, hope crept into me and I felt like breaking into a musical number like something out of a thirties film. Maybe it was his smile that made me think this wasn't going to be bad or it could have been his insane confidence, throwing me off in a good way. Whatever it was, I couldn't wait to see what he had planned for later.

46

It was like a scene out of movie. The patio was empty except for us because it was too cold for most sane people to be outside. Still, Marrano's kept their twinkle lights lit, in shades of white and orange leftover from Halloween, wrapped haphazardly around wooden posts and draped over nearby tree branches, giving the whole place a warm glow.

Kris sat at one of the corner picnic tables, picking at its peeling green paint. The second he saw me, he stood, a relieved smile on his face. "I was wondering if you were going to blow me off for your theatre friends."

I tried to look nonchalant as I made my way across the wooden deck, even though a big part of me wanted to run. Instead, I focused on not getting my heels caught in the floorboards and not looking cold. "It's only opening night. Nothing special." I let amusement flow into my last sentence since both of us knew opening night was always a big thing. I slipped onto the bench opposite him and dropped my keys onto the table. "Besides, how can I pass up a frozen custard blizzard?"

"Good point." He pushed his hair out of his face. His usual confidence seemed a little subdued tonight. "So…"

I waited, and when he didn't say anything, I played nervously with the long twenties-style necklace I wore. "So, I know we talked about it in the atrium, but what did you really think of the play?" I glanced up from studying my necklace, my heartbeat accelerating from fast-ish to staccato. I couldn't believe how much I cared about what he thought.

Kris dropped his elbows to the table. "It was cool seeing you up on stage again. You're so different up there; it's amazing. Kind of like when you made your speech. Except with the speech, you were still you."

His words made me feel shy, maybe even a little bit exposed, so I tried to break in with something lighter. "It's the corset and bustle. Alec thinks I should try to bring them back in style."

"I'd rather see you again in that Italian dance outfit."

"Oh." Heat snaked up my neck and over my cheeks as I thought of that very un-Victorian corset-and-skirt combo, "Well, we're performing another two nights," I said as breezily as I could while trying to not squirm under his smirk.

"I'll have to stay out of the library during that part, then," he teased, then turned serious. "I saw what you meant about bringing parts of you into the part. Everyone, even Nora—expected her to be this shallow..." he searched for a word, then seemed to give up and go with the obvious, "...doll, but she turned out to be smart and fierce and ambitious. And a little wild and rebellious. Sounds a lot like you."

I wasn't sure if that was a compliment or an insult.

Either way, his comment threw me off. "I'm sure Mom and Dad wouldn't like the whole 'wild and rebellious' thing. But maybe you would?" I said, and grinned as, this time, he was the one who squirmed.

"And, with that," he said, "I'm going to get a sundae. What do you want?"

I resisted the urge to stop with the back-and-forth banter and just say, "to kiss you again," but instead said, "A kiddie s'mores blizzard sounds good." At his skeptical look on "kiddie," I shrugged. "I got hungry at the diner and stole some of Dev's fries. And ate before the show. I'm not being cute and trying to play the starving actress."

"I think you are," he said as he made his way towards the ordering window.

"Pretending to be a starving actress?"

"No. Cute," he threw over his shoulder. Oh. My. God, Kris was definitely flirting. And doing an awesome job of it. Who knew that was possible?

I wrapped my fingers around the underside of my bench and leaned back, trying not to giggle and feeling like I was back to being fourteen years old on my first "real" date. This part of Lambertfield didn't have as many streetlights as Main Street and the building blocked the streetlamp, so the stars stood out brighter here than anywhere else in town. I tried to forget about the chill and the fact I should have worn a jacket, and instead focused on looking "cute." Kris came to my show, stayed to watch, invited me out, and just flirted with me. And he'd moved mountains to make my speech as successful as possible.

Maybe years of perception weren't reality.

A mug filled with heavenly-smelling coffee drifted under my nose and I straightened up. Kris slid the mug and a cupful of frozen custard onto the table in front of me, then sat, his tray with a coffee and a giant gummy-bear-covered sundae taking up half the table. "I thought you might want a coffee, too," he said, leaning forward to nudge the mug even closer to me.

I picked it up and took a sip, basking in that smile and the fumes of pure energy. "You know me all too well." As much as I wanted to just sit here and keep flirting up a storm, I steeled myself with another sip of coffee chased with a spoonful of s'mores-y custard goodness and said, "You said in the atrium we needed to talk? What about?" The heat and ice running through me didn't have anything to do with what I was eating or drinking.

Kris' spoonful of sundae was halfway to his mouth, but he slowly put it back into the bowl. "Yeah."

As much as I was dying to hear what he had to say, I couldn't help teasing him for that. "That's an 'eloquent' answer."

He aimed his spoon at my mouth and wiggled it in front of me until I leaned forward and took a bite. The part of me that wasn't getting all swoony over the cuteness realized that gummy bears and frozen custard really were an awesome combination.

"Eat your non-starving actor food and let me talk," he

said. When I silently raised my eyebrow at him and waited, he dropped his spoon on the tray. "It's about Boston."

"I figured as much."

"If you're going to make this hard for me, I can just stop and go back to eating this culinary masterpiece." Kris looked frustrated and tried to push back his hair, which didn't stay thanks to the lack of gel.

I mimed zipping my lips shut and sat up straight, trying to look innocent.

After smiling at my goofiness, he grew serious again, his expression making my own smile melt away in a puddle of dread. "Was it an act?" I tilted my head in confusion as he continued. "The whole thing between us in the museum and at the dinner? Because I know what you said after you kissed me, but I think something was already going on between us way before that."

I dropped my gaze to the table. Kris' straightforward way of talking was refreshing after all the games with Wil and every other guy I'd dated, but it was also frustrating. The strangest part of it all was that he made me want to be just as honest and clear. "It started out that way."

He reached across the table and, with two fingers, pushed up my chin so our eyes met again. "What does that mean?"

Instead of squirming, I decided to turn the tables on him. "Was that really you back in Boston? You didn't act like yourself."

"Maybe you finally spent enough time around me to see

the real me and not just the person you always thought I was. Honestly, going into this, I thought you were a spoiled drama queen who bossed around her friends, but I was wrong." A little smile escaped from him at the offended sound that came out of me, but it disappeared just as fast. "Still, you didn't answer my question. What did you mean when you said it started out that way?"

"I thought you were acting like that just to throw me off my game. You know, act all nice, make me feel like I was nuts for thinking otherwise, maybe make me fall for you and then, bam, crush me right before I have to compete."

"If I was planning that, your ex-boyfriend beat me to it. Great judge of character, Em."

"Don't start being a jerk," I said. He imitated my earlier action, zipping his own lips, and I continued, "So, I thought I'd beat you at your own game. I started flirting and playing nice with you, too."

"It wasn't my perfect smile that drew you to me?"

I pressed my lips together, trying not to smile, and shook my head. "That smile used to irritate the living hell out of me. Honestly, I think things started changing when we hung out on Sunday morning, but I really didn't want to believe it." I rubbed the bridge of my nose and dragged the next few words out. Once I said them, I'd have no way to save myself if he really didn't feel the same as I did. "I lied, back in the hallway. I kissed you because I wanted to, not because you were the closest hot guy."

"We'll get back to the fact that you think I'm hot in a

minute." His spoon tapped against the edge of his bowl but his expression didn't budge. Not even on the "hot" part. "Do you seriously mean to say that you were planning to, what, make me fall for you and then break my heart right before we competed or something?"

"I know, not the best plan, but I never said I was a psychological ninja."

He went back to eating his sundae, the annoying superior look on his face again. "That's pretty obvious." His eyes met mine. "When was it still an act? The rotunda?"

I refused to look away, holding his gaze with an expression as serious as death, even though my heart rate was going through the roof. I could hear my heartbeat like the timpani in band. "No. That was real. You?"

"Real. Was that why you freaked out after…" He waved his spoon about, and a faint blush just tinged his cheeks.

"Yeah. Need I remind you I thought I was going to be getting back together with my ex at that point. I might be diabolical, but I'm not awful. But you kind of short-circuited my common sense for a little while."

"That's flattering, coming from the legendary Ephemie Katsaros."

"Seriously, keep calling me by that name and you'll be wearing that sundae."

"Too bad. It's a cute name. I think it fits you perfectly, Ephemie."

I reached playfully for his sundae and he caught my hand. A thrill ran up my arm and my heartbeat jumped up even more in tempo.

"Not fair," I managed to squeak out. Any flirtiness flew out of my head and I really did feel like this was the first time a boy had ever held my hand. "You're trying to short-circuit me again."

"If you like me," his thumb ran back and forth over the back of my hand and made me shiver, "or at least think I'm hot," I let out an *eep* sound, but he continued, "and if I like you, even though you tried to play psychological war with me, and your ex-boyfriend is now definitely an ex, then why are we avoiding each other like the conference didn't even happen?"

My brain finally started working again and I rotated my wrist to turn the tables on him. Now, I was the one running a finger, whisper-soft, across his palm. I smiled when his eyes shut involuntarily. "It's like *West Side Story* and I'm Maria to your Tony. From two different worlds…"

His eyes shot open and he laughed, breaking the spell between us. "Okay, now you're being ridiculous. Student council and the drama club aren't the Sharks and the Jets." Part of me warmed even more at the fact that he made a musical theatre reference. Kris stood and pulled me to standing so that we were practically toe-to-toe in the abandoned patio. "Now that we've figured out there aren't going to be turf wars if we date, what do we do now?"

I stepped closer and rose onto my tiptoes, reaching my face up to his. "If I remember right, you made the first move at the museum, I made the second at the dinner, so isn't it your turn again?" At this distance, I couldn't tell if it was the heat coming off his body or my own blush that overheated me.

He bent forward so his mouth nearly brushed mine. He was so close his breath tickled my lips. "I don't know. I hugged you after the competition. Does that count?"

I snaked my free hand up his arm and shoulder to wrap around his neck. He visibly caught his breath and his lips parted the tiniest bit as my fingers traveled up, and I smiled my best Lauren Bacall-esque smile at his reaction.

"That wasn't a hug, it was an awkward arm pat," I said, tangling my fingers in the hairs at the base of his head and pulling him even closer. We were just millimeters apart.

"If you're going to argue—" He pretended to start pulling away, then, with a smile, closed the gap between us, catching me off-guard. At first the kiss was desperate, like we were making up for all the time lost between the competition and that moment. It was one of those amazing kisses you see in the movies. *Epic.* I went from live wire to floating and back to electric, like my body was nothing but energy that concentrated everywhere his skin touched mine. The cold and sweet of the ice cream I tasted on him contrasted with the fire that rose up between us.

His free arm wrapped around my waist and pulled me tight against him, trapping our linked hands between our bodies. My legs turned to mush and his arm, along with the magnetic pull between us, were the only things keeping me from melting to the floor.

I broke the kiss by barely moving enough to say against the corner of his mouth, "What were you saying about arguing?" My voice sounded floaty and soft. No kiss had ever done that to me before.

He let go of my hand to cup my cheek with his palm. "This is the only way I can think to keep you from fighting with me." His thumb drew tiny circles under my ear, distracting me.

Payback was sweet and I used my free hand to trace his bottom lip before replacing my fingers with a teasing kiss. "I like the way you think. Let's go with that." He tried to kiss me again but I playfully pulled back and touched my nose to his. "This doesn't mean I'm going to campaign for you or anything."

"Elections were over a month ago. But that's okay, because I'm not coming to your orchestra concerts. The CIA should look into those as a valid form of torture."

He tried to tug me into another kiss but I pouted and turned my head so his lips landed on the edge of my jaw. While I talked, he trailed feather-light kisses back towards my mouth. "You're mean."

Kris laughed. "I'm honest. And I honestly,"—he picked up my hand again, brought it between us, and kissed it before leading me over to a bench—"am happy we figured this out. Because another month of what had been going on would have killed me."

"Hmm," I said, then tangled my fingers in his, let my eyes grow wide, and said, "I think I feel a fight coming on again. Want to stop it in its tracks?"

"Good idea." Kris lowered his head and pressed his lips to mine. And everything was perfect.

It was just us and the twinkle lights and the stars.

47

I peeled the wrapper off a cupcake and took a bite, making a face as the heavy chocolate-pecan-coconut combination hit me. That taste was an all-too-familiar reminder of something I seriously wanted to forget. "Ugh, German chocolate. I don't think I'll be able to eat that or Black Forest anything for a long time." I scanned the bake sale table for something that looked non-German, which was tough because, damn, they made great desserts. One of Phoebe's chocolate sugary things had to be safe—at least they were from a Brazilian recipe.

I'd stashed my purse under the table when I showed up for my shift at the bake sale and Phoebe now reached into it to pull five dollars out of my wallet. She added it to her money tin. "You can't let an ex-boyfriend turn you off an entire country," she said, matter-of-factly.

"Oh, no? Watch me." I tossed the barely eaten cupcake into the trash can behind me, doing a little dance at the fact that it landed inside on the first try. "See? Two points for me."

Phoebe scrunched up her nose. "You know, you could have given that to a football player instead of wasting it. One of those guys would've eaten it."

A familiar hottie passed our table and I reached out to grab the strap hanging from his backpack. Instead of reeling in my catch like I was tempted to, I waited for him to notice my tugging.

"Wouldn't you like to buy something sweet from someone sweet? It's for a good cause." I waved dramatically at the Noelle's Song banner the musical theatre club had draped on the long cafeteria table.

Kris grinned as he freed his backpack from my grip. "But Phoebe's busy." He jerked his chin towards where she was trying to convince some of the guys from the chess club to buy the entire plate of chess squares. "Besides, I usually don't do bake sales." He made a show of studying everything on the table. "They're a little inefficient, you know?"

My eyebrows arched up and I tilted my chin superiorly. "You'll be happy to know that in three lunch periods, we've already raised enough to get twenty beginner practice books for the program. How's that for inefficient?"

"Ask me after the gala next week. It might get a little more media coverage than the school paper." He crossed his arms, imitating my pose. "You're coming, right?"

I shrugged, trying to look noncommittal. "Only if you buy something."

"Blackmail. I like it. You're learning, Katsaros." Kris leaned over the table until we were less than a breath apart. My gaze dropped right to his mouth and I took a shallow breath, trying to come up with a witty response. I swore at that moment all the chocolates on the table had to be melting.

Phoebe cleared her throat, pulling my chair back with both hands. "PDA," she said uncomfortably under her breath "You don't want to get written up by the lunch monitors."

"You're so cute," I said to her, then ignored everything she said and leaned forward to give Kris a kiss that ranked on suspension level for public displays of affection. I turned back to her when none of the teachers came our way, knowing I had to have a goofy grin on my face. "There *are* perks to dating the student council president, you know."

"I doubt not getting in trouble for PDA is one of those perks," she pointed out.

Kris shrugged. "She's very good at corrupting me. But, ignoring the PDA thing, can I steal Em away for a few minutes?"

Even though I was tempted to jump up and into his arms, I looked from Phoebe to him, a wicked little smile spreading across my lips as a plan hit me. "That'll cost you extra. I think buying a whole cake or plate of cookies might cover that and the gala."

Phoebe nudged me with her elbow. "I always said you two were exactly alike."

"Mercenary and giving at the same time, right?" I gave her my best "evil queen trying to look benevolent" look.

"As long as we use our powers only for good, I think the world could use us." He pulled a ten out of his pocket and handed it to Phoebe. Sweeping up a blueberry crumb cake with one hand and catching my hand with the other, he pulled me away from the table. "Thanks, Phoebe. I'll have her back in a minute." As we wove through the crowded lunchroom, he paused to drop the cake off at the table where our school's quarterback sat. "Save me a slice, okay?" Then, he kept going, pulling me through the school's double doors and out into the courtyard.

The student council table outside was deserted. I extracted my hands from his to pull the sleeves of my sweater down to cover my hands and wrap my arms around myself. "So? What's so important that you'll pull me away from my new favorite charity?"

"Well, first," he gently untangled my arms and placed them around his waist, then bent over to catch me off-guard with a kiss. All of my goosebumps disappeared as a new set of shivers that had nothing to do with cold fluttered across my skin. Kris ran his thumb over my cheek, then said, "I'm just taking advantage of a student council perk." He sat on the table's stone bench and I let him pull me alongside him as he draped his arm over my shoulder.

I leaned in, soaking up his warmth. "Yeah, it's so nice of them. You can freeze your asses outside if you want. Or get soaked in the rain. Or burn to a crisp for the other, like, two months of the year."

"Well, you know us student politics types. We're tough, unlike certain weak artsy people." He punctuated his comment by pulling me closer to him.

I narrowed my eyes. "Keep insulting me and you'll have to buy another cake if you want artsy arm candy at that gala."

"Then I guess I won't tell you my good news." Crap. There was that innocent look again. If he started looking off to the side and whistling, I was going to elbow him.

Instead, I slipped icy cold fingers under his shirt and against the small of his back. I suppressed a giggle when he first cringed away, then grew incredibly still. I nudged him with my shoulder to get him to focus again. "Which is?"

Kris reached back and grabbed my hand, pulling it away from his back. "I was in Mr. MacKenzie's office—"

"You really are such a kiss-ass."

He put his index fingers against my lips. "Shh. Like I was saying, I was in his office and overheard them talking about another speech writing competition that's opening up in a few weeks. The scholarship money sounds decent, too."

He had me at "scholarship." Anything that would close the gap between being indebted forever to student loans and just scraping by automatically made my radar. I sat up straighter and looked him right in the eye. "What's the speech supposed to be about?"

"I'm not sure, but does it matter? We're awesome." His eyes lit up and the corners of his lips quirked up in an almost-smile that looked a little conspiratorial.

"Right. If it's about something like the importance of sports in an academic setting, you're not the best advocate for it. Now, me, with my abundance of exposure to football players and cheerleaders and an archery person—"

"Excuse me, but thanks to being forced to spend time with your friends, I'm more sensitive to the needs of our athletic department. I'm incredibly well-rounded. Let me remind you that I gave Mike and the guys my cake." He pointed at the cafeteria windows in the general direction of the jock table.

"You're so altruistic." I grew serious and turned my head so I looked directly into his eyes. "I don't know if I want to compete against you again." The thought terrified me. This was the first time I'd ever felt this strongly about anyone, and putting our relationship to the test so early on was like pouring acid on a base in chemistry class. Things were bound to go explosive in ways I didn't want to explore.

Even for another scholarship. Meanwhile, the commonsense and competitive parts of me wanted to slap me for being so idiotic about it all. Boys came and went, but scholarships that helped me realize my dreams didn't just pop up all the time.

But I really, really liked this boy.

Kris seemed to notice something was off and reached up to smooth his hand over my hair. He'd learned quickly that running his fingers through my curls meant stuck fingers and me complaining about frizz the rest of the day. "Hey, it's just a competition. It's not going to affect *us*." On "us," he kissed my forehead. "We're stronger than that. I promise."

I pressed my lips together. "I know you and I really know me. We get a little cutthroat, especially against each other."

Instead of denying it, like I'd expected, he nodded, his expression incredibly serious. "That's why we should do this again. You make me work to do better than my best if I want to beat you. We raise the bar for each other. Plus, you get all flirty when you want to beat me."

My smile reappeared in spite of my reluctance. "I'll have to change my tactics, then. Keep you on your toes." The thought of standing up on a stage again, giving a speech, made a thrill run through me. It was more fun and energizing than I'd thought, like nailing a character on the first read-through. "Maybe I'll ignore you this time. You know, a 'no-kiss' pact or something."

"Diabolical," he said with a laugh. He smoothed my hair back again, his fingers lightly tracing the edge of my ear and down my neck. I had to fight to keep from closing my eyes and leaning in to his palm. "Does that mean you're competing?"

I nodded, gracing him with a predatory grin. Forget German ex-boyfriends and fake-flirting in Boston. This next competition would be epic. "Bring it on, Lambert." I punctuated my tough-girl words with a kiss that was calculated to melt him into a puddle of goo—and get us both sent to the principal's office if one of the lunch monitors looked outside at that moment.

But he didn't melt. Instead, he pulled back, his face the perfect mix of competitive fierceness and passion that made my heart stop.

"I can't wait, Katsaros."

We were going to kick competition ass.

THE END

AUTHOR'S NOTE

While the "US Change Council" is a fictional scholarship contest and conference inspired by a mix of three or four real programs, there are many student scholarship programs and opportunities to help offset college/technical/vocational school costs, some of which can go as high as 100% coverage. Like Dev told Em, "You can't win if you don't even apply," so I encourage students to reach out to their guidance counselors, local religious and civic organizations, and (for US readers) to use resources like the National Association of Secondary School Principals (NASSP) list of approved student programs (https://www.nassp.org/news-and-resources/nassp-approved-student-programs) to find their own "Change Council" opportunities.

ACKNOWLEDGMENTS

Considering Em loves theatre and musicals so much, it would be an absolute travesty to mention *The Sound of Music* in *Bookishly*'s acknowledgments but not in *Dramatically*'s, so, starting at the very beginning (you know the rest!)— thank you to all my readers. Your tweets, emails, reviews, and comments magically seem to come whenever I need a boost. I've had the joy of meeting some of you, either in person or virtually. I've (literally) cried happy tears over your "aesthetics" posts and fanart. I love fangirling over books, animation, and all sorts of wonderful things with you. You make all the stress, long hours, and rewrites worth it. Thank you for reading and I hope Em's story lived up to your expectations.

Next, to Patricia Riley and Asja Parrish, my amazing editors. Bless you for pushing and challenging me to make this book a million times better. Thank you for helping me to grow as a writer and for helping Em to grow as a character. Thank you for margin smilies at my goofiest lines and for challenging me when I tried to take the "easy" way out in a character conversation (Honest to goodness, I now know more about divergent opinions on NGOs and voluntourism than I ever thought possible. Wheeee!)

To my agent, Carrie Howland, thank you for putting up with my newbie author questions and freakouts after *Bookishly*'s release and during *Dramatically*'s edits. Thank you for being my advocate, guide, and for not blocking my phone number in your phone after my gazillion texts. I still owe you that ice cream.

To everyone at Spencer Hill Press and Midpoint, especially Karen Hughes—endless thanks for your work on *Bookishly* and now *Dramatically*. Thank you for giving me such beautiful books and for dealing with all the curveballs from bookstore computer system glitches to an author who (sometimes…okay, maybe a lot of the time…) kept responding to everything like a project-managing engineer. To Caroline DeLuca, who worked magic in copyedits and had to put up with my "made-up-but-not-quite" Ever After universe brands. And to Eric Kampmann, thank you so much for supporting Spencer Hill Press, myself, and this series.

To Meredith Maresco, the best publicist on the planet, as well as someone I'm lucky to count as a friend. You handle everything I've seen thrown your way with so much grace, creativity, and an epic sense of humor, and I can always count on you for a heart-emoji battle just when I need it the most. You deserve the world for your work and friendship. Please never stop being amazing.

To Veronica Bartles, Stephanie Pajonas, and Deena Graves—three of the most talented writers I know and the first people to read and believe in Em's story. Thank you for your endless suggestions, support, and for helping me to make this.

Despite juggling being a new father, work, election season, and putting out the most EPIC Star Trek: Excelsior episodes on the planet, James Heaney took so much time out of his schedule to help me work through a number of scenes in this book. From the moment I got your email to now, I've been giggling over your "Mao Tse Kris" comment (and will probably giggle about it forever). Thank you, thank you, thank you.

There may have been a point while writing *Dramatically* where I reached out to Madeline Martin in a panic, saying something along the lines of, "Uhm. I have Em saying this thing about a kiss that 'set her panties on fire' but, uhm HELP!" You and your romance writer magic made me push through my inherent fear of kissy scenes and hopefully made the sparks fly between Em and Kris.

Again, always, to all the R&Divas, especially Erika, Lori, and Chris, who bore the brunt of my *Dramatically Ever After* cubicle babble after work and over lunches. To all my friends at both the NJ and PA sites, your support has meant the world to me, especially since I look up to so many of you. Writing can be a lonely profession and to know you all have been cheering me on (and that you read my book... oh, dear. UHM...) has really bolstered me. Thank you, also, for not laughing at my bright pink wrist supports, ergonomic mouse, and latte obsession when I'm on deadline. Thank you for showing up to signings and nearly making me cry at work by asking me to sign *Bookishly*. Thank you for being you and making "the day job" a joy.

Speaking of lattes…this is also for the baristas, especially at Burlap and Bean, who kept me well caffeinated and smiling. There's a reason why my characters talk about fancy lattes all the time.

Writing is hard and finding your path as a writer is even harder without a compass. Eastern PA SCBWI has always been my compass, and the Ever After books will always be the Poconos retreat books to me. There's magic in those cabins at Highlights Foundation. Sending so much love to all of you, especially to Kim Briggs—thank you for all of your support, friendship, and the endless work you (and Alison Myers, sending you also all the hugs!) do for kidlit.

Last, but never, ever least, to my family. To my extended family (including everyone who might not be family by blood but still family by years of friendship) whose excitement and support have made this journey a joy. To Nela and Susie—when we were little, Mom used to tell us, "Your sisters are the best friends you can have." I don't think any of us believed it back then, but now that we're "all grown up," I know it's the truth. You have been my biggest cheerleaders and advice-givers and I couldn't do this without you. To Joey and Dennis, who made me laugh and commiserated with me through all the ups, downs, and edit letters, thank you for being a part of this bookish rollercoaster. To Joey and Sara, for putting up with going to a bunch of TiTi's book signings and keeping me company. And to Mom and Dad: you believed in me from day one, supported me through drafting, edits, being late to dinner as I worked through "one more paragraph," and figuring out how these "grown-up" and "author" things worked. You are the reason why these books are even able to happen. Thank you.

ABOUT THE AUTHOR

Author photo by Rachel McCalley

Growing up, Isabel Bandeira split her time between sum-
mers surrounded by cathedrals, castles, and ancient tombs in
Portugal, and the rest of the year hanging around the lakes
and trees of Southern New Jersey, which only fed her fairytale and nature obsessions. In her day job, she's a Mechanical
Engineer and tones down her love of all things glittery while
designing medical devices, but it all comes out in her writing.
The rest of the time, you'll find her reading, at the dance
studio, or working on her jumps and spins at the ice rink.

Isabel lives in South Jersey with her little black cat, too
much yarn, and a closetful of vintage hats. She is represented
by Carrie Howland of Empire Literary. *Dramatically Ever
After* is Book Two in the popular *Ever After* series.